The Last Night

By
Mark Dunn

JournalStone
San Francisco

JOURNALSTONE
YOUR LINK TO ARTISTIC TALENT

JournalStone books may be ordered through booksellers or by contacting:

JournalStone

www.journalstone.com

ISBN: 978-1-942712-76-3   (sc)
ISBN: 978-1-942712-77-0   (ebook)

JournalStone rev. date: April 15, 2016

Library of Congress Control Number: 2016935545

Printed in the United States of America

Cover Art & Design: Chuck Killorin

Edited by: Aaron J. French

The Last Night

Prologue

San Cristobol, New Mexico—1975

Winter had arrived in the desert, and though it could still be unbearably hot during the day, the cold of the night was equally brutal. On this frigid night in the middle of November, there had been no snow yet, but the clouds seemed so low that a man might reach up and tear off a piece. It was only a matter of time before they ruptured and turned the brown land white, if only until the heat returned the following afternoon.

Pulling his dusty Ford pickup to a stop in the driveway of his house, Doctor Timothy Barron couldn't stop himself from reflecting briefly on how many different ways the desert could kill you. If it wasn't the heat, it was the cold, and if it wasn't the cold, it was the scorpions, the flashfloods, or the goddamned snakes. Already this year he'd had to chase two good-sized rattlers out of his house, and with the first winter chill having now arrived, they'd really be getting ornery.

As he opened the door of the truck and stepped down to the ground, he reminded himself to get the broom from the hallway closet and set it by the kitchen door. The snakes especially liked to crawl beneath the oven. Like so many creatures in this world, they only wanted to be warm.

"I'm home," Tim called out as he stepped through the front door, which was unlocked. You had to worry about a lot of things living in San Cristobol, but robbers weren't on the list. In the five years he and his wife had lived in their house on the outskirts of town—if San Cristobol could even be called a town, with its two stoplights, one gas station, and four bars—the garden had been plundered by armadillos, the trash ripped to pieces by marauding coyotes, and Seymour, the marmalade cat, killed by a rattler, but there had never been so much as a hint of malfeasance from the human sector.

"In here," came the answer from the kitchen, from which Tim could also hear the sounds of cooking. And what was that smell? Garlic? Onions? Tim's stomach growled. He'd spent all day at his office in town without eating. He pushed through the swinging saloon doors into the kitchen.

Isabel, his wife, was standing at the stove, giving Tim a jolt of anxiety.

She said, "Don't worry. I checked underneath with a broom before I started, you silly man."

He put his arms around her thin waist from behind and nuzzled her neck, inhaling deeply of her skin and rich black hair. "What's cooking? Smells great."

"Fajitas." She turned her face towards his and kissed his cheek, rough with stubble.

"Mmm. Hope you're making lots. I could eat a horse."

"Good, because we ran out of steak and I had to shoot Trigger. But I seasoned him up real nice, so you should barely notice." Isabel was half-Mexican, and though she spoke perfect English, the gentle remnant of her accent often made him smile, especially when she was trying to be flip. Trigger, for instance, was *Tree-gurr* from his wife's lips. Beautiful.

"That's very funny, Izzy," Tim said, getting a bottle of beer from the fridge and twisting the top off, "but you shouldn't joke. You know how sensitive Trig is, especially in his old age." Trigger was the oldest of the seven horses Tim and Isabel owned, and the only one she never used to give riding lessons. Over the past several years his attitude had grown progressively worse, until finally the disgruntled horse had become, for all intents and purposes, a well-fed punchline.

"Not 'is,' *mi amor*. Was. Trigger 'was' sensitive. Now he's just a little tough."

Tim sat down at the kitchen table and put his feet up on one of the other vinyl-seated chairs, drawing a disapproving look from his wife. "How was your day?" he said.

She turned the strips of meat she was cooking and said, "Okay. I had Jose this morning and Sally this afternoon. Pretty slow, really, which was fine with me. Who wants to be out in that cold all day?"

"Looks like it's going to snow tonight."

"I almost hope so. If it's going to be this cold, we should at least get some scenery."

Isabel took the griddle off the stove. She opened the oven and took out a foil-wrapped stack of tortillas, then retrieved a platter of lettuce, tomatoes, onions, and peppers from the refrigerator. She said, "You ready to eat?"

It was all Tim could do to nod. He was aware that he was gaping at the food, and made himself close his mouth, which was suddenly watering.

She sat down and they both started preparing their fajitas. Along with the meat, Isabel had chopped tomatoes, lettuce, and an avocado. A bowl of her signature salsa, which she made just about as hot as a man could take it, sat on the table, too.

Tim was about to take a bite when the phone rang.

"Oh, bullshit," he said. "No fair." He set the fajita down and frowned as the tortilla unrolled, spilling its contents all over his plate. He walked to the phone mounted on the wall and snatched it up, feeling irritated and justified in his irritation, which only annoyed him more.

"Hello?"

There was rapid breathing on the other end of the line, hitches and gasps. "*Doctor Barron, es Maria Stanton.*" The words were spoken with such a deep accent as to be nearly indecipherable, but Tim had seen Maria several times over the last few months and knew her cadences well. The young woman was a second generation American whose family spoke a combination of fractured English and Spanish in the home. Her husband, a lanky blond cowboy-type named Steve Stanton, was a transplant from Ohio and as white bread as could be. Tim remembered that the man had bailed on Maria almost immediately after learning that she was pregnant—a sterling specimen of the American male.

After years working in the primarily Mexican town of San Cristobol, Tim was able to make out muddled Spanglish that would have baffled someone else. He spoke to her in Spanish, guessing that in her obviously distraught state, her mind would default to the language in which she'd been raised.

"*Maria, que es la problema?*"

"*El bebe!*" Maria said, the end of the word turning into a breathy moan.

"Maria," Tim said, trying to keep his voice soothing, calm, "*hay alguien con usted?*"

"*No, no—*" Maria screamed and Tim jerked the phone away from the piercing sound. There was a loud bang, as if the receiver had rapped against the floor.

"Maria! Maria!" But there was no answer. Even the screaming had stopped. "Maria!" Tim said one more time, listened, heard nothing.

A thrummy spastickness took control of Tim's body. He felt as if he had just witnessed a murder, or overheard one. Jesus, he'd been present at hundreds of births, and he'd never heard screams like those, not even when a delivery went sour. It had sounded like she was being torn apart.

He thrust the phone out at Isabel, who accepted it like it might bite her.

"Don't hang up. If she starts talking again, tell her I'm on my way. I'll be there in ten minutes."

Isabel nodded, her face serious. "What's wrong with her, Tim?"

"I don't know," he said, driving his arms into the sleeves of his heavy, fleece-lined coat. "Call the hospital in Las Cruces, tell them to send an ambulance to Maria Stanton's house on Albermarle Road, out near the arroyo."

Isabel took the phone. "Go," she said. "I'll give them directions to the house."

Tim suddenly remembered that Izzy and Maria were friends, and that his wife had been to Maria's a thousand times.

"Go," she said again. "Hurry, Timmy."

He climbed into his pickup, which was still warm and ticking from his drive home, jammed the keys into the ignition, and backed out of the driveway.

In five minutes he was two miles out of town, heading into the desert on a dirt road. There were no other cars out at this hour, and the low-flying clouds blocked out any light the moon or stars might have lent the world below. It was dark. Dark and cold. Tim cranked the heat as high as it would go and pressed down on the accelerator a little harder, urging the old truck ahead.

He rounded a corner in the road and Maria's small house came into view. It was right on the side of the dirt lane, no neighbors to either side for at least a mile in either direction. He pulled the truck to a stop by the stairs leading to the front door and climbed out.

And stood there.

Inside he felt a compulsion to rush into the house, to help Maria any way he could, to save her and her baby. But that compulsion was stifled by a deeper knowledge, a certainty he couldn't explain, but couldn't question.

Maria Stanton was dead in there. And not just dead, but dead in a *horrible* way. Tim scolded himself. *She's suffering inside and you're standing here. Stop with this horseshit right now. Get in there and do what you can. If she's dead, she's dead. But if she's not, and she dies because you stood here like a goddamned zombie doing nothing…*

Hefting his bag, he climbed the stairs to the porch and rapped twice on the front door, unable to stop himself from observing the formality.

"Maria!" He tried the knob and found the door unlocked. It swung open, revealing more darkness.

"Maria," he called again, stepping inside. Again, there was no answer, but now Tim could hear a sound coming from upstairs, tapping and scratching, tapping and scratching, almost rhythmic, but not mechanical.

He started to call out Maria's name again, then realized he was only stalling. He didn't want to go up the stairs, not at all. He wanted to stay right where he was—no, strike that, he wanted to be back in his warm house with his beautiful wife and his dinner. He wanted to be anywhere but here, *anywhere*.

Trying to shunt the bad thoughts from his mind, he started up the steps.

The light was on in a room at the end of the hall. Maria's bedroom. During his visits over the course of her pregnancy, Tim had always examined her in the bedroom. She said it made her feel more at ease to be in a familiar place. It was a pleasant room, he recalled, decorated with hand-me-down furniture from her mother's home. There was a patchwork quilt on one wall, a portrait of her and her siblings with their mother and father on another.

Tim reached the top of the stairs and started down the hall.

The sound was louder now. Not clicking and scratching like he'd thought at first, but something else, something…something *wetter*.

"Maria," Tim said, "*es Doctor Barron. Estas aqui?*" The door to the bedroom was closed most of the way, allowing only a sliver of yellowish light to escape into the hall. The sound he'd heard from downstairs was much louder now, and when he stepped into Maria Navarro's bedroom, he saw where it was coming from.

She sat on the floor, back propped against the wall. Her white cotton nightgown was bunched up around her waist and soaked with blood, and a pool of blood was spreading on the bare wooden floor in front of and beneath her. She held her head straight back against the wall, her eyes rolling back and forth sluggishly in their sockets, her mouth opening and closing with a dreadful slowness. Her breathing was rapid and labored; she seemed to be struggling for even the smallest gasp of air. He could hear a sound that was something between a whistle and a gargle, wet and weak, the sound he'd been hearing since he stepped inside the house. In the crook of one arm, she held a squirming baby, its umbilical cord trailing over her blood-streaked thigh and under the bunched hem of her nightgown.

"I'm here," Tim said, rushing to her and dropping to his knees. "Let me look."

One of Maria's hands closed tightly on his forearm and he looked up. She was trying to say something, her lips moving soundlessly. Her eyes couldn't make up their mind what to do; one second they were fixed on him, the next they rolled back in her head, or looked over his shoulder, then back to him.

Tim leaned closer. "What?" he said into her ear. "What are you saying?"

Her lips were forming two words, the first beginning with an O, breathy, the second with a plosive, a P or a B, he thought. *Ot...Bay...* Tim searched his brain for any clue as to what she might be trying to communicate to him. She mouthed the words again, and this time there was the faintest whisper of a voice. *Otro bebe.*

Another baby?

With his free hand, Tim pulled up the bloody bottom of Maria's frock and looked at her pelvis. A tiny foot and ankle protruded from her distended vagina.

A breech, he thought, expecting to feel a fresh wave of panic surge over him. But it didn't. Instead, he felt a calm settle within his mind. He looked into Maria's eyes, and for the first time he recognized what he saw there.

She knew that she was dead. She hadn't been holding on for the sake of herself. It was the unborn baby twisted in her womb that she'd survived for. And although Tim thought that there was little chance the baby could have survived so long in its current position, there was at least a chance.

For Maria there was none. She'd lost far too much blood. Even if the ambulance arrived, she'd be gone long before the vehicle reached the hospital.

"*Entiendo,*" Tim said, and Maria nodded almost imperceptibly, a species of disbelieving relief in her eyes. Her head lolled to the side and Tim thought she had fainted.

He pulled her further onto the floor, so that she was three-quarters laying down. He took the baby from her arms and lowered it to the floor, where it lay on its back, crying and waving its arms.

He slid two of his fingers into her vagina and tried to gauge the severity of the breech. The child was badly contorted, which meant the umbilical cord was likely under severe stress, maybe even wrapped like a noose around the baby's neck. He needed to act quickly. In less time than it took him to realize he'd done so, he'd chosen.

At the bottom of his bag there was a flat black case. With hands that were now streaked with snotty gore and blood, Tim removed the case, opened it, and removed a heavy scalpel. Because it was the fastest way, he used the scalpel to slice Maria's frock down the front, then laid the two halves of it open, exposing her belly. Then he cut a long, wide incision across the brown expanse of her stomach, slicing through skin and fat and muscle and then into the uterus itself.

Tim reached into the bloody red cavity of the woman who had been his patient and his wife's good friend and pulled from the wet hotness of her insides a child, quiet and still.

Far away, he could hear the sound of sirens.

Part I

Chapter 1

Charlotte, North Carolina — Present Day

John opened his eyes and waited for the dream to fade. From the living room, he could hear the TV, turned down low; he'd left it on the night before for the voices. There was a faint smell of freesia from the Glade dispenser plugged into the bathroom outlet. Beneath him, John felt the sheets, damp with sweat.

John realized he was holding his breath and exhaled.

He sat up and pulled on the t-shirt he'd tossed onto the floor when he lay down to read last night.

In the kitchen, he put coffee on and then went back into the bedroom, opened the drawer of his bedside table and pulled forth a thin journal with a black faux-leather cover. When the coffee finished brewing, John poured himself a mug, grabbed the journal and then stepped outside onto the balcony of his apartment, which bordered a green tract of woods. In the distance, he could hear the occasional car zip by on Harris Boulevard. It was warm outside, unseasonably warm, even for spring in North Carolina, and although there was still an hour until sunrise, John began to perspire.

Birds were starting to sing. Someone in another apartment was up and cooking breakfast, bacon and eggs from the smell, and John's stomach churned.

As he sat in one of the weathered Adirondack chairs on the balcony and sipped his coffee, the dream returned to him again and John opened the journal to a blank page, uncapped the black pen nestled inside, and began to draw.

This dream had been much like the rest: violent, dark, culminating in the murder of a young man with a tattoo on his neck—a black sun releasing blood red rays. He'd been dirty, maybe a drunk, someone from the streets, and wore tight, torn-in-the-knee blue jeans, a soiled white t-shirt, and black combat boots worn crooked in the heel. Sometimes the subjects were men, sometimes women. A few times over the years, children, and in the worst of the dreams, a recurring nightmare that came to him at least once a week, it was an infant. Those occurrences were so devastating that they haunted John for hours or even days, leaking back into his mind when he saw children at work, the park, the supermarket.

As always, he found himself marveling through the horror at the detail of the dream, which was more like a very vivid memory than a fabrication of his mind. There had been a bar, bordered by gently undulating palm trees and brightly lit with red and blue and green neon lights. Smoky air, the smell of beer and cheap well-whisky, people all around, crushing him in, the chest-tightening sensation of claustrophobia. Later, the interior of an old car, the seats cracked green leather, the edges of ragged tears sharp against the bare skin of his legs, a man reaching for him, then blood everywhere, warm and salty and thick in his mouth and on his chin.

John stopped sketching and looked down at the page, which was filled now with amateurish drawings of the details he could remember from the dream. As a child, he'd been instructed to do this by a psychologist his parents had taken him to see, and it was a habit with roots sunk deep inside of him. Not only did the act help John to remember his dreams, it also helped him externalize the images, to set them away in a safe place where they weren't nearly as frightening. He capped the pen and tucked it back into the journal, then stepped inside the apartment and tried to shake off the dream.

His cell phone was lying on the Formica counter between the kitchen and living room. He flipped it open and pressed speed dial 2. The phone only rang once.

"Johnny."

"Hi, Mom. I didn't wake you up, did I?" There was really no reason to ask; since his father had taken over the farm in West Chester, Pennsylvania, his parents never slept a tick past five in the morning. Still, calling *anywhere* so early felt strange. John could picture her right now. She would be in the kitchen with a mug of coffee, sitting at the round oak table in the breakfast nook, looking out over the open fields that in a few weeks would sprout the first nascent stalks of corn.

Beyond the fields, near the barn, two long, windowless cinderblock buildings where the mushrooms grew. Before he left for college, it had been his job to harvest the mushrooms from their tightly layered beds of compost. It was work done in the dark, not because the light would hurt the mushrooms, but because the heat the bulbs threw off would. The growing buildings were like cool, dank caves. He was surprised at the wave of nostalgia that washed over him; he used to hate that chore, but God, how easy it all used to be.

"In my dreams," his mother said in her gently accented voice, jolting John from the memory. "I keep waiting for that goddamned rooster to die, but I swear to God, it's immortal."

"Well," John said, sitting down on the flimsy futon in the living room, "it *is* your birthday. I could hire someone to bump him off. Maybe even do the deed myself." He lowered his voice and affected his best New York accent, which was still pretty horrible. "By midnight, he'll be sleepin' wit da fishes, whaddayasay?"

His mother grunted in mock approval. "Don't tease," she said, then added, "fuggedabout it." With the slight lilt of her Mexican upbringing, the New York accent sounded both ridiculous and bizarrely exotic.

"Anyway," John said, "I just wanted to wish you a happy birthday."

"Sixty-three," his mother said. He knew she was shaking her head. "How did this happen?"

"Oh, stop. You never paid attention to age before."

She sighed. "I'll get over it. Your father and I are going to drive over to Kennett Square for dinner tonight. *Chez Maurice.* That'll be fun."

"Is Dad there?" John asked.

"Out feeding the animals."

"Well, maybe he'll kill the rooster while he's at it."

She chuckled. "How are *you* doing, Johnny?"

"You know," John said and sipped coffee, sneaking a glance at the clock on the DVD player, "same same." He didn't want to tell her about the intensification of his dreams; she'd worry about him and ask him if he wanted to come home, and although the answer to that question would be "yes," he'd find a reason not to get on a plane up to Philadelphia. A meeting he couldn't miss, a friend he'd agreed to help move, something, anything.

"Sounds exciting," his mother replied.

"Like I said."

His mother paused for a moment, then asked, "Any more dreams?"

"I don't think they'll ever stop entirely, but nothing too bad."

His mother chuckled wryly. "John, you should think about coming home for a while, maybe the next time you have a break at school. For Easter, maybe. You could help out on the farm for a few days, get your hands dirty. They always say a tired body and a calm mind go hand in hand."

"You should see if Widener offers a PhD in psychology."

"Avoider."

"Nag."

"I love you, Johnny. Let us know if you need anything. We're here for you."

"I know, Mom. Happy birthday. Tell Dad I say hi." He said goodbye and hung up the phone.

* * *

He pulled into the school parking lot at six-thirty. The sun was coming up over the swatch of woods beyond the football field, and John sat there and watched for a while.

Relatively speaking, he'd been teaching at the Denton School for a long time, nearly three years now. Before Denton, he'd worked at independent schools in Pennsylvania, Delaware, and Ohio, spending a year or two in each spot, then moving on. College had been no different. He'd left his home in West Chester and headed off to Boston College when he was eighteen, but within two years a violent wanderlust came over him. The last two years of college he'd spent at

UVA. Immediately after graduation, he packed up his few belongings and had been bumping around from place to place ever since.

His work references were excellent because John was a talented teacher, but sooner or later schools were going to start looking at his seeming inability to commit to a position and stop hiring him. This was part of the reason he had forced himself to stay put at Denton for as long as he had.

From time to time he went home to Pennsylvania, but every time he did, he felt like he was putting his parents in a bad spot. No, it was more than that. When he went home, he felt—he *knew*—that he was endangering his mother and father.

The first day would be fine, an inkling here and there that something wasn't quite right, but nothing he couldn't chalk up to the return to a once-familiar place, to somewhere you'd known so intimately as a child, but in which you were now nothing but a stranger, an interloper. And then night would come, and he would find himself going every five minutes to a window, looking for...looking for *nothing* out in the dark. It was crazy, the kind of thinking that marked not just paranoia, but real mental aberrance. Still, sometimes it was all he could do not to run, to drive away as quickly as possible, leaving the old farmhouse and barn and growing buildings forever behind him in a cloud of dust. As a result, most of his contact with his mother and father was over the phone, a fact that saddened John, especially now that both his parents were in their sixties, his father just south of seventy.

He had become comfortable at Denton, however, though he couldn't deny the constant nagging feeling that he should leave and move on, a sensation that had intensified in recent months, even as the dreams had reestablished their prominence in his life. But so far he had stayed. He liked the people he worked with, the kids even more than the adults, and though he told himself he would leave after each academic year, he hadn't yet. Of course, he *would* leave eventually, but he had no idea where he'd go—someplace completely unfamiliar, most likely, like Iowa or New Hampshire. For now, though, he was here.

On the radio, two local DJs were doing their daily Morons in the News segment, something about a farmer in New Zealand who'd tried to crossbreed a goat and some kind of lizard. Bullshit, no doubt, but not beyond the stupidity of man to attempt.

John turned off the car and, lugging a briefcase full of ungraded papers, headed for his classroom.

* * *

"Hey, John."

The voice jolted him from his skin. He'd been grading freshman essays at his desk. When he looked up, Suzie Clusky was standing in the door of his classroom, a Styrofoam cup of coffee in her hand. From behind her, he could hear the buzz of growing activity in the hall. Not loud yet, but it would be soon.

"Suze," John said. "What's going on?" As always when he saw her, he felt a mixture of sadness and longing. He and Suzie had dated for several months when John first signed on at Denton, and although that relationship had come to a somewhat bitter end, Suzie had, for whatever reason, allowed John to salvage a friendship with her.

"You okay?"

He looked up at the clock over the door and saw that it was almost seven forty-five. The bulk of the kids, most of them bus riders, wouldn't get in for another ten or fifteen minutes.

"Yeah," he said, manufacturing a smile. "Great. Never better." But even as he said the words, he realized what he had been doing, and why she had asked. There was no essay on the desk in front of him. He had been sitting here for the better part of an hour, a pen in his hand, staring at...at what? On top of that, he remembered the way his reflection had looked in the mirror this morning—the dark shadows beneath his eyes, the unusual pallor of the olive skin he'd inherited from his mother. And he felt strange. Not from simple lack of sleep, either. His eyes felt too wide, his nerves raw; the world almost seemed to tremble in front of his eyes, as though it were supercharged. All he could remember was a few snatches of an imagined scene—a candle-lit room, filthy cots filled with moaning men and women. He was prone to these lost moments—had been since he was a kid—but they never failed to make him feel dislocated.

"You look like you could use some shut-eye."

"Tell me about it," he said. "But I'm fine, really. A little insomnia."

She left, giving him a brief smile, and at around eight John's homeroom started filtering slowly in.

Most of the morning went pretty well, considering the fact that John was running on reserves. Sleep had always come hard for him, ever since he was a small child. He was a victim of what his middle-school guidance counselor had called "night terrors," but his hadn't gone away as he'd gotten older. And now, in the past few months, they had suddenly tripled in power and frequency. Still, John figured he'd get through it; he always had before. For a while the dreams would be there every night—vivid, bloody, terrifying—and then, suddenly, they wouldn't be. Until they were again. There was no way he could ever get used to such a thing, but over the years he'd grown accustomed to it, and sometimes that familiarity was the only thing that helped him keep going.

He taught four classes, his three sections of freshman English and a senior elective, so he had plenty to keep him busy. But by fourth period, his last class before lunch, he could no longer ignore the growing feeling of panic in his head and chest, the cool buzz all over his skin. It was something like the feeling he often woke with, a tight-throated sense of...of what John could only define as impending danger. The feeling was sharp and nearly acidic, like what he'd heard some people experience right before a tornado touches down; he almost went into the bathroom to see if his hair was standing on end. There was a tight pressure behind his eyes, as if they were swollen in their sockets, or as if his brain had suddenly expanded to fill the rest of the room in his skull.

After lunch, John had a free period, so he went to the faculty lounge and got some coffee, then sat down on one of the old, saggy couches. Normally, this was the time of day when he would try to catch up on grading or planning, but he knew that if he tried to perform any function that required mental focus, he would end up reading and rereading the same five words over and over. Images and words and physical sensations spun through his mind, but John couldn't latch on to any one particular thing.

The school was situated on the edge of a heavily wooded park, and the best feature of the lounge was a large plate window overlooking the athletic fields, and, beyond those, the rolling expanse of trees that were just beginning to erupt into green life again. When John first came to Denton, he would take advantage of planning periods and walk through the woods on the well-worn paths run flat and wide by fifty years of cross-country teams. It was quiet down there in the mornings and the afternoons; the creek ran sluggishly along its banks behind Denton, not unlike the portions of the Brandywine River and Crum Creek he and his father had canoed when he was young, casting for small-mouth bass and trout.

Down below, on the soccer field, a group of middle-schoolers zipped around in brightly colored pinnies, chasing the black and white ball. All as it should be. But still, it wasn't.

Feeling restless, John took his Styrofoam cup and left the lounge. He took the stairs down to the ground level of the school and had just reached the door to the main office, on the way to check his mailbox, when something stopped him cold. Voices raised, frantic, the sound of something or someone slamming into a locker.

Oh God, he thought, *here it comes*, then immediately: *What does that mean?*

Clarence Drake, the physics teacher, rounded the corner, coming from the building's main entrance, a frantic look in his eyes, his face flushed so deeply crimson that John wondered if maybe he was suffering a heart attack or stroke. John was so shocked by Drake's appearance that it took him a moment to see the wet blood covering both of his hands and soaked into the front and sleeves of his white Oxford shirt. There was a chunk of something wet and glistening on Drake's electric-blue and maroon striped tie and John couldn't take his eyes off it.

"Clarence," John said, feeling suddenly breathless, "what happened? What's wrong?" He looked Clarence up and down for an injury of some kind, but couldn't find one.

Clarence lurched over to John, grabbed him by the shoulders. His fingers were hooked like talons, and they dug painfully into John's shoulders. John flashed back to his childhood, when he had pulled a much younger boy floundering in the deep end of the pool to safety; Drake clung to him in precisely the same way, nearly unhinged with whatever he had seen. *Fuck nearly*, John thought, *he's done. Done and gone.*

"Kyra," Clarence said, and he was sobbing now. "Kyra Metheny. We were out front of the school working on her Doppler Effect project—she must have stepped into the—someone—someone ran her down! Jesus, John, someone ran her *down!*"

"What?" John felt the skin on the back of his neck constrict, felt a flush rising in his face.

"Someone ran her down! Hit her and drove off! Oh, Jesus, her head! It's all over me."

"Call 911," John said, shoving Clarence toward the phone at the back of the lounge, and then he was out the door, sprinting toward the main entrance of the Denton School.

Behind him, he could hear Clarence still yelling, repeating the same two words over and over. "*Her head! Her head! Her head!*"

* * *

There was a crowd of kids, the rest of Clarence's class, John knew, gathered at the side of the road, near the semicircular drop-off/pick-up port at the front of the school.

As John ran toward them, the heels of his scuffed Rockports clapping on the concrete, he realized that he could hear and see everything with a bizarre clarity. He'd heard of the intensification of the senses that accompanied an adrenaline rush, but this was the first time he'd ever experienced it. His head felt like it was stretching to allow all of the sensory details rushing to fill it.

From above, in the branches of the trees that canopied the entrance of the school, he could hear squirrels scrabbling over the rough bark; somewhere far down the suburban street, he could hear a dog whining to be let out; and though I-85 was a good two miles off, he could hear the six lanes of traffic rushing along as though he was standing on the shoulder of the Interstate.

Davey Stuart, a big kid from the football team who anchored both the offensive and defensive lines, turned. His face was completely devoid of color and John knew that he was in severe shock. When he spoke, his words came out slurred, as though he were drunk.

"Mr. B.," he said in a tone so flat he sounded lobotomized, "there's something coming out of her head."

John nodded, amazed at the preternatural calm that was filling him. There was still that acute awareness, but now it was accompanied by the sensation of total and complete control. A sudden thought stepped into his mind: *It's going to be okay. It's going to be just fine.*

"Listen, Davey," John said, taking him by the shoulders, not as Clarence had done to John moments before, but gently, reassuringly. "I need you to do something for me, okay?"

Davey nodded, his eyes wide, the pupils unnaturally dilated, but as John held the boy, he thought he saw some sense of awareness come back.

John spoke slowly. "Go to the office. Tell them what happened. Tell them to call 911. Mr. Drake should have already, but we can't be too safe. Got it?"

Davey nodded, and—it shocked John to do it as much as it must have shocked Davey to see it—John smiled. A small smile, but a smile nonetheless. A thought then, quick and terrible, but not frightening. Not scary.

Something is happening to me.

Davey stumbled off toward the school and John headed again for the side of the road, where more of the students had turned to look at him, the same blank glaze on their mask-like faces as the one that had been pasted onto Davey's. He'd seen a painting by Picasso once during an exhibit at the Tait Gallery in London, *Portrait of Madame Matisse*, that resembled the way the students' faces looked now. Death masks. Pale, unlined, porcelain-like, mouths and eyes expressionless slits, windows not into their souls but into whatever colorless void people's minds accessed when confronted with an experience that is simply too much, too horrifying, to comprehend. John remembered that Picasso, when asked why he'd chosen to paint Madame Matisse's face in the manner of a death mask, had said that he knew the woman far too intimately to see her how she *really* was anymore. The exact opposite was true here; these children had come into contact with something about which they knew *nothing* whatsoever—death—and it had shattered them.

They parted as he approached.

And then, all at once, he could see Kyra Metheny.

The first thing John thought upon seeing the girl wasn't about her at all. Instead, he found himself transported in his memory to a place and time he couldn't identify.

There was a road in this remembered place, too, a straight stretch of new, tarry-smelling blacktop, two vivid yellow lines running down its middle, but all around was nothing but openness, green fields, blue sky. The crayon-bright colors of childhood. And on the grass off to the side of the road, a black cat, its spine twisted back on itself into a revoltingly inorganic L.

He saw small hands reach out, touch the cat, which was dying and unable to do anything besides warn him away with a wet, gurgling hiss. Blood bubbles grew from its nostrils and popped on the cat's nose. In this vision, John saw spatter from the blood bubbles land on the cat's eyeballs and he thought, *this can't be made up. I could never make up anything like that.*

From behind him, a hand on his shoulder, a woman's voice. *Careful, Johnny.* Laying his hands on the cat, feeling the blood-soaked fur beneath his hands, the twisted, crumpled spine, the—

"Mr. Barron!"

Kristy Levinworth stood in front of him. She was crying, but seemed to be the only student capable of normal movement. He felt her cold hand slip around his and let her lead him forward.

"Help her," John heard Kristy whisper. "Oh, please fucking do something. You have to do fucking *something*."

John pulled free of her and knelt beside Kyra.

The girl lay half in the road, half on the curb. Her right shoe, John saw, was missing. Out of the corner of his eye, he saw a Nike running shoe dangling from the branch of a spindly sapling fifteen feet away. It was an image he'd remember on and off for the rest of his life, always completely out of context. One of Kyra's eyes was open, and John saw it fix on him, drift away, then fix on him again. There was no other movement in her body, and it wasn't hard to see the reason why.

The left side of Kyra's head had collapsed inward like a sinkhole, and blood dribbled like thick red ink from her nose and mouth and one of her ears. Her left eye seemed to be missing, and John wondered whether it had come out, or if it had sunken back into her skull somewhere. It didn't matter. The damage had been done.

Something pinkish-gray—part of her brain, John knew, but wouldn't let himself totally comprehend—was smeared on her cheek like a chunk of congealed oatmeal. From the position in which she was lying, her hips rotated almost completely around from the angle of her shoulders, John could tell that her back was broken. In fact, from the way she looked, John would have been surprised to hear that any of her bones had been spared. More than anything else, she looked like a human-sized version of the Raggedy Ann dolls his mother had collected. Limp limbs twisted into all sorts of impossible angles, her bones little more than splinters and white dust wrapped in bruised meat.

"Hey there, sweetie," John said, trying to find another smile like the one he'd given Davey but failing this time. "Everything's going to be okay. There's an ambulance coming. It'll be here any second. Just stay with me, alright?"

One of Kyra's hands was lying on her stomach, and John started to reach for it. She probably wouldn't be able to feel anything, but who knew? She deserved any mercy he could bestow on her.

Just as he was about to take her hand in his own, he stopped.

Careful, Johnny, he heard his mother say from somewhere in the past. Around him, he felt something building in the air, in his head, in his body, an energy he didn't recognize or understand. It was coming from everywhere, flowing into him the way light flows into a black hole. *This is it,* he thought, and felt a rush of certainty and fear plow through the center of his body like a bullet.

John took Kyra's cold, still hand.

There was a moment of growing warmth, almost frictive, in his head, like hands rubbing rapidly together. And then a star exploded white and blue and hot behind his eyes.

John sucked in air to scream and then everything was gone.

Chapter 2

John woke up in a dark room.

From off to his right side, beeping, rhythmic and low. A little further away, voices, muted by distance, words indistinct. He lay still, listening, waiting for his eyes to adapt to the darkness. It was hard to keep them open, though, and they kept drifting closed again. His head hurt and his throat was dry. He felt something crammed down his throat and began to panic, tried to calm himself.

After a little while, a louder voice sounded over an intercom, still far away, but he could make out the words.

"Doctor Nelson to Oncology. Doctor Nelson to Oncology."

A hospital. Of course. He was lying in a hospital bed, and the beeping was the sound of an EEG. Somehow, this knowledge relaxed him, and he felt himself drifting back off.

* * *

He prowled the streets, looking at men and women walking and talking and laughing.

Later, a man named Brett with blond hair and a patchy five-day beard sat beside him at a bar that smelled of smoke and stale beer and, faintly, urine. When Brett smiled, there were black gaps where his teeth were missing. An old, ragged scar ran from his temple to his cheek. A fighter. This revelation did not concern John; he simply filed it away for later reference.

Somewhere dark then. An alley maybe; the smell was awful, like decomposing fish and feces. Brett pressing against him, searching for his mouth with his own lips. There was a throbbing pressure on John's thigh and he knew it was the man's erection.

"Come on, just a little," Brett said, laughing. "You'll like it, I promise."

And then a scream, a man's—Brett's—and a warm, salty, pulsating flood over his hand and in his mouth, his nose, his throat.

From far off, soothing words, over and over. "John, it's just a dream. Just a dream."

* * *

Sometime later, he found himself sitting up, still unable to see other than vague impressions of light. He knew he was awake, that he *looked* awake and was acting as though he was awake, but whatever it was that made him *him* was trapped somewhere behind a wall of glass, like a cop staring into an interrogation room through a one-sided mirror.

The back of the bed had been raised, and a nurse with curly black hair and an unpleasant scowl was feeding him something sweet that tasted of brown sugar and maple syrup.

Oatmeal. *Oh, Christ.*

The nurse tried to put more of the crud into his mouth, but suddenly it tasted not sweet, but fleshy and sour, like blood and spoiled milk.

"No," he tried to say, but his mouth wouldn't work and all he could do was lock his jaws in refusal.

"Come on now, John," she said, and not in a *nice* voice. "Eat up like a good boy." John felt his jaws pried open, more of the brain-tasting oatmeal shoved into his mouth, and then he was throwing up, muscles contracting as what little sustenance in his stomach made its way back up into the world. Fingers poked into his mouth and shoveled it out, and that nasty voice said, "Thanks a *pantload.*"

* * *

He was looking at Monica Rourke, his best student. She wore faded jeans torn in both knees and an oversized Denton basketball sweatshirt. She sat in the chair beside his bed reading a book. *A Separate Peace*. John wondered what Finny and Gene were up to.

"Hey, Mon," John said.

The book flew out of Monica's hands like a startled bird and she screamed breathlessly, then put her hand over her mouth and looked at John, laughing nervously.

"You're awake," she said, looking around the room, as if for assistance.

"It would appear so," John said. "Is there any water around here? My throat's killing me."

"Let me get someone." Monica was up and out the door in a spasm of herky-jerky movement. A moment later a doctor and a nurse trailed her back into the room.

The doctor, an older woman with white hair and startling blue eyes, smiled at John, then turned to Monica and said, "Give us a minute, okay? I just need him for a second, then you can come back in. Cool?"

"Sure." Monica looked once more at John, then left quietly.

"Sweet girl," the doctor said. "She's been here a lot."

"My best student."

"Your parents have been here, too. They were so exhausted that a couple of days ago I had to send them to a hotel, but they're being called. The hotel's just a few minutes away."

The nurse came around the side of the bed with a glass of water. He poked the straw into John's mouth, saying, "Slowly now. You've been intubated for the past several days, so your throat's going to be sore."

John sipped from the straw, shuddering as the glacial water cooled his parched throat. He was still sucking when the nurse pulled the straw away.

"How's that?" the doctor asked.

John nodded. "Better."

"I'm Doctor Barnes. I've been treating you since you were admitted last week."

That took John from the side. "Last week? You're kidding me."

Barnes sat down in the chair Monica had occupied before, leaned back, and crossed her legs. "Things were pretty touch and go there for a while, John. How much do you remember of what happened?"

John thought for a moment before he spoke. "Kyra Metheny." His voice was a dry croak; he felt like he could drink a gallon of water and still want more.

Barnes nodded; her hands were folded neatly on one knee. "That's right. Do you remember what happened while you were with Kyra?"

"The last thing I remember is taking her hand. We were waiting for the ambulance to get there, and I knew she probably wouldn't be able to feel anything...I knew she was dying, but I just thought that maybe if I held her hand...God, that poor girl."

"So you don't remember what happened after—" Barnes paused for a moment, then said, "Well, *after?*"

"No, nothing. What are you talking about?"

Dr. Barnes stood up, came to John and rested her hand on his shoulder. "John, what I'm going to tell you is going to come as a shock, so I want you to prepare yourself, all right?"

John nodded, but found that he did not want to hear what she was going to say.

"Kyra Metheny did *not* die that afternoon. In fact," Barnes paused to smile and shrug, "she's been back at school the last two days."

Chapter 3

Amelia Island, Florida

Rose was cutting it close.

A few minutes after five A.M., and the sky over the Atlantic was streaked with orange and pink. Soon the visions would start, and not long after that... Best not to think about after that. Just get inside.

Dangerous, Rose thought. *Stupid.*

After making a cursory examination of the house from afar to make sure there were no cars in the driveway or lights in the windows, she entered through the basement door.

It had taken her hours and hours of wandering along the beach to find the empty vacation home, but she'd known that sooner or later she'd find one that suited her purposes; she always did.

The key, true to the custom of rich people the world over, had been secreted away beneath a terra cotta flower pot on the deck in back of the house, and there was no alarm system in place to defend against would-be burglars. Not that Rose was a burglar; far from it.

She was just another animal looking for a warm place to sleep.

Rose had no idea how many houses she'd turned into temporary dens, as she would this one. Dozens? At least. Hundreds? Maybe.

Once or twice she'd had owners come home on her, but her luck had remained amazingly constant over the years. The owners of this particular house, she knew, weren't due home for several weeks. On a desk calendar in the study upstairs, a month and a half was marked off in red pen: HAWAII—DOGS AT KENNEL THROUGH APRIL 28.

There was always the chance one of their children would come home from college—from financial documents on the desk in the study, she knew there was a son at Kenyon, a daughter at Haverford—but these kinds of kids didn't come home for Spring Break. They went to Cabo or the Caribbean. Barring something completely unexpected, Rose thought she was secure here for the time being.

Closing the door behind her, Rose pulled the queen-sized box spring in front of it, blocking the only window in this room of the basement. She crossed the gray cement floor to the mattress she'd dragged down from one of the bedrooms in the empty house above and collapsed unceremoniously onto her makeshift bed.

The mattress was covered with a multi-colored patchwork quilt, one of the few items Rose traveled with. Years ago, she had taken it from a foster home, but she could no longer remember which one. There had been so many. She pulled the blanket over herself, exhausted from her night. It wasn't cool enough for the blanket, but it always made her feel better to be under it.

Rose felt herself begin to slip away. In minutes, she would be asleep, or what passed for sleep, anyway.

But not yet.

Even now, worn down to the point of emotional and mental numbness, Rose saw the baby.

The baby.

Girl or boy? It was impossible for Rose to tell. She'd only started seeing it a couple of weeks ago, at around the same time the visions had started and the dreams had intensified. The child was olive-skinned, like Rose, and crowned with a head of fine blond hair. Its eyes were a brilliant blue, intelligent, aware. Its arms held out to her.

She wanted to hold the child, to cradle it to her body, to inhale its smell.

Seeing the infant behind her closed eyelids, Rose curled into a fetal tuck and imagined the baby nestled against her cheek, the soft wind of its breath against her hair…

When she fell asleep, she was smiling.

* * *

By eight-thirty that evening, Rose was back out again. She'd slept fitfully the past several days, her normally undisturbed rest sullied by the goddamned dreams, and her head still ached, even though she'd woken more than an hour ago.

She'd always had strange dreams, but there had never been pain before. That had started with the dream about the dead girl on the street, eight or ten nights ago, and the pain had been the worst on that night, but even as it faded, it continued, and that concerned Rose.

She had no idea where the dreams came from, but they wore her out and made her feel threatened and *disgusted* in a way she didn't understand. Seeing the girl lying in the street, her head crushed in, taking her pale hand, and then the burst of warmth. The last thing in the world she wanted to do after one of the dreams was go out, but her need left her no choice. And the need was bad tonight. Already, she could feel the hunger working in her guts, in her brain, making her weak. Making her vulnerable.

As a general rule, Rose traveled light. Whatever material items she accrued during her tenure in a certain place, she left behind when she decided it was time to move. It kept her from getting too comfortable in any one location, reminded her of what she was: a nomad. A Bedouin traveling the American wasteland.

Tonight, she'd scrounged around in the small pile near her bed and picked out a pair of tight-fitting blue jeans and a simple brown and maroon peasant blouse. On her feet she wore thong sandals.

She'd lifted the entire outfit from a Wal-Mart in Jacksonville, along with razors for her legs, deodorant, and several pairs of underwear. It was a routine she'd repeated who knew how many times as she traveled up and down the east coast, through the Midwest, down into the southern states.

Even without the benefit of a mirror, she knew she looked good in the clothes. Her body was lean and tight, her skin tanned and flawless. She never worried much about what she wore, just made sure to leave as little as possible to the imagination. The peasant blouse fulfilled that function perfectly, allowing what she knew was a generous view of her cleavage.

She wore no make-up, but she never did. Her features were more striking when left alone. Her eyes were dark, her hair a lustrous black, as were her fine eyebrows, which arched inquisitively and narrowed to sharp points near her temples. Another reason Rose rarely looked in the mirror was that doing so always shocked her.

She looked so little like what she actually was. Recently, she even found herself avoiding windows in which she might see her reflection.

Like so many things in her life, she didn't know why she despised seeing herself, but the compulsion to avoid her reflection was undeniable and strong. As with the visions of the baby, it worried her, not only because this newfound discomfort threatened to disrupt her normal pattern, but also because it meant that inside of her, in whatever passed for her soul, something had changed, and that change was an affront.

Growing accustomed to a way of life like hers was no easy task; doing so required nothing less than the sacrifice of one's morality, of one's very humanity. But she had done so, because she had no choice, and although some of the things she'd had to do in the intervening years had made her sick with guilt, she had done what she had to do. It was, she figured, a pre-condition of her survival to act in ways that would drive a normal man or woman mad in hours.

It took her about twenty minutes to walk from the beach house to The Birdcage, a high-class strip joint just over the bridge to the mainland. As she approached, she saw that even though it was still early, business was hopping.

The large lot was almost full, and not with broken-down jalopies and the rusty pick-ups owned by the Mexican migrant orange-pickers. Instead, the cars parked outside The Birdcage were BMWs, Mercedes, and Jags. Rich husbands from the Island getting away from wifey for a few hours of fun with their fellow deviants.

Encouraging, but no guarantee, as Rose had learned the night before when she'd prowled the crowd until even the after-hours bunch had shuffled off to bed. Still, it was a new night. Anything was possible. More than that, she needed something to happen tonight. If it didn't she was going to be in some serious trouble.

Standing at the edge of the parking lot beneath a flickering arc-sodium lamp, Rose held her arm up in front of her face and looked at the underside of her forearm. The veins were a little too prominent, a little too dark. In twelve hours, a day at the outside, they would be nearly black. Then her vision would start to grow hazy, as if cataracts had suddenly spread over both of her corneas. Her strength would wane, and then the bleeding would begin, from the mouth, nose, ears, other places. These were symptoms not unlike those a severely hypertrophic person might experience—she'd researched the symptoms on the internet and had even tried taking blood pressure medications, but they only helped for an hour or two—but even that stage would only last a few hours. Soon after, she would be too weak to do more than pull herself along on her belly like a broke-back snake. She'd been that bad only once, but once had been enough. Tonight, she would get what she needed. One way or another.

As she was approaching the front entrance, the doors suddenly banged open and two enormous bouncers in black muscle shirts carried a flailing man out of the club and dropped him on the concrete.

One of the bouncers—the guy looked like a refugee from some late '80s Schwarzenegger flick—glared down at the leather-clad man, who was covering his head as if he was afraid of being hit or kicked. Which seemed a reasonable fear, considering.

"You even try to come back in here, you'll spend the next week picking your teeth out of the toilet." The bouncer didn't wait for a reply, just trailed his partner back inside. Techno music blared out of the club when the door opened, then died down to bass-heavy thumps as the door swung shut.

Rose stepped back as the man, who was dressed in black leather pants and a black silk shirt and black motorcycle boots, climbed to his feet. He tottered as he stood, and Rose knew he had been drinking heavily.

He wasn't terrible looking, like an aging Jim Morrison with shorter hair. Jim Morrison meets Wall Street. Brown hair and eyes, a couple days' worth of stubble on his face, which was smoothly skinned if too tan. He was the kind of guy who liked to cultivate tough when he went out, but who rubbed Neutrogena moisturizer on his face before bed each night, and maybe a dab of Pond's under-eye lotion to get rid of all that pesky pouching.

Maybe, Rose thought.

The man turned and saw Rose staring.

She watched as something stupid, maybe *what the fuck are you looking at*, or *why don't you take a picture* or something equally brilliant came to his mouth, and then she watched him take her in and wonder, *wait a minute, do I have a chance here?* Finally, he said, "Funny, huh?"

Rose put on her most sympathetic face, pooching her lower lip. "Are you okay? That looked like it hurt."

The man mumbled something she couldn't really hear over the heavy bass from inside, though she made out the words "faggots" and "pussies."

She nodded and tried to look interested, which must have worked because the guy smiled and stepped closer.

"Hey, you know what?" Rose said and put her hand on his arm. "I'm not really in the mood for this place. Do you want to go for a ride or something?"

He was drunk and stupid but not brain dead. His eyes narrowed suspiciously and he said, "I'm not in the market, baby." He started to push past her, but Rose kept her hand on his arm.

"I'm just looking for a good time," she said, looking him directly in the eye, "and I'm not going to find anything better in there." She nodded toward the club. "I'm going home with someone, one way or the other. It can be you if you want, but it's your call."

She watched him fight and lose a two-second battle with himself. "Let's go," he said.

Rose smiled. "Good."

They walked to his car, a black Infinity, and got in. Ten minutes later, maybe five miles from the club, the guy pulled the car onto the side of the road and turned to Rose. His face was flushed and fatter than she'd originally thought. The flesh of his cheeks and neck quivered as he spoke.

"Look," he said, obviously flustered, "I gotta tell you something. We can't go to my place. My wife and kids—"

Rose slipped a hand around the back of his head and ran her fingers through his hair. He was sweaty and oily, and Rose felt her stomach turn over with revulsion. Touching this creep was like fondling an undercooked slice of bacon.

"Oh, Christ," he said, and whatever small fragment of nobility had been trying to assert itself inside his head was bumped aside by lust. "Can we just—you know, here, in the car? I have rubbers." He looked to Rose like a little boy who had just asked mommy for a popsicle.

"Sure," she said. "Come here." She licked her bottom lip.

He leaned in to kiss her, but when he was close enough, Rose dropped her mouth to his neck and, with one snakelike motion, tore it open.

The man screamed and flailed out at Rose, but she was stronger and faster and with one hand slammed his head into the driver's side window. The glass cracked in a web-like pattern and bulged out slightly but held. The same couldn't be said for the flabby man, who slumped unconscious in his seat, bleeding from his neck and, now, from his head as well.

Rose spat out the hunk of skin and flesh from her mouth. His skin was greasy and salty and Rose thought the idiot probably hadn't showered for two days. Another trait he shared with Jim Morrison. But she dipped her head back into the hollow of his neck and drank, at first tasting only the sweat and ordure from the man's neck. But then, as always, the blood pumping into her mouth began to do its work, and Rose felt the warming, euphoric heat emanating from her stomach, spreading to her limbs, to her brain, to her groin, bringing her a sense of unspeakable relief. She pulled away from the man and wiped her mouth and waited for the world to come back into focus.

Leaning back in her seat, head tilted to the side, she watched as blood seeped from the man's ruined neck. At first it came in sluggish gluts, but after a few seconds those died down into dribbles. Soon the flow ceased altogether and Rose knew he was dead.

She got out of the car and walked around to his side, opened the door, and dragged the corpse out onto the side of the road. In his wallet, she found a hundred dollars in twenties. Not bad. She shucked the platinum-plated Rolex from his wrist and plucked a diamond-studded wedding band from his pocket. He wore a gold chain around his neck, and Rose took that, too, dropping all of the valuables into her shoulder bag. In a week or a month, whenever she was far away from here and out of the range of the local authorities, she'd pawn the jewelry. She kicked the man's body down the embankment into a soggy drainage ditch, then turned toward the car.

The driver's side seat was a mess. Smeared blood glistened on the black leather, and Rose saw that small ponds had formed in the seams, an especially deep pool in the spot where the man's significant weight had pressed the leather down into a reservoir. There was no way she'd be able to clean it up. Not quickly, anyway.

"Shit," Rose said. She'd hoped to get some mileage out of the car, but looking like this…if she got pulled over, she'd have to kill the cop. Even if she managed to get most of the blood off the seat, she wouldn't get it all, and if there was one thing she'd learned about blood over the years, the stuff *smelled*. Not much at first—just a little tang of fresh copper in the air—but within a couple of hours, when the blood started to turn…it would be like riding in the back of a garbage truck.

Beneath the driver's side seat, a pistol. Rose was no pro with firearms, but she'd seen enough to recognize this one: a Smith and Wesson .32.

"Look at this," she said. "Naughty, naughty." She flipped open the cylinder and saw that the pistol was loaded. After checking to make sure that the safety was engaged, she tucked the gun away in the bag, too, secreting it away underneath everything else.

She used a rag from the trunk of the car to wipe the remaining blood from her mouth and chin.

Five minutes later she was a quarter-mile away, whistling to herself as she walked along the shoulder of the highway in the direction of the beach house.

Chapter 4

Suzie Clusky gave John a ride home from the hospital ten days after he'd been admitted. In actuality, he had been cleared to leave the hospital before that, but what should have been a happy moment turned into a nightmare.

John had said goodbye to his parents before they left for the airport. His mother cried as she kissed him on both cheeks, and his father had done everything but pinch himself to stop his own tears from coming. It was one of the small points of light in the ordeal since Kyra's accident, that he had been able to spend an extended period of time with his parents; stuck in the room as he was, they'd had little to do but talk, and John felt closer to them than he had in years. He'd as much as decided that he would take the rest of the year off from work and head back up to Pennsylvania, maybe work on the farm for a few months, get his feet back under him.

Several times during their stay, his parents had tried to get him out of bed, out of the room, but from the television coverage, John knew the scene outside the door was the last thing in the world he needed to see.

This was another reason the rolling country of West Chester County drew at John so powerfully; the idea of the news media invading quaint Kennett Square was ludicrous, impossible to imagine. Now, it looked like John might be forced to go to just those lengths to avoid the tabloids and television reporters.

Two days after she had been run down in the street, Kyra Metheny had gone on a daytime talk show. John was still unconscious at this point, so he'd been unreachable for comment, but that was okay; the host had brought not only Kyra but also several members of her physics class, the kids who had seen the accident and the aftermath, onto the stage, and over tears and Kyra's repeated avowals that she had been saved by an angel, John's legend was immediately cemented.

Flipping through the channels of the TV in his room, John had seen clips of the interview replayed on several recap shows. He had stopped and watched each time, not because he wanted to hear one more word about what had happened that day, but because of what he saw before him: Kyra Metheny, alive and talking. He searched her head, her posture, for any sign of the grievous injuries she had sustained in the accident, but there was nothing. She was the same girl, the same Kyra he'd taught each day in ninth grade, the same Kyra he'd watched with half-attention as she flipped and tumbled during halftimes at Denton basketball games.

It made no sense. As many ways as he tried to explain it to himself, he couldn't get his mind around what had happened. He replayed what he could remember. Clarence Drake bursting into the lounge, covered in blood; rushing out to the street; the electricity in the air; and then Kyra's shattered body, half in and half out of the street, her only remaining eye rolling up to look at him... These things, he knew, were *real*. He knew that because someone—he had no idea who, but if he ever found out, he would be hard pressed to hold his temper in check—had clicked several photos of Kyra's prone form with a high-grade camera phone. The pictures weren't professional quality, by any means, but John could make out the details just fine.

So what had happened? It was the question that plagued John, and the one he did everything he could do to avoid answering. So far, he had turned down interviews with reporters from the Charlotte *Observer*, the New York *Times*, the Boston *Globe*, and the Philadelphia *Inquirer*. His mother also told him there had been phone calls from several talk shows and from *Good Morning*

America. It was surreal. Surreal and stupid and something he wouldn't be able to sidestep for much longer.

That morning, John was propped up in his bed reading Donna Tartt's *The Secret History,* a novel he'd loved since he was a kid, when the door opened to admit a fifty-ish woman dressed in blue surgical scrubs that didn't even come close to fitting her nearly skeletal frame. Her hair was tied back into a gray-streaked ponytail, and her face was heavily lined with wrinkles. John had become familiar with most of the staff in this part of the hospital and didn't recognize her.

Dr. Barnes had told him that security had been beefed up after the news stories had run last week, and that it would be all but impossible for anyone to sneak into the hospital, but the imbalance in her deeply recessed eyes spoke for itself.

He dropped the book and patted his hand along the bed until he found his panic-button and clicked it, then looked back up just in time to see the woman lock the door behind her and lean back against it, her arms braced against the wood as if waiting for someone to slam into it from behind. John hadn't seen it at first, but there was a smear of blood on the back of her right hand, and another on the bottom hem of her scrub top. It looked fresh.

She's a patient here, he realized. *Not from the outside at all.* She'd seen his picture on the TV the same as everyone else, heard the reporters when they named the hospital.

"What do you want?" John said, trying to keep his voice confident and assertive. It was a ridiculous question, but he had to say something. He kept his eyes on the woman but tried to recall what was on his bedside tray. Books, a pen, a glass of orange juice. Nothing that could help him here.

The woman stepped into the room, toward the bed, eyes locked on John. "I need your help," she said. "Help me."

"I can't do anything for you," he said.

A nurse's face appeared in the small window on John's door. Over the woman's shoulder he saw the nurse, a pretty girl named Becky, try to push the door open then realize it was locked. She found John's eyes with her own and held up a finger. *One second.* Then she was gone and John was alone again.

The woman was closer now, halfway across the room, holding out her hand. "I saw your picture on TV. They said that if you touch someone, they won't be sick anymore. Touch me," she said. "Touch me and make me better. I don't want to die."

John pushed himself as far away from the woman as he could. The railing on the bed was up, but he reached down and lowered it. "I can't help you," John said. "None of what you've heard is true. It was all made up." He was shaking, and when he lowered one leg and then the other down to the cold tiled floor, his muscles trembled from fear and lack of use.

"That's not true!" the woman screamed. She had reached the bed and now it was all that stood between her and John. She put her hands down and left a bloody smear on the white sheet.

John backed into the wall. "Please," he said. "Just go away. I can't do anything for you."

There was a rattling from the door and John saw a uniformed cop through the window. *They have a key,* he thought. *They have to have a key. Just buy another couple of seconds.*

"The police are outside," John said. "Stop this. You're only getting yourself in trouble."

The woman had come all the way around the bed and stood mere feet away from him now, close enough for John to see her bloodshot eyes. There was a stench radiating off of her, something like rancid body odor crossed with ozone. *This is the way crazy smells,* John thought.

His right hand, which had been flat against the wall, encountered something metal, and it took a minute for him to realize what it was. His walker. The first couple of days he'd been up and around, they'd wanted him to use it, just to make sure he didn't hurt himself. He grabbed it now in both hands and held the aluminum contraption up in front of him, pointing the rubber-capped feet at the woman.

"I don't want to hurt you," John said. "Stay back."

Just as he finished speaking, the door opened and the woman turned to look as the cop entered the room, followed closely by Becky and two other nurses. The cop stepped forward and the nurses clustered behind him in the doorway.

"Ma'am, don't move," the cop said. He was a young kid, no older than twenty-five, but big through the shoulders. Slowly, he drew his gun, but held it pointed at the ground. John silently counted his blessings that the young cop seemed completely uninterested in using his gun in the line of duty. Through the cop's eyes, John saw what the young man was seeing: a sick woman not in control of herself—not someone to be feared, only to be pitied. He was thinking, *this could be my mother.* John could almost hear those words running through the young cop's mind. "Stay still."

There was a brief moment where John thought it might end there, with no real incident to speak of. The woman looked from the cop back to John, and he could see the tears in her eyes, and the fear, the primal and mind-dissolving fear. "I'll be dead in a month," she whispered, then lunged toward John. He held the walker out to ward her off and felt a jolt as one of the feet connected with bone, a rib or her clavicle. She grabbed the bars of the walker and tried to jerk it out of John's hands; her strength was shocking. He stumbled as his feet got tangled, then went to the ground with a grunt, elbows and knees banging hard on the floor, the bars of the walker slipping from his hands.

For one vivid second, John saw her loom over him, arms stretched out, fingers reaching, but then the cop engulfed her in a bear-hug from behind and lifted her emaciated frame off the ground and carried her from the room. John could hear her screaming incoherently as the cop hauled her down the corridor.

John climbed to his feet, his knees scraped and burning from the fall, and Becky stepped forward to help him back to bed. "In a second," he said, holding up his hand. "I don't think I'm ready to lie back down right now. What the hell was that all about?"

Becky bent to pick up the walker and said, "She hit a nurse over the head with a cane in the oncology unit and took her scrubs."

"Is the nurse—"

Waving a hand, Becky said, "She'll be fine. Scalp laceration and a mild concussion, nothing that won't fix itself in a week."

That explained the blood. "What's wrong with her?"

She set the walker back against the wall, then stopped and looked at John for a moment before answering. "Late-stage lung cancer. What she said about dying in a month, well, she'll be lucky to make it a week. It's hard to believe she had the strength to get all the way up here."

John nodded. "She seemed pretty strong to me."

A few items from John's bedside tray had been knocked to the floor, and now Becky stooped to pick them up. She set his book back on the tray, then noticed the blood on the sheet where the crazy woman had rested her hand. "Is that yours?"

"No."

"I'll get someone to come and change those. You know—" Becky had been walking toward the door, but now stopped and turned back.

"What?" John said.

"If what they're saying about you is true, that you can heal people—" John started to say something, but Becky held up her hand. "Hey, all I mean to say is that if it's true, and if you've been kept here for so long to protect you from people who want your help, it's just...funny. That might not be the right word, but keeping you locked in a hospital, where all the really sick people are, it's just the dumbest thing I've ever heard."

John laughed. "That never occurred to me. Where were you three days ago? I could have used that logic."

Becky pulled the door open. "Minding my business, like a good little nurse. Don't tell anyone I said that, okay. Just get out of here as soon as you can. When the news gets hold of this, it's going to happen again."

"Yeah," John said. "Tomorrow. First thing. Thank you, Becky."

John sat down in the cushioned chair near the window. Outside, the day was bright, the sky a crystalline blue, the trees below a vivid, eye-popping green. John suddenly wanted very much to be back out in the world, but now had to wonder whether it was a world that would ever allow him to be who he had been.

* * *

During the drive with Suzie from the hospital back to his apartment, John's sense of unreality was only amplified. Though he had known Suzie for three years, he felt as though he was riding with a stranger. She was jumpy and quiet and John couldn't really blame her. Their exit from the hospital had been a circus; the hospital's entrance was thronged with reporters. To avoid them, Suzie picked John up in the hospital's parking garage. Even so, there were dozens of flashes inches from the windows as they exited the multi-level deck. As they made the turn onto Hawthorne Avenue, several vans and at least two reporters on motorcycles had given chase. When Suzie stopped at traffic lights, the vans would pull up beside them, sometimes even in the lanes for oncoming traffic, and well-coifed men and women would hang out of the vehicles, tapping on John's window with the ends of microphones. It was only a piece of swift thinking on Suzie's part that got them free. Without signaling, she took a sharp left across traffic into the parking garage of a shopping complex that boasted signs for Target, Marshalls, and Circuit City. Never slowing to see if she had lost their pursuers, she wove in and out of rows of parked cars and then took the ramp down to the lowest level of the structure. Quickly, she backed into a space and killed the engine.

"Down," she said to John, and they both slumped in their seats. A few moments later, a lone news van, this one with Channel 6 News tattooed in a rainbow of colors across its side, hurried by, and then nothing.

John glanced over at Suzie, hardly aware that he'd been holding his breath. "Jesus," he whispered. "Nice driving, Dale." They both broke into a fit of giggles and when Suzie was able, she pulled cautiously out of the parking spot and navigated her way out of the parking garage.

Soon, they were driving in total anonymity along Pecan Avenue, headed north toward John's apartment complex.

"You okay?" Suzie said, glancing over at him.

"Sure," John said. "I appreciate you picking me up."

Suzie smiled. "This might be my one chance at celebrity. You never know. Maybe my photo will even be in the *Observer*."

"Next to a caption that reads, 'Barron and Mystery Woman Sneak out Back Door of Presbyterian Hospital.' Jesus, I hope all this dies down soon."

"It will," Suzie said. "I give it a week more, tops. Then there'll be some natural disaster or we'll stick our noses into another war and it'll be 'goodbye, John Barron, hello new…whatever.'"

"You're probably right." John rubbed his temples softly, trying to soothe the low-level headache that had never truly left since the day he woke in the hospital. Doctor Barnes had told him that the headaches probably would have abated more quickly—they had been terrible at first, real meat-grinders that turned his vision red and wreaked havoc on his equilibrium—but there was an issue with the quality of sleep he'd been getting at the hospital. When she'd told him that, John had laughed.

Barnes told him that whatever was upsetting his sleep was so powerful that none of the usual dream-inhibiting drugs had been effective in stopping it. No matter what they gave him, his brainwaves were unaltered. In fact, Barnes said, his brainwaves didn't come anywhere close to resembling the typical pattern of a human in dream-state.

Normally, when a person is dreaming, Barnes had said, the majority of the brain enters a phase of relative inactivity—a state of rest that allowed the brain to recharge. The only part of the brain where activity would actually *increase* was a tiny area called the limbic system, the area also credited with controlling emotion.

Only in John's case, this wasn't happening. Instead, when John was asleep, his brain appeared to be fully awake, at least for long stretches of time. There was no REM that might signify entry into deep sleep, no deviation of his alpha or beta waves that would signal relaxation or excitement in disparate zones of John's mind. Although his eyes were closed and John appeared, for all intents and purposes, to be sleeping, the routine brain-scans he had undergone while hospitalized showed him to be wide awake. More than wide awake, really. The firing in John's brain actually intensified during the nighttime hours, as if he were being asked to process immense amounts of raw information.

And the strangest part, Barnes said, was that it had become nearly impossible to wake him up once he'd fallen into this seemingly fallacious sleep state. From dusk until dawn, John was all but unresponsive, except, of course, for his periodic attempts to sleepwalk. Those the staff had impeded with straps, confining John to the bed.

Amazing, Barnes had said. A new type of sleep disorder. If it could indeed be called a "sleep" disorder at all.

Swell.

"Hey," Suzie said, jolting John from his thoughts. "Did it really happen like they said on the news? She just came in and locked the door? That must have been scary as hell."

"It was," John said, then paused. "But I understand where she was coming from. She's dying, and she thought I could help her."

"Could you have?" Suzie asked and sneaked a look over at him.

"Are you asking me if I'm really a 'healer'?" John made quotes with his fingers. "If I could have touched her and made her cancer vanish? Just, poof, you're healed, go get an ice cream cone?" John heard the edge in his voice and tried to hold it down.

"Yeah, I guess."

"No," John said and looked back out his window. "I don't know exactly what happened at school that day, but it had to be some kind of mass delusion. Someone saw Kyra get hit by a car and reacted hysterically, then everyone else kept stepping it up until we were all seeing something that just wasn't there."

"There were those pictures."

"Photoshop," John said. "I bet they came in hours after the accident. Some asshole cheating a couple bucks out of some magazine. Whatever."

"That wasn't just some asshole," Suzie said. "It was Jerry Soames. He's been driving a new Jetta to school the past few days."

John grunted. "Jerry Soames. Figures, the prick. Still, if anyone would be good with Photoshop, it would be that little perv."

Suzie nodded and kept her eyes on the road. After a moment, she said, "When that woman came into your room yesterday, why didn't you just touch her and prove that it was all bullshit, then?"

John could think of a dozen things to say in response—that he'd felt attacked, cornered like a wounded animal trying to protect itself; that in spite of himself, he'd been disturbed, even disgusted by the woman; that if the cop hadn't grabbed her, he *would* have done what she wanted—but instead he let the silence stretch out. The truth was that, in the very first moment he had seen the crazy woman come into his room, John had known that whatever else happened, he *must not* allow her to touch him, that doing so would kill him, without question. Where that imperative had come from, he didn't know, but he couldn't deny that he had felt it. He had no answer he wanted to offer, and so he chose instead to say nothing.

They parked in front of John's apartment building. His car was there, which meant someone had driven it here from school.

Suzie saw him looking and said, "I hope you don't mind. We thought it would make things easier for you."

"It's great," John said, feeling absurdly touched that he'd been thought of in such a considerate way. "Thanks." They grabbed John's few belongings, mostly t-shirts and underwear his mother had purchased for him at Target, and headed up to his floor.

In front of his door stood five or six reporters with their cameramen in tow. When the first saw John, he tossed aside the cigarette he'd been smoking and closed fast. "Hey, John," he said, the others now falling in behind him. "Want to make a comment, get your side of the story out there? I work for CBS, man. You know what that means? *Big money*. Whaddayasay, partner?"

John pushed through the crowd, pulling Suzie along behind him. He could hear the reporters' tones changing from quiet faux-respect to out and out irritation. John was an America and

Americans loved money and being on TV. They couldn't understand why he didn't want those things.

John felt his irritation growing and knew that if he didn't get away from them soon, he'd say something he might regret. Somehow, he managed to get his key into the lock and then he and Suzie were inside, the reporters just a smattering of muted voices outside the door. John leaned against the wall and exhaled.

"Well, this place has really gone to shit, hasn't it?" Suzie said as she glanced around the stale-smelling apartment.

A thin light shone in through the drawn curtains and revealed a fine layer of dust on the coffee table in the living room and on the bookshelves along the wall. It looked like no one had lived in the apartment in months, not ten days. John tried to remember the last time he'd cleaned and couldn't recall.

"I wasn't expecting company," he said. "I think *you* might have been the last person I had in here."

She looked at him with an eyebrow raised. "Are you serious? All this time and you've never been with anyone else?"

John shook his head and dropped his bag in the living room. "Nope. Not much the ladies' man, I guess."

Suzie looked at him for so long he began to feel uncomfortable.

"What?" he said.

She shrugged. "Nothing. I guess I just always figured you were full of crap, you know? That you just wanted to get rid of me because something better had come along."

"No," John said quietly. "I meant what I told you." Three years ago, John had broken off a six-month relationship with Suzie. He'd had two relationships in his life, two that meant anything to him, anyway, and both had ended the same way— one day, he just knew it had been too long, that he was putting someone he cared about in a bad situation, and that things had to end. The sensation wasn't unlike the one he got while home in Pennsylvania with his parents, a tingling, nagging feeling that if he didn't move, leave, jump, *whatever*, things would get ugly and people—people he genuinely *loved*—would get hurt.

And had he loved Suzie? In a way. She was perhaps the kindest and most selfless woman he'd ever known, always the first to offer help, a ride, anything that might make another person's life easier. When John had arrived at Denton, he had come off a string of moves and was hoping to settle down, at least for a couple of years, in a single place. He had just been *tired*. His relationship with Suzie had taken shape organically, growing out of long talks in the teacher's lounge and over lunch in his room. There had been dinners and movies and long, leisurely breakfasts eaten in bed, the crossword spread between them. Then Suzie raised the idea that they move in together. Within days, John had broken up with her, not cruelly, but firmly. He counted himself unbelievably fortunate that Suzie had chosen to stay in his life; he wouldn't have blamed her if she'd never wanted to talk to him again, but after a brief cooling off period, she'd begun talking to him once more, understanding, perhaps, that what he had done was not his choice at all.

"Are you going to be okay here?" Suzie said. Her concern sounded sincere, and John wondered what he'd done to deserve it. Regardless, he appreciated it.

"I'll be fine," he said, thinking: *will I? Because I don't think so. I don't think so at all.*

"Okay, then," Suzie said. She hugged John tightly, pecked his cheek, and then headed for the door. "I'm glad you're okay. Call if you need anything." She slipped out and had closed the door before he could respond.

* * *

John went around the place with a can of Pledge and a rag, dusting, straightening. Though he was tired, his legs shaky with the lack of use over the last week and a half, he even managed to vacuum before collapsing on the futon.

Twenty minutes later, he realized that he'd been staring at one point on the wall, seeing nothing.

He got up and walked outside to the mailboxes. There was nothing in his box but a handwritten note that said: *Your mail is being held in the clubhouse.* As he turned to head in that direction, a voice called out, "Hey, John, how 'bout a couple of words?" He looked toward the gate separating the complex from Harris Boulevard and saw five or six reporters with cameramen in tow. He dropped his head and picked up his pace.

The woman at the desk in the clubhouse did a double-take when John walked in. He'd seen her a dozen times before and didn't know why she'd react so strangely. He handed her the note that had been in his box. She plucked the note from his fingers, making sure her fingers never came within inches of his.

"I think you have some mail for me," he said.

Without a word, she went into the back room of the office and returned with an orange plastic milk carton full of haphazardly jutting envelopes.

John was dumbstruck. "You're not serious," he said.

The woman nodded, her eyebrows raised archly. "Hold on. There's more." She walked once more into the back room and this time returned with an actual Postal Service sack, USPS stamped in fading letters on the side. This too she set on the desk and then sat back down and looked pointedly away from John.

"Thanks," John said. He slung the bag's strap over his shoulder and hefted the milk crate, then left. He could feel the woman's eyes boring into his back as he walked out. The twinge in his belly blossomed into a full-blown ache.

Back in the apartment, John cleared off the coffee table in the living room and sat down on the futon with the mail and a Diet Coke from the fridge. He chose an envelope at random from the crate, tore it open, and pulled out the yellow legal-sized sheet.

Mr. Barron,

Only you can help my little girl. She has cystic fibrosis and will die unless you heal her. Will you help her? Please call (761) 555-4585 and ask for Bob or Ellen. God bless you.

Bob and Ellen Greenburger

John put the sheet down and opened the next envelope.

John, kill yourself before it is too late. You are a devel and need to die. Buy a gun or hang yourself from a rope. It's the right thing to do. If I dont read about you dieing in a week, I'll come to your house do the job myself.

There was no signature on the second note, only a mark that John thought was a plus-sign at first. Only several minutes later did he realize, *not a plus-sign, dummy. A cross.* The go-to signature of the Holy Crusader, especially when the Holy Crusader in question seemed hard pressed to spell one of every two words correctly.

For the next two hours, John worked his way through the letters; they broke down into two general categories. *Help-me/help-this-or-that-person,* or *kill yourself,* with the "help me"s jumping out to a sizeable two-to-one lead.

By the time he reached the last envelope, John felt dirty and guilty, though he didn't know why. He'd prepared himself for the eventuality that something like this could happen, but had never really believed that it would. Not like this.

He turned the final envelope over in his hands and read the front. The script was neat, the postage mark from Kennett Square. That stopped him. Then he saw the name of the person who'd sent it. Constance Pelham. His fingers felt suddenly numb, and for a long time he just sat and stared at the envelope, wondering if his mind might be playing with him.

Chapter 5

Rose woke at seven-thirty in the evening and went upstairs to shower in the bathroom of the master suite.

As she climbed the stairs, she shook her head, trying to clear it of the scene she was seeing, the one she always woke to: a small, neat apartment. Moving around in it, making dinner, pouring a glass of red wine. She shook her head again. Goddamn if these fucking hallucinations weren't creepy. Mundane, even prosaic, but *creepy*, like being two people at once. But it was starting to fade now, thank God.

Like the rest of the beach house, the bathroom was garish, painted a shimmering gold, a gilded gold chandelier hanging from the vaulted ceiling, purple towels draped over the towel-bars. The shower itself was done in the Mediterranean style, open to the rest of the cavernous bathroom, no shower doors, floored with rough-hewn marble.

She turned the water on as hot as it would go and let the steam build up until the bathroom was tropical, the air nearly opaque. Then, her bare skin already beaded with perspiration, she turned the water down to a tolerable level of warmth and stepped into the shower.

The water sluiced over her shoulders and down over her breasts and stomach. She felt a river running down her back and between her buttocks, felt the hot water beating hard on the back of her neck, knew she'd be red there when she got out, reached behind herself and turned the dial further toward HOT.

She groaned with commingling pleasure and pain.

In front of her closed eyes, the baby. Beautiful. Rose smiled.

She took the child in her arms and held it to herself, felt the water running down between the baby's skin and her own, savored the heat of the infant's tiny body against her breast.

Its mouth found her nipple and the baby began to feed, making soft sounds. Rose cradled the tiny life in her arms and rocked gently back and forth, humming a song she'd heard in the car last night before she had—

Rose started from the episode and gasped.

The hot water had run out and freezing cold water flowed over her. She grappled frantically for the knob and shut the water off, snatched a purple towel from the towel-bar and wrapped it around herself, shivering.

* * *

Later, she walked along the shoulder of the road, her bag slung over one shoulder. Inside was the quilt, neatly folded, and a single change of clothes, purchased from a Wal-Mart with the money from the dead man's wallet.

Rose didn't know what she was doing, just knew that she had to *move*. It didn't feel right here anymore, though she didn't understand why. Always in the past she'd stayed as long as possible in one place; when you didn't know when someplace new to stay would come along, you stretched what you had as far as it would go. It was part of the loose code by which she'd lived so much of her life, a code that had allowed her to live as long as she had.

And that's why she knew what she should do now: head back to the beach house. But still, here she was, walking away from safe, reliable shelter. *Why?* This was stupid, reckless. She didn't do things like this, never had. But then, things had been changing recently, hadn't they?

For as long as she could remember, there had been an insistent, constant pulling deep inside of her, almost a yearning, as though she were magnetized in some abstract, unidentifiable way, *drawn* to something. Even as a girl, when she'd lived first at the orphanage and then at any number of foster homes, she had felt the pull, the urge to leave the place where she was and make her way out into the world. But if she was being honest with herself, it had always been more than that. The urge hadn't been simple wanderlust; it had been more pointed, more specific.

She could remember one time in particular, when she had been living with a nice family in the suburbs of Wilmington, Delaware, when the urge to bolt had been almost too strong to resist. A girl of only eight or nine at the time, she had come from school each day to the sprawling suburban home her foster parents owned, dropped her books in her room, and then made herself a snack in the well-stocked kitchen.

This was years before the changes going on inside of her had advanced to the point where she could no longer enjoy food. Back then, as a little girl, she loved the taste of peanut butter and jelly sandwiches, marshmallow fluff, grapes and oranges, apple juice. Living in the new foster home, it had become her ritual to arrive home, deposit her belongings in her room, and immediately make something to eat and devour it at the kitchen counter.

Until one day, when she never got out of her bedroom.

Putting it back together in her mind later on, Rose imagined that the fugue—if that's what it was—took her just after she dropped her books on her bed, since they were there, neatly stacked, when she finally got around to homework that evening. Instead of heading downstairs for her snack, however, she had felt drawn to the window, not to anything in particular, not to something she had seen or heard, but to something she *felt* deep inside of her body. Or rather, to something she very pointedly *did not feel*. It had been as if a part of her was missing—had *always* been missing—and was calling out to her to come find it, to unite with it.

This was a sensation with which she had become familiar over the months and years of her childhood, but in the past the killing—whether of a stray cat or dog or even, once, a homeless man in a local park—had always held it at bay. This time, however, the feeling had been stronger, more potent, totally enthralling.

Hours later, her legs and back aching with a dry, throbbing heat, she had come back to herself standing slightly bent, forehead pressed against the glass of the window, eyes unfocused, staring not at anything in the front lawn or in the street, but at something far beyond. The incident had scared her, but not in any way that would have stayed with her if it had been an isolated event. It wasn't.

As the days went by, Rose found herself drawn to the windows in her room, and at school. When her foster mother took her on trips to the supermarket, she would wake from a trance when the car jolted to a stop, forehead firmly pressed to the car window, head aching from the vibration of the car's engine through the glass.

Gradually, she took to sitting outside on the front porch of the house since the ache—and if it hadn't been a physical ache at first, it grew into one quickly—abated the slightest bit when she stepped out of the house, as if whatever it was that had captivated her was rewarding her for even this miniscule progress toward it.

It was at this same time that the need to kill had also advanced from a compulsion to an obsession. Where once she had been a child—a *dark* child, certainly, one who needed to keep secret her forays into the back alleys and woods—she began to recognize within herself an essential difference from everyone else around her. And this was when the need to run, to move, move, move had truly set upon her, and it had never gone away.

A car swished by on the highway, stirring a brief dust storm. Rose squinted her eyes and covered them with a hand, coughing a little as the dust got in her throat. *This life,* she thought. *This goddamned life.* There had to be more than this, didn't there? Had to be something else, something new, something better. Even the simple techniques she'd developed in order to keep herself alive were failing her now, and that was somehow the ultimate insult.

Always, she had been able to resist the force tugging at her, to moderate its effect. When she began to feel out of control of her own urges, especially the urge to move, she had killed and fed, and for a while the urge abated somewhat. That had changed now. If the pull before had felt like a fisherman reeling her in with a spin-caster, this time it felt like she was being yanked forward by a chain affixed to a bulldozer.

Deep inside, she knew that there was a link between her unease, the impulse to up and leave, and the things she'd been seeing lately. The baby. The visions just before she fell asleep and after she awoke. They were tied together somehow, had to be. As a creature that had lived the lion's share of its adult life on the road, Rose knew the value of instinct, intuition. She also knew the danger of trusting it too much. Now, she needed to find the middle road between what she felt, the need to move, and what she *thought*, that leaving when she still had a place to stay for several weeks was a mistake. The compromise, she'd decided: head north, stop at the first place that looked safe, take no chances, then reevaluate.

It felt right. But it felt stupid, too. Rose wanted to slap herself, to climb out of her body and scream at herself. It wasn't just that she was leaving a safe place, a shelter, it was what her leaving represented. For the first time in her life that she could remember, she didn't trust herself.

Behind her now, the sound of an approaching car. Rose turned and saw headlights coming, raised a hand and waved. The car passed by, and Rose kept walking.

She caught a ride half an hour later with Big Bob Bartok, a fixture salesman out of Jacksonville, on his way up to Atlanta. He seemed glad for the company, smiled toothily at Rose, looking over at her frequently as if to reassure himself that she was really there. Rose needed the ride, so she played along, smiling back, talking when he stopped. When he said something funny, she touched his leg just above the knee and giggled. The next time she touched his leg, she saw the bulge in his crotch and sighed inwardly. *Men.*

They got into Atlanta at around three in the morning, and there was an awkward silence when the salesman pulled his Subaru Outback into the hotel where he was staying. He turned the car off and coughed nervously.

"Don't worry," Rose said, putting her hand back on his knee, firmly now, giving a slight squeeze, raising an eyebrow. "I don't bite."

*　*　*

She spent the next day sleeping in the hotel room. Twice during the day she woke from her sleep but felt so miserable that she couldn't force herself to rise. She had never liked the day, didn't feel *safe* during the day, but recently that sensation of insecurity had blossomed into something much more intense, a potent feeling of dread mixed with something she couldn't quite define but which she understood on a deeper, intuitive level. The closest she could get to putting the feeling into words was that she felt incomplete during the day, out of place. It was as if she was going through the accelerated final stages of a change that had been lingering half-completed for most of her life. Finally and inarguably—and, she felt, irrevocably—she was becoming a creature of the night.

A knock woke her. She looked at the clock on the bedside table. 7:22 PM.

"What?" she called, rolling over and bumping into the cold hunk of flesh that Bob Bartok had become. After killing Bob the night before, she had showered and slipped into a white terry-cloth bathrobe hanging in the bathroom. She stood now and cinched the belt more tightly around her waist.

"You staying another night?" A man's voice, sounding unhappy. *Shit*, Rose thought with some alarm, Bartok had paid just for the one night. As far as the desk was concerned, they'd missed the checkout time by half a day.

"No," Rose called, sitting up. "Give us ten minutes."

"Five," the man rumbled, "and only because Bob's a regular. I should charge you for another night anyway."

"Fine," Rose said, "five."

There was grumbling from beyond the door, but Rose heard footsteps leaving. She stood, dressed quickly, and looked at the corpulent salesman lying on the bed, still dressed in his jeans, flannel shirt, and cowboy boots. The side of his neck was a bloody crater. What was she going to do with him?

"Shit," she said. She needed to delay their finding him and calling the police for long enough to get out of the immediate area. Looking around, she weighed her options.

Underneath the bed was out. It was one of those modern ones with the drawers built in underneath. No space. Bathroom?

Rose went into the bathroom. There was a small closet that housed a miniature water heater, but there was no way beefy Bob was fitting in there. Bathtub? She tossed that one out immediately. That would give her, what, two minutes? Not nearly enough time to be sure of eluding detection. Something else...

Walking back into the bedroom, wringing her hands, she saw the window and walked over to it, parted the curtains and looked out.

The third-floor room Bob had rented backed on a line of trees. Beyond them, Rose could see the twinkling lights of the highway and McDonalds' golden arches. But below was dark.

Rose slid the window open and popped the screen out, dropped it, waited for someone to yell up, "Hey, fuckin' watch it!" or something equally charming. No one did.

Well, okay, she thought.

Bob was heavy, but Rose was strong as five men Bob's size. She wrapped him in the bloody sheets from the bed and dragged him to the window, heaved him up to the sill where he lay face down, half-in and half-out. Praying that there was nobody staying in the ground floor room directly below, she took the toes of his boots in her hands. She was about to give him the heave-ho when something suddenly occurred to her.

Aware that she was pushing it time-wise, Rose quickly patted the man down, found his keys in his front jeans pocket, his wallet in his back pocket. *Almost blew that one,* she thought.

She lifted Bob's feet and he went quietly out the window. There was a bat-wing flapping from the sheets as he fell and then a whoofing thump when he hit the grass below, but that was all. No screaming, no yelling. She heard the crunching of leaves and knew he had rolled into the underbrush.

Counting her blessings, Rose flipped the mattress upside down so the bloodstains were hidden and then slipped quietly out of the room and down the back stairs.

* * *

As the sun was just beginning to brighten the eastern horizon, Rose prowled a quiet suburban neighborhood. Finding a safe place to bed-down was always more difficult in the city, and if she didn't find somewhere soon, she'd end up wandering around, half-addled with the day, just trying not to get hit by a bus.

Ah, here.

The back door of a brick apartment building was wedged open with a book. She entered the building and followed the stairs to the basement.

She glanced around. Not much in the way of cover. Washers and dryers on one side, storage on the other. Rose headed over to the storage area, a ten-by-twenty rectangle sealed off by a chain-link fence. The padlock hanging off the clasp was open.

Rose opened the gate, stepped in, closed it after herself. She found a spot out of sight behind a row of high-piled boxes and lay down, wrapped in the patchwork quilt, the bag of clothes her pillow.

Ten minutes later she was asleep.

Chapter 6

Sitting outside Dr. Barnes's office, waiting for the first of what was bound to be dozens of check-ups, John worried the edges of the folded sheet of paper he held in both hands. He hadn't spoken to Connie Pelham in ten years, and he'd gradually come to the conclusion that he would never see her or hear from her again. And now this. He assumed that Connie had sent the letter to his parents' house and that they'd forwarded it to him—not having spoken to her in so long, she would have no idea how to reach him directly.

Connie's letter had been short, barely one full page in her neat cursive script. Seeing her writing was nearly as bad as getting the letter in the first place, and John's mind was flooded with the feel of her, the way she looked and smelled and sounded. Sitting on his lousy futon in his lousy apartment, John had felt an alternate future grab hold of him, one where he had stayed in Boston with the only woman he'd ever truly loved, married her, raised children with her... But that wasn't the way things had happened, of course. Instead, he had left her crying at an Amtrak station in south Boston, wondering why the one person who was supposed to love her more than anyone else was leaving her behind as if she'd been nothing more to him than a one night stand.

Sitting in the anteroom of Barnes's office, John unfolded the letter and read it again, his eyes skittering over text he had already memorized.

John,

I can't really believe I'm writing you this letter, not just because it has been so long since we've seen each other, but also because I feel...selfish for doing it. I saw on the news what happened to you, what you did for that girl who got hit by the car, and it was like some connection I'd been trying to make forever finally came together in my mind. Ever since I saw you on that newscast, I've been thinking about this a lot, you see. And what I've finally come to understand is that everything the newspapers and the talking heads on TV are saying about you, all of the hype about how you healed that girl, it's true.

If I know you, you're fighting this thing tooth and nail, rationalizing the whole thing in your head as some fluke, some mistake. Before you go too far down that road, please listen to what I have to say, and then to what I have to ask.

A couple of weeks after you and I started dating, my sister Lisa came to stay with me for a few days. Her making the trip up from New Jersey was a big deal, much bigger than I ever let on to you, because a few months earlier she had been diagnosed with ovarian cancer. She had been through all kinds of treatment for it — radiation, chemo, the works, and things were starting to look up a little bit. That was when she decided to come visit me at school. The day before she left home, she found out the cancer had metastasized, and my mom and dad wanted to keep her home. The doctors were giving her next to no chance to live. The cancer was just in too many of her organs. She insisted on coming to see me, though. It was only for a couple of days, she said, and she wanted to meet this guy I'd told her so much about. She would go to the hospital when she got back. All she wanted was to see me and have a day or two of peace before starting in on treatment again.

You never knew any of this, but do you remember meeting her? I think you do, and I think you remember winding up that night in the emergency room with the worst flu I'd ever seen. A flu that came out of nowhere, with no warning. I know my sister remembers it; we talked about it last night over coffee.

John, I need you to call me. I believe you saved my little sister that night. I need you to do something for me now. I know how all of this sounds, but I hope you'll hear me out before deciding I'm crazy.
   —Connie

Below her signature was a phone number. John folded the paper again and stuffed it into his pocket, his mind cloudy and reeling. It was all too much. For ten years, he'd kept his memories of Connie partitioned off in a room of his brain that may as well have had DO NOT OPEN: TOXIC stenciled across the door. Still, even as he'd gone about what had come to pass for his life, John knew that a part of him—the part of him that was both the best and, perhaps ironically, the weakest—had wanted to open that door and sort through those memories. Connie in denim cut-offs and a bikini top on the stony Maine beach at Ogunquit, where they'd spent a few passion-filled nights one summer; Connie nestled deep beneath the flannel sheets and down comforter on the bed they'd shared as soft snow drifted down onto the frozen Charles River outside; Connie sitting at the breakfast table in their tiny one-bedroom walkup, doing the crossword from the *Globe*. Connie...

John took a deep breath and let it out, trying to dismiss the sudden ache in his chest.

A few minutes later, the phone on Dr. Barnes's secretary's desk bleeped and she told John that Dr. Barnes was ready to see him. John stood and walked into her office, then shut the door gently behind him.

The office suited the woman. Like her, it was edgy and modern, emitting an air of confidence and self-knowledge, but not of cockiness. The walls were an institutional cream color, a fact Barnes had probably had little ability to alter, but the décor was warm. Facing the desk were two plush leather chairs—the kind of chair in which one would want to be sitting, John thought, when receiving difficult news. On the walls, a smattering of framed photographs, mostly of Barnes with a man and two college-aged kids John assumed were her children. A good looking family, all in all. Happy. Barnes's various diplomas were mounted on the wall, also, and John saw the names Johns Hopkins and UCLA.

Barnes was sitting behind her sleek black desk, a pile of folders half a foot high in front of her. She took one look at John and said, "What's wrong?"

"What?" John said, unprepared for the question.

"Your face." She gestured for John to sit down in one of the chairs across from her. "You look like someone crapped in your shoe."

"Wow, crapped in my shoe," John said. "There's one I haven't heard before. Thanks."

She smiled tightly. "So are you going to tell me?"

He regarded her thoughtfully for a moment. "It's kind of personal."

"You'd led me to believe you didn't have much of a personal life."

"I don't," John said. "It's from my misspent youth, when I *did* have a personal life. I was more fun then."

Barnes clapped her hands. "Well, enough of the chitchat. Let's get down to business."

John spread his hands. "What do you want to talk about?"

"Dreams," she said.

"What about them?"

"How long have you been having these dreams? Not the run-of-the-mill ones, the ones you described as 'night terrors,' but the real doozies."

John thought about the question. He'd always had bad dreams, but these ones...

"A month and a half," he said. "Maybe two. There have been times in my life before when they've gotten worse, but then something changes and they ease up."

"What changes? What makes them go away?"

"Easy," John said. "They go away when I move."

"Hence your colorful employment record."

"Hence that, yes."

Dr. Barnes sat back in her chair, fingers steepled. "Can you remember them?"

John nodded. "Almost always."

"Same dream, or different ones?"

"Different, but similar in ways. Why?"

Barnes shrugged and ran a hand through her short gray hair. They were sitting in her office, and she was obviously comfortable here, surrounded by her things. "This really isn't my area of expertise, but I know that recurring dreams can be a symptom of certain medical conditions."

"But not different dreams?"

"Like I said, I don't really know that much. If anything you say raises flags, I'm going to run it by a shrink I know, an expert. What happens in the dreams? A typical one."

John thought for a moment. "Killing. Very violent killing. Murder."

"Do the dreams *always* involve a murder?"

"No," John said, "sometimes—not often, but *sometimes*—the dreams are almost peaceful, but…lonely and sad. And even where there is no killing, there's always the feeling of underlying aggression, the feeling of a *need* to be out doing those things, to be out killing."

Barnes paused for a moment, then said, "Is it you committing these murders?"

He shook his head emphatically. "No, that's the strange thing. I know it's not me. But it feels like it is. And not like a dream at all, but like it's really happening."

"Do you ever recognize the victims?"

This question shocked John; he hadn't ever thought about it. *Could he even remember their faces? So many…*

"No," he said, "I'm pretty sure not. No."

"And this strange sleep pattern, your grogginess at night, it developed at around the same time as the dreams began?" The medical staff at the hospital had been mystified at finding John all but unresponsive during the nighttime hours. For John, this was nothing new; he'd been living according to this strange cycle for weeks, but he'd always figured it was something his body and mind were going through and that eventually it would remedy itself.

"Yes. One night a couple of months ago I stayed late at school, trying to get some grading done. I got something to eat at Burger King, and after I ate, I decided to take a walk down to the river behind the athletic fields. It wasn't quite dark yet, but the sun was going down, and the next thing I knew, I woke up from a horrible dream where I had ripped someone's throat open. When I tried to stand up to go to the bathroom, I realized that I wasn't in my bed at all, but lying on the grass, my head about a foot from the edge of the river. A few more inches and it would have been *syonara.*"

"And the same thing happened the next day?"

John nodded. "I was freaked out, so I stayed at home, watched some TV. I remember seeing the local news, and then it was suddenly six in the morning. Same thing has been happening ever since. It's not that I collapse at first dark or anything—I'm not Cinderella at the ball—but even when I can stay awake, I feel...I feel like half a person, like something inside of me is...missing."

"That must be very hard to live with."

John thought, *not really,* surprising himself. "It stops me from going to some of the late games at school," he said, "but other than that..."

A long pause, then, from Barnes, "Would you say it's fair to presume a link between your fatigue and these dreams, John?"

"That would seem to make sense."

She nodded. "And other than the dreams, can you think of anything...*unusual* that you've been feeling lately? Strange pains? Physical issues like nausea, dizziness?"

John started to respond, but then stopped himself, realizing he wasn't sure what he'd been about to say.

Barnes arched an eyebrow. "Yes?"

He chuckled softly. "Strangest damn thing. I hadn't really thought about it until now, but every once in a while I have these little...daydreams, I guess you'd call them. They're like flashes— nothing developed, just images, sensations."

"Of?"

"It varies. Streets, bars, rooms in houses. Whatever. For just a moment or two, it'll feel like I'm in two places at once."

"And you didn't think to mention this."

John shrugged. "My mother always told me I had an overactive imagination. To hear her tell it, I've been spinning crazy stories since I was a little kid."

Barnes paused to consider, then said, "Then do you mind if we talk again in a couple days? I want to do a little research, see what I can find out. Maybe I'll uncover something that'll help. If not, at least you'll have someone you can talk to about all of this."

"That would be good," John said. "I could use all the help I can get."

* * *

During his drive home, John thought about what had happened with Kyra Metheny. It was something, he'd discovered, that he was exceedingly loathe to do, and to date he hadn't allowed himself to get deeper into the memories than recalling individual smells, images, sounds. He remembered the look on the kids' faces, the glob of stuff on Clarence Drake's tie that had almost certainly been part of Kyra's brain, the sounds of squirrels scrabbling around in the trees above. But thinking about it all now, John found he truly had no recollection of the "event" itself, just of kneeling down beside the girl, taking her hand, and then, nothing. Until he'd woken up in the hospital. For better or worse, the rest just seemed to be missing.

John shook his head. This was impossible to think about rationally, especially with everything that had been in the papers.

Though John hadn't been conscious during the time most of the articles were printed, by now he'd seen them all. One of the many envelopes that continued to arrive in his box had been stuffed with them, maybe fifty, from papers all over the country. It had even been in the *New York Times*, though they had been wise enough to drop the story after the first couple of days. There were wars going on, after all; how silly did it look to a supposedly serious-minded audience to keep running stories about some purported healer in Charlotte, North Carolina? *The National*

Inquirer was another story, however. They continued to run stories whenever some new nugget of information reared its head.

Some of the headlines in the past couple of weeks: HEALER RELEASED FROM HOSPITAL; METHENY RETURNS TO SCHOOL, EARNS 'A' ON MATH TEST; JOHN BARRON: LEGIT OR PHONY? And his personal favorite: IS JOHN BARRON AN EXTRA TERRESTRIAL? Even through the shock and disgust, he'd been able to laugh at that one.

There had been so many phone calls at John's apartment in the last week that he'd changed the number, but they got the new one somehow and the calls started all over again. Finally, John simply unplugged the phone and reconnected it only when he had a call to make. If anyone he knew really needed to get in touch, they would find a way.

The letters, which continued to arrive in a barrage, he dropped into the orange milk crate, which he'd stowed away in his closet. He didn't have the heart to toss them, but neither did he want to have them lying around where they could eye him. Right now there was only one letter he had any interest in, and that was Connie's, not that her re-entrance into his life at this particular moment had come without its own load of guilt and — somewhere deep down where he didn't want to look too hard — a kind of anger.

Fuck, he thought, turning into his complex, *healer*. He laughed ruefully and pulled in to collect the mail.

* * *

Someone had been by to see him.

As John pulled open the screen door at his apartment, he saw the card stuck beneath the knocker. He pulled it free and looked at it. There was just one word, neatly handwritten.

Call

Beneath that was a phone number with a 704 area code. Local.

"Right," John muttered, tucking the card into his pants pocket. "Let me get right on that."

*   *   *

He was preparing for bed after a dinner of Raisin Bran and toast when he found the card in his pocket. Wearing pajama bottoms and a tee-shirt, he plugged the phone in, then took the handset and a glass of red wine outside onto the patio.

The sun was sinking down into the tall pines to the west, and John felt a sudden, poignant longing for the night sky. God, how long had it been since he'd seen the stars? Since he'd really sat out and *looked* at the stars?

A flare of anger bloomed in his chest as he punched in the number on the card. The other line was picked up after one ring.

"Hello?" A woman's voice, groggy and a little slurred, like she'd been sleeping.

"You were at my apartment today," John said, a wave of emotion rising inside him. Yes, *this* was why he'd called. A reasonable voice inside him said to cool his jets, this wasn't *him*, but he ignored it. "What do you want? To tell me that I should cut my wrists? Maybe put a shotgun in my mouth? Drink a glass of Drain-o?"

"God, no," the woman said, waking up now.

"Well, what then?" John was shouting now, knew he should stop before one of his neighbors started wondering what was going on. "Do you want me to make your fucking doggy feel better? Does Junior have diaper rash?"

"I want to help you understand." Calm, placating, as if expecting these hysterics. That just pissed John off even more.

"Under-*fucking*-stand *what*? That I'm some kind of *witch doctor*?"

"Do you want to know what I have to say or not?"

"Not!" John yelled. "And never call me or so much as come within a mile of where I live again or I—"

Click.

Feeling ridiculously satisfied and still riding the crest of his outburst, John threw back the rest of the wine in his glass and went inside to get ready for bed.

Chapter 7

Rose prowled the nighttime streets of Atlanta, her bag slung casually over one shoulder. She'd broken into an apartment on the second floor of the building where she'd slept and had taken a shower and changed her clothes, so she felt fresh and clean. Her nerve endings were raw and active, picking impressions up from the very air.

God, she felt *good*. Despite her previous reservations about leaving the beach house in Florida, Rose couldn't deny the sensations of pleasure singing in her blood. Here she was, a predator, following her predator's instincts, moving according to impulses being relayed to her from some source even she couldn't fully understand. And why did she *need* to understand? Always before, she'd been well served by her hunches. Doubting them had been nothing more than simple fear of the unknown and, as always, it was a fear she'd confronted and conquered.

All around her, people milled on the streets, talking and laughing, going in and out of shops and bars and restaurants.

Rose found a bench in a grassy park and sat for a while, watching. It was a warm night, but there was a cool breeze blowing from the east. In her knee-length muslin skirt and tank-top, Rose felt wonderfully bare and unrestricted.

The park was well lit and clean. A group of young men and women kicked a soccer ball around on one side, and on the other, several couples and families sat on the grass or on blankets.

Someone had brought a radio along, and the Counting Crows played softly behind the sounds of voices.

A young couple walked by Rose hand-in-hand. The guy whispered something to the girl and she laughed and slapped him lightly on the arm. He said something else and she stopped him, put her arms around his waist, kissed him, and then laughed again.

In Rose's stomach, something tightened. She stood up and walked on.

*   *   *

After another fifteen minutes of looking, Rose found what she wanted, a chintzy bar and grill called Frederick's. It was lit up like a Christmas tree and boasted a spacious deck with a bar of its own.

Rose sat at the bar and ordered a beer. She sat drinking it, waiting for a fish to bite.

As always, one did.

He was a nice guy named Mike Clover. Not the kind of man who typically came onto her in places like this. She looked at his left hand and saw no ring, no tell-tale tan line. She finished her beer and he bought her another, and after maybe half an hour, Rose found herself utterly unable to look away from his face.

He was maybe thirty and tan, but not that fake n' bake tan so many yuppies went for now. His eyes were deep brown, the skin crinkled at the edges from smiling or from some grief that didn't come through otherwise in the way he carried himself. His hair was brown, too, though a bit of gray had just begun to salt his sideburns. In all, Rose found him gorgeous and caught herself staring more than once at his eyes, which seemed to suck her in.

Once, he caught her staring and laughed. "Are you all right?" he asked.

Flushing, Rose looked down at her hands, then back up, a smile on her own face. "I'm fine," she said. "Just...I don't know."

"You looked *lost* there for a second."

"Lost? Maybe..."

"Is something wrong?"

Rose thought for a moment. How best to handle this? Normally, she'd just play the part and edge her way out. Then again, normally she'd never found herself so infatuated with a man, especially one she'd only just met. She wanted something from this man, but what? She had to say something; he was starting to look worried. *God, what was she going to say?*

"Not wrong," she said, or rather heard herself saying, "just strange. Really, I don't know—I just think you're beautiful."

Inside of her head, she screamed and felt her face turning red. She looked down.

Silence for a second, then he said, "Wow, thanks. That's a new one for me. Beautiful, eh?"

Rose's face felt like it had been doused with lighter fluid and set on fire. She put her hands up to cover it. "Oh my God," she said, "I'm sorry. I didn't mean to say that out loud. "

He was laughing, not in a mean way, but embarrassed almost. He said, "Well, don't apologize. You just made my year."

Rose took her hands away from her face and ventured a glance at him. He was grinning, and when he saw her looking, he raised an eyebrow, then licked a finger and touched his chest with it.

"Tsss," he sizzled at her. "On fire."

"You're laughing at me?"

He leaned closer and shook his head. "No. Well, maybe just a little. But for what it's worth, I think you're beautiful, too."

* * *

When they finished their beers, Mike asked Rose if she wanted to take a walk and she said yes.

It was the deep of night now, and as they made their way along the crowded streets, Rose found herself falling into a place she didn't understand, but which she welcomed. Talking with Mike about his job, his life, was...pleasant. It felt good and natural. She wished she could stop time and keep this feeling forever.

"Where are you from?" Mike asked, looking over at her. He'd lit a cigarette and took a pull from it. He smoked like a man who loved to smoke, but who almost always denied himself the pleasure.

Rose held up a hand and said, "Mind?"

As he passed her the cigarette, his hand brushed hers and she felt a shiver throughout her entire body. Her skin felt hot and cold all at once. She took a drag and decided to be as truthful as was possible.

"Here and there," she said, handing the cigarette back. "I was in Florida for a while, but there was nothing for me there."

"But originally?"

She shook her head. "I don't know." It was the truth. "I was orphaned and lived with a bunch of different families when I was young. New Mexico for a while, then Pennsylvania for a while, then I think a couple of foster families in New Jersey. When I fourteen I ran away and I've been moving around ever since. Never one place for very long."

He'd stopped and was looking at her. "So are you living here now, or just passing through?"

What to say? "I'm not sure. But I never am."

He started walking again and she fell back in beside him.

"What do you do?" he asked after a while. "I mean, for work?"

There was no good answer to this. Rose had never worked in her life, except at staying alive. "You know, this and that. Restaurants, bars. That kind of thing."

He nodded, dropped the cigarette on the street, crushed it out. "Want to sit for a while?"

Rose hadn't been completely aware of her surroundings for some time now, and when she looked around, she saw the same park where she'd sat earlier on. "Sure," she said.

They sat down on the same bench, close, but not touching. Rose turned toward Mike and drew one of her legs up, tucked it beneath her, laid her arm atop the bench-back.

An enormously powerful feeling was building inside of her. She wanted to be close to this man, to touch him, to feel his strong arms around her, his breath in her hair. She wanted to smell him and put her hands on his body. She ached between her legs and suddenly, more than anything, wanted to have him inside of her. She shivered as a flush of heat went through her, a flush that found its center at her sex.

"Cold?" Mike asked.

"No," Rose said, then, "well, maybe a bit."

He looked down at his shirt and said, "I'd offer you my coat, but—"

"Then come here."

Mike scooted over until he was touching Rose, put his arm around her.

"That's nice." Rose said. She leaned her head against his shoulder and smelled a mild cologne mixed with deodorant and something else that excited her. The smell of a man. Rose exhaled and felt her body relaxing.

She looked out at the park.

The soccer players were gone, but a few of the families remained, parked on their blankets beneath the lights.

Rose leaned back and tilted her head up toward Mike.

He was looking down at her, a slightly bemused expression on his face. "Are you about to kiss me?" he said.

She ran her fingers gently through his hair and brought him closer.

Chapter 8

A lot of bad had come out of the Kyra Metheny situation, but John's new relationship with Iris Barnes was anything but. When he arrived at her office a little after lunch, Barnes's secretary showed him right in and, after asking if he'd like coffee, hurried off to fix a cup.

As before, Barnes sat behind her desk, John in a comfortable chair across from her. Beyond that small nod to formality, though, talking to Barnes was as easy and pleasant as chatting with an old friend, only one who had something he badly needed: information.

"So, what did you find out?" John said. "About my dreams."

Barnes nodded. "Yes, let's talk about those." She gestured at a couple of books stacked on her black desk and said, "I've done a little reading—no hardcore research, so there may very well be facts and theories I know nothing about—but what it all boils down to is that...no one has the slightest damned idea what dreams are. I guess I'd heard that before, that there was no one good theory that explained everything, but Jesus, there are *thousands*. It's amazing. If you read Freud, he'll tell you that dreams are a safe place for your subconscious and repressed desires to come out, that your dreams are actually trying to *tell* you something about what's going on inside of you. But that's just one theory. There's also the idea that dreams— the things that happen in them, the people in them, everything—are representative of the dreamer. These people would say that, if you're having a dream about a fight with your best friend, it's got nothing to do with that friend, it's just that something inside of you is in conflict.

Both you and your friend represent components of *you* at war with one another. It's interesting."

John nodded slowly. "So what does it mean, then, when your dreams are all about killing?"

"I thought about that," Barnes said, leaning back in her chair. "If you listen to the second camp, the 'components-of-yourself' people, let's call them, your dreams could stand for an unarticulated need, something you don't even know you're feeling, to kill— metaphorically speaking, of course—something within yourself, for the need to eliminate a *part* of you."

"It's hard to argue with that," John said. "Who really likes everything about themselves? I mean, shit, I'd love to kill the slob part of myself, or the lazy part of myself, but that seems like a pretty insignificant reason for these dreams. And plus, their duration... I've been having these things in one way or another since I was just a kid. I wasn't stupid when I was nine, not by a long shot, but I don't think I was advanced enough to generate those kinds of thoughts about internal conflict. You know?"

Barnes was nodding now. "That's what stopped me, too." She leaned forward and put her elbows on the desk, drummed her fingers for a moment on the leather blotter. "You're an only child," Barnes said abruptly. "Correct?"

The tangent took John by surprise. "Yeah. My mother couldn't have kids after me. Why?"

Barnes looked at him almost apologetically. "It's going to sound a little crazy," she said, "but the *only* thing I found that bore the slightest resemblance to your case was a chapter on twins I found in this book." She tapped a thin tome with a finger. The spine read *Dream Theory*.

"It resembles my case how?"

"Basically word-for-word. Well, minus the murder angle, of course. We've all heard the stories about twins separated at birth who still somehow shop at the same stores, eat the same brands of cereal, marry women with the same first names. This guy just talks about the dream component. He has documented cases where twins separated by hundreds and even thousands of miles have been able to describe the furniture and objects in their sibling's homes."

"Because they saw the other house in their dreams," John said quietly.

Barnes nodded, one eyebrow raised.

"Okay," John said, pushing forward, resting his elbows on his knees. "Let's take this one and run with it for a sec. If we take—" he looked down at the spine of the book Barnes had indicated "—Martin Harris's theory and project it onto my situation, what we're basically saying is that, A, I have a twin I know nothing about, and B, said twin is a serial murderer." He paused for a moment, then added, "And a precocious one at that, to be scaring the shit out of me since we were kids." He looked at Barnes.

She smiled. "Hey, I said it *sounded* like your case. That's all, smart guy."

John grinned ruefully. "I know you're trying to help," he said. "I'm just tired of trying to figure out—"

"How it all ties together," Barnes finished for him.

"I'm wondering how I can get back to my life. Back to teaching, going out at night, not worrying about whether I'm going to turn into a vegetable at the stroke of seven PM."

"So you don't think the whole thing with Kyra Metheny is related?" Barnes sat back and appraised him, head slightly tilted.

John blew air out. "That's complicated."

"Why?"

"If all of this other stuff—the dreams, etcetera—had started *after* the thing with Kyra, whatever that really was, sure, I'd say it's all probably related, but that's not the way it is. It's not like this is all the result of what happened that day, some kind of psychological repercussion, trauma, whatever. The dreams were around twenty-five years before I even met Kyra."

Barnes thought for a second, apparently weighing whether or not to say what she wanted to. "There's something you're not saying. Why don't you just say it and get it out there."

John laughed because she was right. "What if I don't want to?"

She shrugged again. "Your choice. But I'm not going to say it for you, and we can't go any further with this until it's been said. Looks like we're stuck." She pursed her lips and looked around casually, glanced down at her wrist, tapped a watch that wasn't there, hummed a few bars. John watched, thinking, *why not?*

"Fine," he said, feigning annoyance, and Barnes grinned. "All of this can't be related because that would mean…it would signal some kind of…"

"Look at you," she said softly, "afraid to even say it. Tisk tisk."

"I'm not afraid of anything. I just don't know how to put it."

"Then just say it. Don't worry about how it sounds. No one here but us birds."

John closed his eyes. "If all of these things were interrelated, it would mean that the dreams and my trouble sleeping were somehow...*anticipatory* of the thing with Kyra, some kind of build-up to what happened that day. But I don't even know what happened that day."

"What do you think happened?" Barnes asked, her voice low but insistent.

"I don't know. Not what people have been saying, anyway."

"You didn't heal her?"

John made a harsh, ugly sound that he barely recognized as a laugh. "*Heal* her? Christ, listen to how ridiculous that sounds! As if that's even possible."

"You don't believe in that sort of thing? In miracles?"

"No."

"You say that as if you have some stake in it. You're not religious?"

"This isn't about religion."

"What's it about?"

"Nothing. I don't know."

"Obviously, you do. You said 'this' isn't about religion, which implies that there is a 'this' and that it's about something besides religion. Semantics, John."

John put his hands to his head and squeezed, said, "Oh God, my brain's going to explode. You should have been a shrink."

Barnes chuckled, then said, "Just think about it, okay. There are places you're not letting yourself go, for whatever reason. Why not? When you come up with some answers, we can talk about them and compare notes."

"Man, and here I thought we were just going to talk about my dreams."

"Jeez, John, what do you think we've been doing?"

* * *

John glanced in his rearview mirror again.

Ever since leaving Barnes's office fifteen minutes ago, he'd felt as though he were being watched, the hairs standing up on his arms and on the back of his neck. As he made the turn into the complex, however, he'd looked around and seen no one suspicious-looking.

But the feeling of paranoia still hadn't subsided completely, and he couldn't stop searching the sea of cars and pedestrians for...for what? Nothing back there but cars, and none that looked particularly threatening. Of course, what *would* make a car look threatening? Fangs on the grill? A bloodstain on the windshield?

Still, he felt it.

* * *

Back in his apartment, John sorted through his mail. The flow of pleas and threats was already tapering off somewhat; today there were only seven or eight, a drop in the bucket when compared to the hundred or so he'd received every day for the first week. He opened them all and scanned through. A child dying in Indiana, a wife sick in Arkansas, another wife who'd lost an arm in a factory accident, her husband wanting John to help her "re-grow it." John grunted at that one and re-read it just to make sure he'd read it correctly the first time.

And a brown envelope with a Charlotte postmark.

John tore it open and pulled out the single sheet of paper inside.

It read: I KNOW WHAT YOU ARE. IF YOU WANT TO KNOW, CALL ME.

There was no phone number, but it only took John a second to understand.

"Son of a bitch," he said, and walked into the kitchen, dug though the odds-and-ends drawer, pulled forth the card he'd found stuck beneath his knocker yesterday. He grabbed the phone and dialed the number, waited impatiently as it rang.

Nobody answered, but a machine picked up after seven or eight rings. John almost hit the TALK button on his phone to hang up, but instead he listened as a woman's voice, recognizably the same voice he'd yelled at, said, "You've reached Doug and Mary Ann Shaw. No one's in to take the call right now, but leave a message and one of us'll call you back." There was a long beep and John hung up before it ended.

He was still frustrated and angry, but at least he had a name now. That created a certain type of equity, didn't it?

Mary Ann Shaw.

* * *

That evening, after a dinner of fish sticks and rice, John poured a glass of wine and called Connie. As the phone rang, he opened the sliding door and walked out onto his porch. The air smelled clean, and a soft breeze played rustling music in the treetops. The phone rang half a dozen times and then Connie picked up and said hello. The sound of her voice froze him and it took a moment to recover.

"It's me," he said. "John."

"I wasn't sure you would call," Connie said, her voice low, as if trying not to wake someone in the room with her. "Thank you."

"Of course," John said. "Things have been a little hectic or I'd have called sooner." A question that hadn't occurred to him earlier now popped into his head and he said, "Where are you?"

There was a prolonged pause. "You mean you don't know?"

"Why would I know?"

"I thought your parents might have told you," she said. "I've been staying with your mom and dad the last two weeks."

What the hell?

"Alright," he said slowly. "We're going to have to take a step back for a second. *Why* exactly have you been staying with my parents? They never said anything about this. They never even told me they'd talked to you."

"I begged your mom not to tell you, but I thought she would anyway. I know how close you two are. I told her that I would tell you, but that it had to be the right time. Don't be mad at her, John. She never felt right about it, but I told her I'd be in touch with you soon, and that it would all come out then. I got here just a day or two after your parents left for Charlotte, when you were in the hospital. We needed a place and they were nice enough to say yes."

John sat down on a plastic chair and stared out over the lush green thicket of trees between him and the highway. "So, why? The last I heard, you lived in north Jersey. You were working in New York, I think."

"That was a long time ago," she said. "Almost ten years now. I got married a couple of years after college and moved to Ohio. And then, when I got divorced, I moved back to Boston. That's where I've been ever since. Well, until now."

"What's this all about?" John said.

Connie was silent, as if bracing herself. "I have a daughter," she said. "Her name is Katie, and she's eight. She...she's sick, John. Very sick. We've been through every treatment option in the past two years. It's been hard on her. A couple of months ago I ran out of money and couldn't pay the mortgage on our house anymore. The bank finally kicked us out last month and we've been moving around since then. Until we got here."

"I'm sorry," John said. "What's wrong with your daughter?"

"You got my letter, obviously," Connie said. "Well, it's our family thing. Cancer. Not ovarian, though. Katie's cancer is in her bones."

John didn't know what to say that could possibly mean anything. "What's the treatment?"

There was the soft sound of a restrained sob on the other end of the line, then Connie said, "At this point, nothing. If the radiation and chemo were going to kill it, they would have by now. Her doctors all agree on that. And it makes her so sick, John. If she is going to—to *die*," John could hear her forcing herself to say the word, "then I don't want her last days or weeks to be spent that way."

"And so it's down to me," John murmured.

John half-expected Connie to equivocate, to plead innocent to the charge he had just leveled, but instead she simply said, "Yes."

John closed his eyes. A significant portion of him wanted to hang up, to click the phone off and disconnect it from the wall, maybe throw it in the trash for good measure. This wasn't his fight, after all. Even if he did have some power, some ability to heal with a touch, what right did this woman, this woman he hadn't seen in a decade, have to ask him to sacrifice himself for her—not even for her, for her *child*? Wasn't his life difficult enough? Hadn't he paid his dues already?

For thirty-odd years, his life had been a rushed frenzy in the service of nothing. He moved from place to place, making few friends and fewer lovers, staying only as long as his paranoia would allow him to. In the beginning it had been hard, but he'd learned to live with his problems, he had learned rules. And yes, he knew this existence wasn't a fully realized one, knew that there was a world he was missing, but that could not be helped. Giving in to his desires for love and stability could only harm others, could only hurt those around him, as he had hurt Connie all those years ago.

So yes, there was that part of him. The rest of him, however, knew that part was bullshit. On the other end of the phone line was the woman he had loved—the woman he *still* loved and always would, if he was being honest with himself—and she was asking him for help. He could say no to her. The simple act of saying the word was nothing; he had become so adept at turning his emotions off that he frequently scared himself with his dispassionate refusals of comradeship and affection. The only people he allowed himself to love fully were his mother and father, and he couldn't even bring himself to visit them for fear of placing them in some kind of danger he didn't even understand. Look what he had done to Suzie, a beautiful and caring woman who had only wanted to know him better.

Sometimes, he barely recognized himself as human anymore.

So was he going to tell this woman he loved that no, he wasn't going to try to save her daughter?

"I'll come," he said and he heard Connie inhale sharply. "I'll be there as soon as I can—a couple of days, tops. There are a few things I need to do before I leave."

Connie was crying now, no longer able to hold the tears back, and the hope he heard in her voice twisted in his gut like a rusty knife. "Thank you so much, John. So, so much."

"As long as you understand that—"

"I know," she said, and he could hear her trying to get herself under control again. "I won't get my hopes up. Not too much anyway. What I said in that letter, John…it's the truth. I really do believe you saved my sister's life, and the same part of me knows you can do that for Katie, too. I don't know if it will work, but I feel that it *could* work. That's—well, that's everything to us right now."

"We'll see," John said quietly. "Either way, I'll see you soon. Will you do me a favor and tell my mom and dad I'm coming home?" As an afterthought, he added, "And can you tell my mom I'm not upset with her? For not telling me you were staying there? I know she was just trying to do…the right thing."

"Of course," she said. Then, "Thank you, John."

And then she was gone.

Chapter 9

Rose needed to shop.

She found a mall not too far away by looking in a tattered phone book in a phone booth at a gas station; she called for their hours then hitched a ride with a couple of college kids. They let her off at the main entrance of the mall and powered off in their pickup, music blaring.

The night before had been unlike any experience in Rose's life. From the park, she and Mike had walked the three blocks to his spacious loft apartment. The building was a mixed-use structure, and from below there was the sound of late-night drinkers reveling at a hip wine bar.

Standing at the window, Rose had shivered gently as Mike approached her from behind and stroked her, then wrapped his arms around her, his hands warm and strong on her stomach, her hips, her breasts. He kissed the back of her neck and then she was helpless. She turned and found his mouth with her own, driving her body against his with an urgency she hadn't felt in her life.

The lovemaking was gentle and when it ended, Rose lay on her back, breathing deeply, the skin of Mike's arm warm—nearly hot— on her belly. The second time had been more urgent, exhausting, and hours later, Rose had found herself wanting to wake Mike for another go. Instead, reclaiming herself to some measure, she crept quietly from his bed, showered and dressed.

As she sat down on the edge of the bed to pull on her shoes, Mike stirred and then woke. They made plans to meet for dinner the next night, and then Rose left, hurrying to beat the rapidly approaching dawn. She'd spent the morning and afternoon sleeping in her makeshift den from the day before, and when she'd woken up to the evening, she set off looking for somewhere to shop.

There was an information kiosk just inside the doors of the day-glow shopping mall, and Rose stood there for a minute, looking at an absurdly colorful map of the two-story structure.

She had a pretty good idea of what she wanted, but she didn't want to spend any more time in the mall than she absolutely needed to. Being around this many people in a confined space made her nervous. Too much opportunity for something to go wrong, especially considering her reason for being here.

Her first stop was The Gap, where she purchased a pair of black cotton panties and a matching bra using the cash she'd stolen from Big Bob Bartok's wallet. When the clerk started to put her buys into a small bag, Rose stopped her and said that she had a lot of shopping to do, could she have a big bag? The clerk smiled and dropped the undergarments into a larger blue bag with GAP printed in white on the sides. Rose thanked the girl and left.

Next, she visited the Saks Fifth Avenue on the second level and walked around for a while, checking out the security situation. Not very tight.

There was a crimson silk dress she liked on a mannequin, and after covertly slipping one in her size into the Gap bag, she took another of the dresses, this one several sizes too big, and asked a pimply-faced female clerk where the dressing rooms were.

When she was done trying the dress on, she gave it back to the clerk, shaking her head disappointedly.

"Must have dropped a size or two," she said to the teenage girl, who smiled and then tried to push the sale.

"Do you want me to get you a smaller one?"

"That's okay," Rose answered. "It looked funny anyway. My boobs were on display." The young girl laughed.

There was a brief moment of anxiety as she was leaving the store when she realized there might be a security mechanism attached to the dress somewhere. But no alarms went off.

Ten minutes later she walked out of Rack Room Shoes wearing a pair of comfortable black leather medium-heeled sandals, her old ones stashed beneath the dress in the bag.

On her way out the mall door, she looked at the black marble clock mounted over the entrance. 8:06 PM.

Plenty of time, she thought.

* * *

She walked to another gas station near the mall and went into the ladies room and locked the door.

Alone, she shucked off her clothes and put on the new underwear and the dress, which fit, but not as well as she had hoped. The spaghetti straps were too long, and even when she adjusted them, the dress hung low, exposing the top of the black bra. She'd been kidding when she told the young clerk in Saks that the dress made a show of her tits, but *shit,* she thought. Chalk it up to karma.

"Hell," she said. "Just hell."

Reluctantly, she reached behind herself and unhooked the bra, slipped the straps down one arm, then the other, then looked at herself in the mirror.

Better, she thought, but kind of trashy. Her nipples pushed against the silk and were entirely too noticeable. This was *not* the impression she'd wanted to make, not after last night. Mike probably already thought she was a slut...

Goddamnit.

* * *

Mike Clover was waiting for her at the bar when she arrived at the restaurant.

He looked fantastic, dressed in crisp tan slacks and a dark blue shirt open at the throat. He hadn't shaved that morning, and a day's worth of growth darkened his cheeks. He was looking at the door when she walked in, and his unselfconscious smile when he caught sight of her made Rose flush.

She was in uncharted territory with all of this. Never in her life had she felt attracted to a man the way she felt drawn to Mike. All day, the strangest thoughts had been going through her head, not only sexual—though there were certainly some of *those*—but other things, too. Things she'd seen in magazines and on television, things that she'd read about in books, but that she had never been confronted with herself. Suddenly she was thinking about how she looked, not because she was worried about her effectiveness as a predator, but because she wanted...wanted what? His approval? Maybe. His acceptance? That this new ground was not only unfamiliar but inherently dangerous occurred to her, but as she'd been doing for the past two days, she pushed the thought from her mind.

Be careful, said the part of her that regulated her survival-drive. *Just be careful, Rose.*

Shut the fuck up, the new part of her countered. *I'm tired of being careful.*

"Wow, is it nice to see you again," he said, standing to greet her. Then he stood back and looked at her again, slowly, feet-to-face, and said, "On second thought, I'd like to amend my prior remark: it's very nice to see you again. You look perfect."

"Thanks," Rose said, proud of herself just for getting the word out. What was *wrong* with her? She wanted to feel angry with herself for being so irrational about Mike, but another part of her, this new and increasingly more powerful part, demanded that she go with it. Her thoughts felt fuzzy, unfocused, a feeling she recognized, but that seemed out of place here for some reason.

The hostess sat them at a seat near the floor-to-roof window that was the outer wall of the dining room. The restaurant sat atop a low bluff over the slow-moving Chattahoochee; below, lights twinkled. Rose felt a powerful stab of longing for the streets. But it passed almost before it had begun.

"What did *you* do today?" Mike asked.

Oh, you know, Rose thought, *shoplifted this dress and some underwear, the usual.* "Some sightseeing," she said. "You?"

"Boring stuff. Work. I've been looking forward to this all day." He leaned toward her. "You are impossible not to think about, Rose."

She blushed again and said something witty back, and it went on that way throughout dinner. Only as the server was clearing away the dishes did Rose realize her gaze had returned to the lights below.

She felt anxious and penned-in. *No*, she thought, *not now. Not now.*

She forced herself to look away and found Mike staring at her.

"Got another date?" he joked, smiling.

"Sorry," Rose said. "Got lost there for a minute."

"I could do a dance, maybe on the table, spice things up."

"You're perfect," she said, and found herself putting her hand over his. But it was a token gesture. More and more she felt her gaze, her entire self, drawn outside. And then she understood why, what that fuzzy feeling was that she'd been feeling since she'd arrived. She didn't feel weak yet, not yet, but it wouldn't be long now. How long? An hour, maybe two, and then she'd be in trouble.

The last time she'd killed had been almost three days ago, Big Bob in the hotel. She'd gone longer in the past, but she always started to feel it at about this stage.

God, why hadn't she taken someone last night after leaving Mike's loft? Or tonight at that mall, some kid in the parking lot, or maybe in the bathroom? She could have killed one or both of the college kids who'd given her a ride to the mall. She'd have been doing the world a favor. What had she been thinking, letting it get away from her like this? Rose was furious with herself, and it must have shown in her face.

"Are you alright?" Mike asked.

"Fine," Rose said, standing. "I just need the bathroom. I'll be right back."

In the bathroom, Rose stood at the mirror, looking hard at her reflection. *It's happening,* she thought. Already, she could see the veins in her chest and arms were a shade darker. Mike may not have noticed yet, but that wouldn't last.

"Fuck," she muttered, and then a laughing woman burst through the door and Rose left the bathroom. As she approached the table where Mike sat, he saw her and stood.

"Everything okay?" he said, extending a hand toward her.

She stopped short of him. "I have to go," she said. The need, the *hunger* was growing. Now that she'd recognized it, she wouldn't be able to stop herself from fixating on it. She needed to get out of the restaurant. Away from all of these people. In her mind's eye, she saw herself rushing to the next table over, ripping some old woman's throat open with her bare hands. Something bad was going to happen, and soon.

She needed to get away, now, before something happened that she couldn't control.

"Rose?" Mike reached out for her.

"Don't," she said, then turned to leave and walked directly into a server carrying a tray loaded with drinks. Somehow, the man managed to keep all of the glasses on the platter, but liquid sloshed off the side and onto the front of Rose's dress.

"I'm so sorry," the server said, "are you—"

But Rose was already headed for the door, and was outside before the flustered man could finish his apology.

Mike burst out the door a step behind her.

"Hey," he said, "what's going on, Rose?"

Rose kept walking, out into the parking lot. Mike followed.

"Rose!"

She stopped and wheeled. "I have to go." It was impossible to keep the edge out of her voice, and he heard it, backed off.

"Can't we—"

"No!" she said. No, hell with that, *fuck* that, she wasn't *saying* anything. She was goddamned yelling, and why not yell? Why not scream? Because she might scare off some man? What did she need him for anyway? What could this man give her that any other couldn't? If she wanted a cock, she could get one any night of the week. If she wanted dinner, clothes, money, she could have that, too. What had she been thinking? *Weak girl*, she thought, *stupid girl*.

"Don't follow me," she spat, hearing the crisp acidity of venom in her voice. "I need to go right now." She turned again to leave and was halfway across the parking lot when she heard the car behind her.

Mike pulled beside her and the window of his black Mercedes buzzed down. He put one arm out the window, reaching out to her.

"Rose, come on, what's happening here? Talk to me."

She stopped, turned to him. Heard herself talking, knew that it was too late not to say what she knew she was going to.

"Okay," she said and smiled, then went around to the other side of Mike's car and got in. Still smiling sweetly, she said, "You want to see what's going on here, Mike? Drive."

"Where?"

"Just go," she said, "into the city. I'll tell you when to stop."

Five minutes later they were driving through crowded city streets.

Rose watched out the side window, waiting. There was something smug sitting in her head, something that blocked her brain, a blanket. *I'll show him*, the thing said, *I'll fucking show him something he's never seen before, never even suspected.* And then it hit her, one of the flashes that sometimes accompanied the hunt, a nearly hallucinatory image of a darkened city street—but not the street of a *modern* city. This street was packed dirt, the buildings lining either side fashioned of rough-hewn stone. Here and there, the flickering flames of torches illuminated the scenery and cast deep and jumping shadows. Ahead, someone moved in the darkness and Rose—or *whoever* was seeing this ancient city scene—closed in for the kill.

And then as suddenly as the hallucination had come, it was gone and Rose was back in her own body, riding in the Mercedes with Mike Clover.

The car passed through an area dominated by stores and bars, then into an upscale residential neighborhood. A few blocks later, the neighborhood started deteriorating, and then they were driving through a slum.

Mike had been silent, but now he said, "Where are we going? This isn't a great part of town, Rose."

Rose didn't answer, but a few seconds later she saw what she'd been looking for, felt a jolt of electricity in her chest. "Here," she said. "Stop." Mike pulled the car to the side of the road and Rose got out.

There was an old woman or man—it was impossible to tell because of the tattered trench coat—pushing a shopping cart along the uneven sidewalk.

Rose started across the street, saw Mike hadn't gotten out of the car, and went back, knocked on the window. "Coming?" she said, and smiled.

Grudgingly, Mike climbed out of the car and followed her.

When they were about ten feet away, the homeless person heard them coming and turned around. It was a woman, Rose saw, but it didn't matter—she didn't care, not about this, not about anything.

"Whaddaya want?" the shopping cart lady said, and Rose grinned disarmingly. The woman relaxed, and then Rose was on her.

She grabbed the woman by the arm with one hand and tore her throat out with the other. It was an easy move, rehashed and rehearsed in her mind a thousand times, executed almost as many. There was a gush of liquid warmth over her hand, and the dirty woman teetered for a moment, her free hand going to her throat, probing almost delicately at the crater Rose's fingers had created. Comprehension flared in her eyes, and she tried to scream, tried to plug the hole in her throat with her fingers, failed.

Rose watched all of this for a moment, then dipped her head and drank; for a little while, she wasn't there at all, was just…swimming, floating in her mind, at peace. Here, for the first few moments, there was nothing but a sense of pure wellbeing. She could feel life flowing into her, filling her with light, blue, brilliant light, almost too much for her body to contain. Once, in some book or other, she'd seen this feeling described in a different way. *Loving kindness.* That's what she felt now. Free, centered, powerful.

Then she came back and remembered: Mike.

Rose dropped the old woman to the ground and turned around. She felt the warm blood dripping from her chin and tracing lines down her neck toward her breasts.

Mike was slowly retreating, back-pedaling toward the car. His face was ashen, and he looked like he was trying to say something, but nothing would come out of his mouth.

"Hm?" Rose said, cupping a hand to her ear. "What's that, Mike? Still want to talk?" She wiped her mouth with the back of her hand and it came away streaked with gore. What had she been thinking? That this man was her savior? Ha! Savior from what? This was life, this was living. No man could give her anything that would compare. No man.

But the new part of herself wouldn't go away so easily. *Go to him,* it said, *explain that this is just the way you are. Maybe he'll still take you, maybe he'll understand.*

Ha! Putting on this dress, these ridiculous shoes! Stupid.

A new swell of rage and Rose screamed, screamed at Mike, screamed at the world for making her into what she was, for making her what she couldn't help but be.

Mike had reached the car and groped behind him for the door, got it, fell into the car, rapping the back of his head on the roof as he did.

Seconds later, his taillights were red dots down the road, then he turned and they were gone altogether.

Chapter 10

John had intended to leave for Pennsylvania soon after he woke up, but he found that there were a couple of things he still needed to do before he could go. One of those was to see Dr. Barnes for a final check-up, and he hadn't been able to get an appointment until five that evening. The other was more personal in nature. Pennsylvania—and Connie—would have to wait until tomorrow.

Finding out where Doug and Mary Ann Shaw lived was easy. Too easy, John thought. Just a few years ago, it would have been difficult or even impossible to find out the kind of information you could uncover on the internet in just a couple of minutes. In this case, it was just a matter of surfing over to WhitePages.com, typing in their last name, reading down the list, and selecting an address.

Fifteen minutes later, he was sitting in his idling car, drinking a cup of Starbucks coffee as Mary Ann left the house, got into her car and headed off to work.

* * *

Mary Ann Shaw was younger than John had thought she'd be. From the voice on the phone, he had pictured someone middle-aged, old even, and for some reason, overweight. Someone who had nothing better to do than pay uninvited visits to the homes of people she didn't know. But she was none of those things. This woman was around John's age, dark-featured, pretty in a solid, unremarkable kind of way. She wore jeans and a white tee-shirt and seemed to favor everyone who spoke to her with a genuine smile.

It also came as a shock to him that she was a teacher, or at least an assistant to one. What he was feeling wasn't what he had expected to feel, or what he'd wanted to feel. Instead of the pent-up anger John had been preparing to release on this woman, he felt nothing but curious. Here, after all, was the only person in this whole crazy situation who seemed to be *offering* him something instead of asking for something. Whether that offer contained anything of worth was open to speculation, of course, but John found that he was growing more and more curious about what she might have to say.

Sitting in his car, John watched as she pushed a second-grader on a swing in the playground of the J. Murray Alfred Elementary School, which wasn't far from John's own school, Denton Academy, maybe two or three miles down the road.

All this time, they'd been this close.

Another child approached Shaw and tugged on her hand, said something John couldn't hear from his spot under an elm tree a block away. She smiled and ruffled his hair, then pointed back at the school building and the child ran off.

John started his car and made his way slowly down the road. As he passed the playground, he glanced over at Shaw, who was pushing the kid on the swing again. She was laughing and smiling.

Not what he'd expected at all. This wasn't his week for fulfilled expectations.

* * *

He pulled into the parking lot of a shopping complex and left his car, then walked over to a bar called the Wine Vault and took a seat outside. It was a nice day, and he ordered a beer and drank it while he thought.

When he was certain, he went inside and made a phone call.

* * *

There was a park not too far from John's apartment, and at three o'clock he arrived and sat down on a bench underneath a big elm.

Mary Ann Shaw pulled into the parking lot at around three-twenty and made her way over to him.

John watched her as she walked, a smooth, self-assured motion that John couldn't help but find attractive. She was wearing what she'd had on at school, jeans and a tee-shirt, but over that she wore a light, lavender cardigan with the sleeves pushed up on her forearms. Her skin was olive-tinted and her hair jet black, but John couldn't quite place her extraction. Somewhere on the Mediterranean, he thought. Spain or Greece, maybe. He knew from their phone exchange that her voice contained just the barest hint of an accent, the kind one might pick up from a parent, but not long-term immersion.

He didn't stand or say hello as she approached, but she didn't seem bothered, just sat down beside him and stared straight ahead. There was a long silence.

Finally, she said, "You were at my school today."

That caught John off guard. "Yes," he said.

She nodded. "I saw your car down the road. It was either you or a pervert watching the kids—we get those sometimes. I was hoping for you."

Another silence.

"Do you want to hear what I have to say now?"

It wasn't why he'd asked her to meet him here. Really, his only reason had been to intimidate her, to let her know that he was onto her, knew where she worked, where she lived. But there was a normalcy to Shaw, a solidity, that was making John doubt himself. This didn't look like a woman who would spend her time looking for people to persecute. She didn't *sound* like a crackpot or a psycho. She just seemed...like a nice person. All of the anger John had been storing up inside of his head and heart was suddenly gone. The only thing left was a numbing fatigue, defeat.

"Okay," he said. "Whatever you have to say, please say it."

* * *

"Some of this is going to be impossible for you to understand," Shaw started. "Just let me finish. I don't expect you to believe it now, but you will in time. You won't have a choice. Things are starting to happen now." Her confidence lent her an air of authority, and John felt himself *wanting* to believe whatever she was going to say. He had started to sweat lightly and realized that he was nervous.

Shaw took a breath and looked down at the ground, as if organizing her thoughts, then began.

"You are a very special person, John. You're blessed with an ability to heal just by touching, a gift that can be traced back as far as Jesus Christ himself."

John started to raise a hand and object, but Shaw continued. "Don't worry, this isn't going to turn into a lecture on Christianity, but it is important that you understand that your ability has roots beyond just yourself. Where does this gift come from? I don't have an answer for that. Some people would say from God, but I don't claim to be any great authority on religion. Why you? Again, I don't know. But I *do* know that once a generation, a child is born with the ability to heal. From time to time, there is born into this world a soul so white, so purely *good*, that its bearer can even take back death, though the sacrifice that soul makes when it performs such an act is...ultimate."

John waved her off and leaned back tiredly. Anger flashed in Shaw's eyes, and when she resumed, her voice was tight with impatience.

"The flip side of the coin is that, in nature, one extreme demands a diametric opposite. You are a healer, a life-giver, but you are only one side of the equation. On the other there is a—"

"A what?" John said and shook his head. "A life taker?"

"Yes," she said. "A person driven to take life in order to survive. Like you, this person doesn't understand what they're doing or why they're doing it; they just feel compelled to kill, to murder, to feed off the act of taking life. And as with you, this is a compulsion that has gradually grown in strength over the years. It may have started off small, with stray animals, but as she grew older...it wouldn't take long before the urge to take a human life would be too much to resist."

Shaw sat impassively, apparently waiting for John to laugh or walk off.

But John had been thinking. "If what you say is true, and I'm the exact opposite this...this life-taker, if I'm a healer, wouldn't that mean that I would need to heal in order to remain alive? Wouldn't I be *compelled*, to use your own word, to heal whenever opportunity presents itself?"

Surprised by John's earnest-sounding question, Shaw answered in kind. "It's a different kind of situation, but you're right. Think about this for a second. When you saw that girl lying in the street in front of your school, what was your thought-process? Did you panic, like the rest of them must have been doing? Did you run to the toilet to throw up, or just let someone else deal with it—pass the buck, so to speak? Most people would have. It certainly would have crossed my mind to shuck and run."

She paused, and John rewound to that afternoon, put himself on the street, saw the kids, blank-faced, shocked, remembered thinking about that painting by Picasso, the one with the death-mask, and then, seeing Kyra...

And what after that?

A remembered calm washed over him, a sense of peace.

He saw himself kneeling down next to the girl and reaching out, then pausing, hand in midair—

Careful, Johnny.

A whisper from the past. Then taking Kyra's hand, that same calm like a cool, silky breeze.

"Do you remember?" Shaw said softly, snapping John from the memory.

John nodded, his mouth dry, each shallow breath clicking in his throat.

"*What* do you remember?"

"Peace," he said, "calm. I remember knowing that everything was going to be just fine. My mind was telling me that she was going to die, that she probably couldn't even feel me holding her hand, but still, I knew...I *knew* that she was going to be okay."

"Did you ever, for one second, think about leaving her there?"

John shook his head and looked up at her, feeling suddenly cold.

"That's because leaving her was never an option. No more than it would be an option for your opposite to stop taking lives. When that poor girl was struck by that car, you saw that a life was in danger of guttering out, so you re-lit the wick. It's what you are, whether you want it or not."

Despite an overwhelming desire to refute what Shaw had told him, John found himself recognizing himself in her words. He searched desperately for a loophole, some kind of caveat in the story she'd laid out. He could find only one, and voiced it. "But this is the first time anything like this has ever happened," he said. "I've never felt anything like I did that day, and I've certainly never *healed* anyone before. If I have this need to heal in order to survive, then how can you explain that?"

Shaw laughed, a light, musical sound. She wasn't laughing at him, John knew, and her laughter didn't cause in him the sort of defensive anger it might have just moments ago. Instead, he just felt tired.

As John watched, Shaw leaned over her knees and plucked a dandelion from the grass, raised it to her nose, smelled it. "John," she said after a moment, "do you get sick a lot? I mean, more than you think is normal?"

"Yes," John said. "Never anything too bad, but sometimes I feel like I'm sick—run down—for months at a time."

"Is it especially bad during the school year?"

"I guess, but that's true for all teachers. Kids are basically just incubators for every type of virus in the world. It's impossible not to bring that crap home once in a while."

"Maybe a little worse for you?"

He thought about it. How many days of school had he missed this last year? Twelve? Fifteen? He routinely went over the maximum number of absences allowed for a teacher, but he was so good at his job otherwise that the administration never gave him grief about it.

"Sure, I miss a little school," John said. "But I don't think it's—" John stopped, realizing what she was getting at. "Oh Jesus, you can't be serious."

She shrugged, hands to the sky. "I didn't say anything. But doesn't it make sense? If you went to school tomorrow and checked student attendance records for the past several years, I bet you'd find that there have been *far* fewer absences at Denton than at any other school in the area."

"This is nuts," John whispered. "I told you, I *never* felt anything like I did that day with Kyra. I never felt like anything...significant was about to happen, nothing big."

"Not at the same level, maybe," she responded. "But then, curing a cold and healing a girl on the doorstep of death are slightly different animals, wouldn't you agree?"

John put a hand over his face. "Insane," he whispered.

"Fine, maybe, but tell me this: do you feel content at school, at peace with yourself, like you're doing what you're meant to do?"

"Sure, but I've always loved teaching. It's all I really thought about doing, ever since I was a kid."

"Did you ever wonder why? Ever wonder why you wanted so singularly to surround yourself with young people each and every day?"

John just shook his head tiredly. No, he had never wondered, but seeing it now, placed so unavoidably out in front of him, it was all too easy to trace every major choice he'd made over the course of his life to this one seminal fact. Of course, the thought entered his mind that his still-exhausted brain—hell, his *injured* brain—might be searching for sense, creating sense, in a place where none existed.

When you got right down to brass tacks, John was exhausted. More than that, he was fed up with not understanding his place, where he *fit*, and all the recent drama had brought the fear and confusion he'd been feeling since he was a child to a roiling boil. It was entirely possible that Shaw's comfortable demeanor and calmness was causing him to hear her words with more credence than he might listen to words from another, more agitated mind. The most convincing lunatics were always the ones who could put their crazy ideas out there as if they were the most rational things in the world.

But he didn't think that's all it was. He didn't think so at all. "How do you *know* all of this?" John asked.

Shaw blew out forcefully and thought for a moment. "When I was eight years-old, my cat was run over in the street outside my house. We lived in Pennsylvania, out in the country. By the time we found him—his name was Charlie—he was almost dead. Stupid asshole who hit him never even stopped. I don't know what people think sometimes."

John had felt chilled before, but now an icy fear twisted in his guts. A brief but powerful wave of bright static washed over his vision. "Oh, God," he whispered.

Shaw continued. "There was a little boy who lived across the street. I used to play with him sometimes. He was over at our house when we found Charlie. He was my age, and I was crying my eyes out, but the little boy, he didn't cry at all, even though Charlie was bloody and had a broken back. He just knelt down in the grass next to my cat and—"

"Your mom said, 'Careful, Johnny.'" John looked at her for confirmation, though he didn't really need any.

Shaw nodded. "And then you put your hands on Charlie and he got better. That cat lived another ten years, and only died the year after I left for college."

"Oh, man," John muttered, covering his face with his hands. His brain was raw, like someone had put a cigar out in it. "Oh, man."

"After that," she said, looking off into the park, "I couldn't get it out of my mind. My mom, either. When we moved away, she used to look in the papers to see if there was any mention of you. She did that for years. Before long, I started doing it, too. It was just always, you know, in the back of my mind, what you did to my cat. When I was a little older, I went to the library and did some reading on the subject of healing. Most of the stuff was religious, faith healers and such. But some of it made sense. I even wrote a paper on it when I was in college." She laughed humorlessly. "Sounds obsessive, I know, but seeing something like that, it changes you, gets inside you. What I found was a pattern, a pattern that I couldn't argue with, and that you fit perfectly. More than anything, it's that pattern I needed to tell you about. It's why I moved here two years ago, to be closer to you. So I could help you understand when something like this happened."

Although he'd sensed where she was headed, the admission that Mary Ann had moved here to be close to him stopped John cold. "Crazy," he said, shaking his head. "You have to see that. You have to see that…I'm not some fucking *prophet*, Mary Ann. I'm a man. Just a man."

She nodded and put her hand on his. "I know that. And I know what this must sound like. It's…stalkerish. I get it, and I'd be creeped out, too. But try to understand. This gift you have, this ability to heal, it's evidence of something greater than we are, John. I'm not making a case for God, or for anything else. I'm just making a case for *something*. Do you understand? I'm a Catholic. I go to church every Sunday, and I say prayers before bed. I believe in God. I believe in Jesus Christ. But I've never *seen* them. What I *have* seen is you. So what was I supposed to do? Go back into the world, forget you existed, never think about you again?"

She shook her head. "I couldn't do that. No," she said, reconsidering her words. "I didn't *want* to do that. Even following you the way I have, my life is full. I have a man who loves me. I have a job I can't wait to go to each day." She shook her head and locked eyes with John. "So yes, I know how it sounds, but please, please try to understand. This is something I had to do."

John looked up at the sky. It was edging towards four. In another hour or so, he'd start to feel groggy, slow, and then an hour after that his vision would start to double and that other reality would start to filter in. Soon after, he'd be incapable of driving, a total menace on the roads. Thankfully, home wasn't far. "You mentioned a pattern," he said.

"Once every so often—there's no set period that I can see, and trust me, I've looked—there are a spate of what seem to be legitimate healings, not the ones you see reported in the tabloids, but the ones that make the big papers. And I'm not just talking about the New York *Times* and Boston *Globe*. When I was doing research, I found references from a hundred and fifty years ago in places like the Dublin *Evening Standard* and the South Africa *Cape Times*. Those are places people don't want to admit the legitimacy of miracles without some irrefutable proof, so it's hard to dismiss them out of hand."

She paused for a moment to think, then continued. "At the same time, there's a rise in the incidence of seemingly *patterned* killings. Mostly, the people who are murdered are alone: transients, traveling salesmen, etcetera. You can actually chart the movements of the killer, your opposite, if you can find a starting spot."

"People get murdered all the time," John said. "I could pick up copies of newspapers from ten cities right now and come up with some kind of goddamned pattern. 'Look, stabbings in Baltimore, Philadelphia, and New York. Must be a *pattern*.' It's impossible."

She shook her head. "These killings are a little more distinct than stabbings, or shootings. Once you start looking for it, you can't miss it. The police know about it. So does the FBI. The last two times the pattern has sprung up, there have been full-scale investigations. Before that, communication was so primitive that law enforcement never would have had the chance to see what was going on right under their noses."

"Okay," John said. "Give. What makes these murders so distinct?"

Shaw locked eyes with him. "I think you already know."

John started to say that he didn't, but suddenly a series of disconnected images flashed through his mind. *The man with the black sun tattoo releasing blood-red rays in the back seat of an old car; the kid, Brett, a fighter with a mashed nose in the back alley of a bar; the aging Jim Morrison look-alike outside the strip club; the burly salesman in the hotel room*...so many more...

"Their blood," he murmured. "Whoever it is killing these people, she—she drinks their blood."

Shaw nodded. "Literary and film treatments aside, what we're talking about here is a...well, we're talking about a *vampire*, John. A vampire who is as privy to your thoughts and dreams as you are to hers."

John felt his mind drifting, as if his rationality had been cut free from its moorings. "And I—*we*—fit this pattern?"

"Perfectly. The last so-called healer died about thirty-five years ago, just before you were born. His death also marked the end of one of these killing sprees in the Midwest. He—" She bit off whatever she'd been about to say.

"He what?"

She shook her head, then looked at him frankly. "He was murdered. When I read that, it seemed like too big a coincidence, so I looked back at the obits of the three or four other seemingly legitimate healers I'd discovered—the ones who shunned the spotlight and tried their best to live normal lives."

"And?"

"And they'd all been murdered also. At the same time, the ritualistic killings came to an abrupt stop. The healers are always the last ones to die, and then...nothing. For a while."

"What does that mean?"

"John," she said, her voice barely above a whisper now. "This is what I really called you for, to tell you this."

"What?"

"The other one, the life-taker, she—and it *will* be a she—she'll be coming for you. For whatever reason, and I wish I could tell you something specific about why, she needs for you to die."

Part II

Chapter 11

Boston, Massachusetts

If there was one thing Phylum hated, it was a pussy, and if this motherfucker wasn't the biggest pussy Phylum had ever seen, he didn't know who was. He hadn't even touched the guy before he'd dropped to the floor and soiled himself, an act that had been accompanied by some pretty revolting liquid sounds, like a toilet being plunged.

He hefted the man by the armpits and dropped him into a chair, grimacing at the smells of piss and shit wafting off Tom Cavanaugh, who was now whimpering like a distressed puppy.

Pathetic, he thought, *fucking pathetic.*

"Shut up," Phylum said, but Cavanaugh was blubbering, snotty bubbles forming and then popping all over his mouth. Taking a steadying breath, Phylum said, "If you don't cut that shit out, I'll do things to you that you won't believe." He bent and lifted Cavanaugh's chin with a finger. The man's eyes rolled, so Phylum slapped his cheek, then grabbed his face with one mammoth hand, squeezing his cheeks.

"I'll stop, I'll stop," Cavanaugh said, sniffling. "I'm sorry, I'll stop."

Phylum stepped back and wiped his hand on his jeans. His patience was running thin; behind his eyes he could feel a dangerous buzzing. He closed his eyes and breathed deeply. *Hold it together*, he told himself. *Just hold it together for a little longer.*

Looking down at Cavanaugh, Phylum could see that the man was trying to collect himself—to get his shit together, so to speak. And as frustrating as this kind of behavior was from a grown man, Phylum had to take into account the man's unique point of view. He'd gotten into bed with the wrong people, borrowing fifty thousand dollars from a loan shark for whom Phylum sometimes did recovery work, and now, one way or another, he was about to pay up. "I take it you know why I'm here," he said.

Cavanaugh nodded, his eyes fixed on Phylum's shoes, his hands clasped between his knees. Phylum could see Cavanaugh coming to the humiliating realization that he had gone to the bathroom in his pants like a child.

"Say, 'yes,'" Phylum said.

"Y-yes," Cavanaugh whispered.

"And I take it, from your excretory reaction, that you know who I am."

Cavanaugh nodded.

"Say it."

"Yes, yes," Cavanaugh said, cringing. "I know who you are."

Phylum let the silence hang for a moment. He was coming back to himself a little bit; he could feel his emotional horizon returning to level. He liked this part, where the sheep was cowering, the wolf in control. It was the natural order of things.

"Are you going to tell me what I want to hear?" Phylum said. "Or are we going to have a problem?"

Cavanaugh started crying again, the tears running fast and fat down his cheeks and into the scruffy facial hair coating his jaw. Phylum felt his patience slipping.

"You're making me mad," he whispered.

"I don't have it," Cavanaugh sobbed. "I don't have it. I need more time, just a couple of weeks. I can get it. I can. I swear."

Phylum nodded, then reached into his pocket and pulled out a switchblade. He pressed the button near the top of the handle and the blade, bright and razor-sharp, flicked forth with a *schnick*.

Cavanaugh's eyes fixed on the knife. "Ahh, God," he croaked. Phylum could see the man's survival instincts kick in, could see him begin to evaluate the various escape possibilities.

"I wouldn't if I were you," Phylum said, and Cavanaugh's eyes shot up to Phylum's face. "You might make it to the window, but by the time you got your hand on the lock, the blade of this knife would be lodged between the third and fourth vertebrae in your spine. I can do that, and trust me, it's no party for you."

Cavanaugh's eyes slipped toward the door and Phylum's followed. He smiled. "The door? That's cute. I can hear what you're thinking. Did you lock it behind you when you walked in? That's a big question, isn't it? If it's unlocked, all you have to do is pull the door open and you're home free, right? But what if you locked it? Then you have to turn that deadbolt, don't you? That could take, what, half a second?"

He moved his head from side to side in a considering gesture. "By that time I could have done a dozen different things to you. Not things that would kill you. No, there would be no point in that. But things that would change your life forever? Definitely." He locked eyes with Cavanaugh. "My advice? Just sit there like a good little boy and tell me what I want to hear. You could still get out of this with…a minimum of damage. I won't say none, because that would be untrue, but it doesn't have to be much, not in the big scheme of things. Do you understand what I'm saying?"

The man shut his eyes and nodded.

Phylum blew air between his teeth. "Say the *words*, fuckface."

"I-I understand," Cavanaugh said.

"Good. Now, the situation is this: Mr. Prince obviously wants his money back from you. It's been three months, and he's starting to lose faith that you're going to make good on your promises. With interest, you now owe him…" Phylum thought for a moment. "Something along the lines of fifty-five grand, give or take a few Gs. I understand from your scatological release that you don't have the entire amount. Can you give me anything, as a gesture of good faith?"

"No," Cavanaugh said. "I don't have anything. I'm totally broke. I have like three bucks in my wallet."

"Alright. I believe you. But I can't go back to Mr. Prince with nothing. Put out your right hand."

"Wha-What?"

"Put it out," Phylum said. "If you make me ask again—"

Cavanaugh slowly lifted his hand and held it out, gingerly, as if he and Phylum were getting ready to play a game of slap-hand and he'd have the chance to yank it back to safety. It was a nice thought.

Phylum's own hand shot out whip-quick and grabbed Cavanaugh's wrist. The man squealed and bucked, his eyes rolling in his head.

"Fucking chill," Phylum growled. "I haven't even done anything yet."

* * *

Fifteen minutes later, Phylum left Cavanaugh's house and dropped a ziplock baggie into the trunk of the Toyota Corolla he'd driven up from New York. In the ziplock were the pinky and ring finger from Cavanaugh's right hand. And actually, it had been a difficult choice.

Phylum always liked to do things right, especially for employers like Mr. Prince, men who really appreciated quality work, so when he made these little social visits he liked to go the extra mile. That meant two fingers instead of just one. But taking two fingers complicated matters. For example, did he take two fingers off the same hand? That always seemed a little mercenary. The last three fingers—well, *two* really, since the world now maintained that the thumb was not, in fact, a finger at all, the way it now maintained that Pluto was not, in fact, a planet anymore—always looked so *fucking* sad. It was like manual deforestation. But if you took one finger off each hand, that really fucked the pooch, too, now didn't it? One hand you could hide—tuck it in your coat pocket or something—but *two*? How would you hold your drink at a party? Sign checks? And then there was golf. Phylum loved golf, and he'd been told that Cavanaugh did, too. That had definitely been a factor in his decision tonight.

But in the end, he'd mostly been swayed by marriage.

Phylum was no romantic, but he could appreciate that a fucking pathetic loser pussy like Cavanaugh might one day find a woman who could look past his innumerable faults and see the man sheathed inside that blubbering cocoon of pussy-meat. And if he did, if this hypothetical pussy-meat-loving woman decided that she wanted to marry this quivering piece of shit, he would need to wear a wedding ring. Taking all of that into account, liberating the last two fingers of Cavanaugh's right hand had just seemed like the *right* thing to do. Better for Cavanaugh's love life.

And better for Cavanaugh's golf game, too, since any old duffer knew the left hand really controlled the swing.

* * *

Phylum's cell phone rang—the first few bars of Orff's *Carmina Burana*—and he picked it up off the passenger seat.

"Phylum," he said.

"It's me," said the voice on the other side of the line, circumspect as always. Never, "Hey, it's Dan," or "Hello, this is Steve, is Phylum available?" Always, "It's me." Three years of these calls and always the same damned thing.

"Ah," Phylum said.

"How was your conversation with Mr. Cavanaugh?"

"Good," Phylum said. "We had a…a couple fingers of scotch."

A considering pause. "So our mutual friend can expect to hear from him soon?"

"Safe to say."

"Good. I have another job for you."

Driving at exactly the speed limit, Phylum said, "Hold on," dug his earpiece from his pocket, plugged it into the ass-end of the phone, and removed his notepad from his breast pocket. He took a pen from the glove compartment and said, "Go ahead."

The voice on the other end of the line spoke for thirty seconds while Phylum scribbled notes down, and then the line went dead. No goodbye, nothing.

Phylum sighed and shook his head. "Prick."

Chapter 12

Once again, she was moving north.

The truth of that fact occurred to her as she sat in the back seat of a black Pontiac Firebird, wedged between two sleeping Mexican children, a boy and a girl.

She'd picked up the ride about three hours ago, in the northern part of Atlanta. The driver, a Mexican man named Pablo who spoke only broken English, smiled and said, "Charlotte," when Rose asked where they were headed. She'd already passed up two rides by the time the dented Firebird happened along, a trucker headed south to Florida and a college kid on his way out to Ohio, and now she knew why she'd waited.

Why north?

She'd never spent much time up north, and her travels had never taken her further up than Pennsylvania. What's more, the feeling that she was being...*directed* somewhere was powerful, which disturbed her greatly.

For her entire life, Rose had been a creature in charge of her own destiny. There were limitations to what she could do and when she could do it, sure, but in the overall scheme of things, she made her own way, the rest of the world be damned.

And now this.

She thought of Mike Clover, now a hundred and fifty miles behind her, and felt anew the contrary emotions the man had provoked in her. The raw, animal attraction, the *need* for him in a way she couldn't explain.

And the hate that had risen in her last night when she'd murdered the homeless woman in front of him.

Why had she done that? If she had protested long and hard enough outside the restaurant, he would have let her go eventually, even if he didn't want to. He was a nice man. And he had cared about her. Even after a couple of days, he had cared. The part of Rose that depended on reading people and their emotions knew that.

If she had just let things be, she could have gone back to him the next night, and he would have welcomed her. She was sure of it.

But she hadn't done that, had she?

Instead, she had very carefully chosen the one thing that would expel him from her life forever, and then she had done it, almost thoughtlessly. Between the time she climbed into Mike's car and when she killed the bag lady, there had been a distinct absence of thought, of consideration. A *forced* absence of thought, more like it.

The worst part was that, looking back now, she thought she knew why she had killed the homeless woman. There had been the need to kill, that feeling inside of her head and chest that she'd experienced hundreds of times before, but she could have held off, could have stopped herself for long enough to get far away from Mike before...before. But her need to take life, to refill whatever horrible and constantly lowering reservoir existed inside of her, had nothing to do with what she had done. But she thought she knew why she had.

Mike Clover had become a weakness for her. He made her vulnerable. Rather, he would have done so if she'd pursued things with him.

Sitting in the back of the Firebird, she thought about that. Yes, it made sense. Living the way she did, the only way she *could*, being attached to anyone else opened her up to danger. Alone, she could move as she needed, leave any place at the drop of a hat.

She could listen to her instincts, which had kept her alive this long.

What she had done in Atlanta had nothing to do with Mike. It had to do with her nature, what she was, and what she had to do to survive. Move, kill. Being with a man had never been a part of her life; having a child...

Rose leaned back into the leather of the seat and heard springs squeak like mice behind her. She closed her eyes, tried to relax, opened her eyes again.

To each side of her, the children, young, maybe eight and ten years old, breathed softly in sleep.

Rose had been sitting with her shoulders tight, her hands in her lap. Now she raised them and draped one around the shoulders of each child. The girl slumped over into Rose's lap and rested her head there, muttered something in Spanish, something that ended with *papa*. Rose lowered her hand to the girl's black hair and stroked it softly.

As she did, she thought of the children whose lives she had taken. Not many: fifteen, maybe twenty, over the years. Killing never gave her joy, but she had learned to anesthetize herself to it. Had to. Killing children, though... There was nothing worse than that. Rose shuddered and looked down at the side of the sleeping girl's face. Smooth, dark-skinned, deeply-dimpled cheeks.

She tried to stop it, but the memory came. Only months ago, just before her wandering had brought her to Florida, she'd found herself stuck in the harsh winter of the Kansas prairie. For a while her time in Kansas had gone well; she'd found a quaint town and no end of barns in which she could spend the days, her sleep undisturbed, deepened even, by the sounds and smells of horses and other livestock. Then, one night while she was preparing to head out for the hunt, a gentle snow had evolved into a full-fledged blizzard and Rose had been stuck, stranded, in a barn miles from the closest town.

She shivered now, thinking about it, the warmth of the car so contrary to the cold of that winter landscape.

For hours she had tried to relax herself, striven to deny the burning need inside of her body, in her stomach, her brain, but finally it had been useless. Almost before she knew what she was doing, she had found herself standing in hip deep snow outside a window of the farmhouse. On the other side of the glass, lit by a bulb burning in the hallway, a little girl of seven or eight lay nestled beneath her quilt, hands holding bunched fabric beneath her chin.

Rose shuddered. She could feel the cold of that night on her skin, in her bones. She could remember the thrumming, frantic need zipping its way through her veins, throbbing behind her eyeballs, bulging in her throat. And then she remembered feeling surprised at how easily the window slid up in its frame…and how sweet the little girl's blood had tasted sliding through her lips, coating the inside of her mouth, slipping like salty, coppery wine down her throat and into her stomach…the relief, the *power*.

Rose felt a sudden swell of anger, was caught off-guard by its force, felt her body tense with it.

Why did she have to be like this?

And if she had to be, why was she feeling these new pressures, these strange urges. Seeing things all the time. The baby, then Mike, the visions. How could nature have made her this way, have filled her with these revolting needs, and then torture her with such profound and inescapable self-loathing for what she had no choice but to be?

Rose wasn't like other people—would *never* be—and she had come to a grudging peace with that fact. But if that was true, then she shouldn't have to live her life controlled by the same needs as everyone else. A man, a family. Not her! It was impossible, ridiculous. She may as well have been a wolf let into the pasture, and then told to starve to death.

She tried to picture the life with Mike Clover, but it came out like something from TV. Her and Mike sitting in a living room in matching recliners, reading the Sunday *Times*, drinking coffee from matching mugs that read #1 MOM and #1 DAD in happy pink letters. A child, a boy, playing with wooden blocks on the floor. Some insipid daytime talk show playing on the television.

Ha!

But her anger grew and she felt it getting away from her.

"Stop the car," she whispered, fists clenched.

The man, Pablo, didn't hear.

Rose was shaking. "Stop the car," she repeated, louder, and this time Pablo swiveled his head to look.

"*Que?*" he said, a kind smile on his face, a smile that vanished quickly when he saw Rose's expression.

"*Dios,*" he said, and whipped the car onto the side of the road, brought it to a screeching halt. Rose opened the door and climbed over the sleeping boy, stepped out of the car, closed the door behind her. Pablo was staring out the window at her, waiting for something, waiting, perhaps, to see what he could do to help. His kindness made Rose even angrier.

"Get away," Rose said, "before I kill you and your children."

Pablo may or may not have understood, but he jammed his foot down on the gas and the car took off.

The rage abated quickly once she was alone, and after a few minutes, she started thumbing at passing cars.

* * *

Rose had walked for a half hour or so when she saw the sign.

CHARLOTTE 21 MILES.

Hunger for the hunt, for the kill, stabbed at her stomach, but it wasn't bad yet.

She'd kill someone when she reached the city.

Chapter 13

When John woke up the next morning, he showered, dressed, and ate a bowl of cereal, and then headed into school to complete the first of his errands, picking up his planner, some books, and some other odds and ends before he left for West Chester, a drive that would take him about ten hours.

Though he felt fine for the most part, John had struggled to fall asleep the night before. Where he would normally nod right off, he'd found it all but impossible to stop thinking about what Mary Ann Shaw had told him in the park.

And then, once he had finally drifted off, his dreams had been disturbing. There were no murders this time, but at one point he had found himself in the back seat of a car, nestled between sleeping children, aching to tear their throats out with his teeth. He had an appointment later in the morning with Dr. Barnes and was hoping she could help him get control of his racing and scattered thoughts.

Trying to shake off his fatigue, John parked his car in his usual spot in the teacher lot and went inside. The visit did not go as he'd hoped.

* * *

He arrived near the end of second period. The halls were oddly quiet and empty; even the air seemed still, and as John stood in the second floor hallway, looking down toward the huge picture window that overlooked the athletic fields, he could see particles of dust hanging almost motionlessly in the wide beams of sunlight filtering through the clouds on the horizon. The feeling the sight inspired in John was familiar, but in a way he couldn't immediately identify. Only as he started to walk down the hall toward his classroom, the rubber soles of his sneakers squelching softly on the black and white tiled floor, did he place it. This was the way he'd felt upon returning home to his apartment after his stay in the hospital—the feeling of being a stranger in a place where he used to belong.

A loud sound exploded near John's head and he recoiled before realizing, with a sheepish cringe, that it was just the bell signaling the end of the day's second period. It was a noise he'd heard every fifty-five minutes of every school day for the past decade of his life, and one that he rarely even *noticed* when it had gone off over that time, but a few weeks away had rendered it unfamiliar. Funny the way the mind worked. The sound died down, and, after a delay of perhaps two seconds—as long as it took for the kids to shoot up from their desks, grab their books, and reach the door—the halls flooded with students.

Ten or twelve came over to him and said hello, but none of them offered a hug or a hand, not the way they had always done before. The looks on their faces were appraising and careful. It's not that they considered him dangerous, he knew. It was just that he hadn't turned out to be what they'd always thought he was, and kids had a hard time dealing with that. Adults did, too, of course, but they were so used to being lied to that they actually came to *expect* that people weren't what they seemed. What had happened with Kyra was just one step in the lifelong pattern of disillusionment these kids would experience, but John hated being a part of it.

When the kids had headed off toward their next classes, John turned toward his room, which was located near the end of the hall.

"Mr. B!" he heard a girl's voice yell, and then Monica Rourke was hugging him.

"Hey, Mon," he said, putting his arms around her and giving her a quick squeeze back. "How you doin', kiddo?"

Monica stepped back, blushing. "I'm okay," she said. "Wish you were still here."

"Yeah," John said, "me, too. Speaking of which, how's my sub doing? I was just on my way down to find out."

Monica frowned, then tilted her head to the side, then smiled. "Permission to speak frankly?"

"Granted," John said. This was an old routine for them, and it was comforting to John to know that not *everything* had changed.

"She's a Nazi," Monica whispered, leaning closer to John so none of the students who were milling all around them would hear, "and she's a little *slow*, if you know what I mean. Like today, we were talking about *Macbeth* and I asked, 'So why do *you* think Macbeth sends hired killers to bump Banquo off?' She looks at me like I'm an idiot for a second, then says, 'Monica, sometimes great men need to learn how to hand certain duties off to the little people.' It was the funniest thing I ever heard. Honestly."

"You didn't laugh, did you?"

Monica smiled, her eyes gleaming. "I said I had to go to the bathroom and then laughed my butt off for about five minutes." Her eyes took on a sudden serious cast. "Have you seen Kyra?" she asked, her voice low.

"Not yet," John said. "How is she?"

Monica shrugged. "Fine. She placed third in the cross-country meet against Corinthian Prep a couple of days ago."

A horrible thought suddenly occurred to John, something vague, centered around Stephen King's book *Pet Sematary* and an old story he'd read as an undergrad at UVA in a course on the uncanny in literature. "The Monkey's Paw," he thought, the one where the dead boy comes back.

"But how *is* she?" John asked, holding Monica's gaze, trying to communicate to her something that he couldn't bring himself to put into words. And what *do* I mean? he thought. Does she stumble around, always just a little off-balance? Is there a smell about her, something you can't quite place, something earthy, fetid, rotting? Is there a distant, not-quite-dead look in her eyes, something hateful?

"She's fine, Mr. B, really. She's just the same as she always was, ditsy and flirty. Don't worry."

John felt a load lift off his shoulders and he exhaled a breath that he now realized he'd been holding for a week. "Thanks, Mon," he said, feeling suddenly very near to tears. "Look, I've got to go get some things from my room, but I'll see you later, okay?"

"Sure," she said, favoring him with a smile, "I've got to get to geometry anyway. Bye, Mr. B."

* * *

John was walking out of the school half an hour later when he saw Kyra Metheny sitting on the grass with Peter Travis, a sophomore John had come to like a lot over the past two years. For the briefest of moments he entertained the idea of going over to say hello to both of them, but then the moment passed. *No need to remind her*, he thought. *Hasn't she been through enough?* She looked normal, though. There was no sign of what she'd been through. As he watched, Kyra laughed and leaned into Peter's shoulder and pecked him on the cheek, then giggled once again.

When John reached his car he looked back at the school, its faded brick mutedly red against the lush green grass that surrounded it.

A voice inside his mind, one he didn't know or particularly like, spoke.

You'll never see this place again.

It wasn't a voice he liked, but it wasn't one he questioned, either.

John unlocked his car and dropped his armful of books onto the back seat, took one last look at the school, an ache low in his gut, and then climbed in behind the wheel.

* * *

John's appointment with Iris Barnes started at ten. He made it to her office a little early and spent twenty minutes in the waiting room leafing through an old issue of *Garden and Gun* magazine.

He was reading an article about window treatments when Barnes opened her door, leaned out, and said, "John?"

* * *

She started it off a little differently.

"We've been talking all this time about your dreams and your problems, but I just realized, I don't really *know* anything about you. Tell me about yourself," she said, then leaned back in her chair and crossed her legs. She was dressed in a black pantsuit, an electric blue blouse underneath her crisply-pressed jacket, and she radiated an air of calm confidence that John could feel setting him immediately at ease. She wasn't here to study him, or to probe at painful places for the sake of doing so; Barnes was here to help, and he could tell that she knew he was here to *be helped*. It was a reassuring thought.

"What do you want to know?" He sipped from a Styrofoam cup of coffee Barnes's secretary had brought for him.

"Anything," Barnes said. "Whatever you think is important."

"Important."

"You know, vital to the essence of who you are. Tell me what makes you *you*." A slight smile.

"Oh. Well."

"What's the problem?"

A good question. What was the problem? "Just don't know where to start, I guess. That's a big question. What if I turned it around? Who are you?"

"I'm the daughter of an Iowan bricklayer and a Montessori school teacher who was originally from Montreal but moved with her family to the States when she was nine. I went to Johns Hopkins undergrad, then Harvard, where I met my husband. I have two kids, Kimberly and Douglas, both in college, and two dogs, a sheltie and a black lab. The lab I love, the sheltie I could do without. I like reading, thunderstorms, and long walks on the beach. Two thirds of that last is true; I'll let you figure it out."

"Cute," John said. "But that doesn't make it any easier."

"Try the beginning. Where were you born?"

"Pennsylvania," John said. "In a town called Springfield, not too far outside Philadelphia."

Barnes nodded, made a note on the pad in her lap. "What about your childhood? What was it like?"

"Happy. I don't know. Fine. Typical. Bikes, football, games of guns in the woods with my friends."

"Where did your family live?"

"In the country," John said. "West Chester. They own a farm, raise cattle and some chickens. Some horses. They used to grow and sell mushrooms to local stores. I'm headed back up there later today for some r and r."

Barnes clicked her pen. "Why 'they'? Not 'we'?"

John straightened in his chair, felt a little hot all of a sudden. He found himself wanting to yank at his collar but didn't. "What?"

"Talking about your family just now, you said 'they,' not 'we.' I was just wondering why." She'd been leaning back, but now she sat forward, her eyes sharp and inquisitive, like a college kid with a crush on the professor.

He sighed, put his hands to his face, laughed ruefully. "You don't miss much."

"That wouldn't do, would it? Not when I have patients lying out their asses to me all day."

"I guess not." Blowing air out, he slapped his knees, then said, "I'm adopted. Was adopted. Whatever. My birth mother died during delivery."

"Who adopted you?"

"This'll getcha. The doctor who delivered me."

She looked confused. "I thought you said you were raised on a farm."

John nodded. "My dad stopped practicing medicine when he and my mother took me in. He bought some land, read some books, and basically started a completely new life."

"Any idea why he quit medicine?"

"I never asked," John said. "And he never brought it up. For as long as I've known him, he's been a farmer. His father was a farmer, too. I guess he figured he'd had enough of doctoring and wanted to do something he felt really connected to. I just don't really know."

There was a moment's silence, then Barnes asked, "Any difference between your childhood bad dreams and the ones you have now?"

"Yes and no. The ones now are more intense, I guess, and when I was a kid, they weren't nearly as frequent. Maybe once a month, sometimes not even that often. Not as vivid. But still, similar, I guess. There was always that sense of violence. Maybe that's why these new ones didn't alarm me so much."

"What about the anxiety? This new sense of foreboding you've been feeling?"

He shook his head. "No, that's recent. Like I said, my childhood was, as far as I can tell, pretty normal. Playing with my friends in the woods, too much candy. No tears of blood dripping from my eyes, no stigmata on Easter or Christmas." He meant for the last to sound joking, but it came out harder than he'd intended.

But Barnes just grinned. "Defensive much?"

He felt himself flush.

"Funny," she continued, "people don't tend to be defensive about things that they think are unimportant. You might consider that. But back to your childhood. Nothing ever happened that might have foreshadowed what happened with Kyra Metheny?"

John paused for too long and knew immediately that if he lied, she'd know it. *Shit.*

"Shit," he muttered.

Barnes raised an eyebrow, said, "Well, let's hear it."

For the next couple of minutes, he sketched out for her what had happened all those years ago with Mary Ann Shaw's cat.

He left out that he had met with her.

When he was done, Barnes thought for a moment. "If she's seen the stories in the paper, she might remember what you did back then and try to contact you."

He was silent and thought to himself: *I am an open fucking book.*

"John?" Barnes, waiting for him to respond. "Did she get in touch with you?"

He gave a guilty shrug. "Maybe."

"What exactly does 'maybe' include nowadays? Phone conversation? Face to face meeting?"

"Both."

"And?"

"And she told me some things."

"Just random things, or was there a common topic?"

"Oh, Christ," he said. Though his conversation in the park with Mary Ann had gone a long way toward convincing him that her interpretation of his life might be legitimate, the prospect of relating Shaw's story to Dr. Barnes made him feel childish and gullible. Still, he also knew that his main reason for keeping this appointment with Barnes was a hope that she would talk him out of buying the bill of goods Mary Ann had so convincingly pitched the day before, so he braced himself and quickly filled Barnes in on everything Shaw had related to him. When he'd finished, she was still looking at him evenly.

"Shouldn't you be laughing your ass off right about now?" he asked.

"Why?" she said. "Is the existence of a 'life-taker' any more difficult to accept than the existence of a *healer*?"

"I should have known."

"John," she said, "there's a commonly accepted world-view which explains that nothing proves the existence of anything so undeniably as the existence of that thing's diametric opposite. In other words, *you* are, so it, your opposite, *must be*. If you're a fan of math, think of it in terms of an if-then statement. If a healer, then a…well, let's call a spade a spade…if a healer, *then* a vampire, a thing that depends on taking lives to remain alive."

He felt his eyes narrow with skepticism. "What's with you?"

She sighed. "Nothing is *with me*, John. I'm just trying to help. You can't work your way through issues you won't even admit exist, and you are refusing to do that."

"That's not true," he said.

"No?"

"No."

"So now you think you're a healer? You've accepted the fact that you can heal wounds and even take back death?"

John shrugged, found himself squirming in his seat. "Well, it just sounds stupid when you say it like that."

"But you think it's a possibility."

John sighed. "If I say yes, are men in white coats going to burst through the door, put me in a straight-jacket, and trundle me off to some asylum?"

Barnes shook her head. "Of course not. No one wears those coats anymore."

John chuckled ruefully. "Okay then, yeah, after talking to Mary Ann and after thinking about it for a while, I'm not willing to say that all of this is just…"

"Bullshit?" Barnes volunteered.

"Bullshit," John agreed.

Barnes tossed the pad and her pen onto her desk, then looked at the door and clapped her hands twice sharply.

"What are you doing?" John said.

Barnes smiled. "Just messing with you, John. But…" She was quiet for a moment. "When you were brought into the hospital, I was in the ER. That's why I got your case and ended up taking care of you while you were here. I was also the first doctor to examine Kyra Metheny when she was admitted and…" Barnes shook her head, eyes turning up slightly as she remembered that morning. "There was blood all over her clothes, John. There was brain matter on her cheek, and flecks of bone on her clothing and matted in her hair. But there was not one single mark on that girl. Not a scratch. I'm going to be honest with you, so stick with me for a second."

Barnes closed her eyes and thought for a moment, then spoke again. "I'm not a shrink, and I'm not spiritual by nature. I don't go to church and, if I'm being completely honest, I don't believe in God. But what I saw that day, John...it terrified me. It shook something inside of me, not just in my head, but in my heart. What if I'm wrong? What if there is more to the world than what I can see with my own eyes? Yes, I'm trying to help you through this, but I'm also trying to help myself." She chuckled. "People always say, 'Anything's possible.' Most of the time it's just a toss off, a nothing statement. But what if that's *true*? What if it's true that *anything* is possible? It's an amazing thought. And a terrifying one."

John nodded slowly. "Yes," he said, looking out the window at the slowly moving clouds, "it is."

* * *

Leaving the hospital, John noticed a black van parked across the street. He would never have given it any special consideration—it was just a black Ford Econo-line van, one of thousands just like it—but when he saw the van, he also saw the driver's face through the window. And the driver gave him the creeps.

In almost every way the man looked normal—square-ish head, strong jaw, crew cut hair—but there was something about him. His lips were too pouty for the face around them, too pink and moist-looking. As John watched, the man raised a cigarette to his lips and tucked the filter between his lips almost daintily. John thought he looked like the kind of man who might enjoy licking dead people. He pictured the inside of the van and saw soiled, bloody blankets, half-used rolls of duct-tape, empty fast food wrappers, moldy chicken bones on the filthy floor.

John very pointedly looked away and turned right down the street.

Behind him, he heard the sound of an engine firing up and then the squeal of a vehicle low on power-steering fluid.

Glancing back over his shoulder, he saw the van pulling away from the curb. His heart jumped in his chest and he picked up his pace, turned the corner.

And ran his face directly into the chest of one of the largest men he had ever seen.

"Sorry," John said, backing up a step, breathing hard. "I wasn't looking." He looked up at the man's face, but the sun was directly behind his head, and all he could see was a dark profile, like the moon during a lunar eclipse. Though he couldn't see the man's face, he got the impression that he was black.

"Don't worry about it," the man said, his voice rumbling, like two enormous slabs of rock grinding.

John glanced back and saw that the black van had nearly drawn even with him.

"Sorry again," he said, and tried to move past the enormous man, but the hulk moved slightly and blocked his path.

The van pulled to the curb beside them, and a moment later, the side door slid open, the moist-lipped man hunched within, still smoking the cigarette. He smiled at John, exposing bleach-whitened teeth.

"I'll hit you if I have to," the huge man said, his voice a deep rumble. "Better you just get in. Easier all around, right?"

So John did.

Chapter 14

The interior of the black van didn't live up to John's first impression of the vehicle.

Instead of the moving garbage pit he'd pictured, he found himself riding in the lap of luxury. Deep, black leather seats, a full wet-bar on the side without the door, a plasma-screen television and all of the hardware to go with it: DVD player, VCR, even what looked to be some kind of game system. Mounted beside the TV was a rack of movies and compact discs. A mini-fridge was tucked neatly away in the joint of the L-shaped seating area. All in all, impressive. And confusing.

"Who are you?" John asked. He was shaky and felt like he still might faint. Instead of settling back into his seat, he perched up on the edge, ready to bolt at any opportunity.

The big man, who *was* black—almost midnight black, in fact—yawned and settled back into his seat. "Just relax, man. No need to rush with that stuff. You'll find out soon enough."

John felt the van ease into motion. The other man had gone back up front and was driving. Smoke from his cigarette drifted back.

"Are you going to kill me?" he asked.

The big man didn't answer, but crossed his legs. For a long moment he said nothing, then he uncrossed his legs and leaned forward, opened the door of the mini-fridge.

"You want a beer?" he asked. His expression was friendly, his tone matching.

What the hell was going on here?

John shook his head. "No," he said, "but if you'd just—"

"Do me a favor and shut the fuck up," the hulk said. He twisted the cap off a bottle of Honey Brown and took a deep drink. "Ahhh," he breathed out, satisfied, then looked back at John and smiled. "You might as well sit back, brother. We're gonna be in this baby for a while. Speaking of which, you want to watch a movie or something? We could play some X-Box."

* * *

Two hours later, the van pulled to a stop.

John's two abductors hadn't talked much during the ride, but he'd been able to pick up their names: the thin one with the wet lips was Curt, and the man-mountain was named, of all things, Percy.

Although John's first thoughts after the abduction had been for his own safety, he now understood that these men had no intention of harming him. There was a strange species of relief in that knowledge, but as they'd driven, John's thoughts had drifted elsewhere, to Connie and her daughter. He had told Connie that he would be there in a day or two. What would she think when he didn't show?

There were no windows in the back of the van, so John couldn't see where they had stopped, but he heard Curt climb out of the vehicle and crunch around the outside. A couple of seconds later, he heard the gas tank cover being unscrewed, and then the pulsing flow of fuel into the van's belly.

As he listened to the goings-on outside, he felt Percy watching him intently. Probably the big man was wondering when John was going to make a break for it, and to be truthful, John had been wondering the same thing himself. If he moved quickly, could he get into the cab of the van without being collared by Percy? He thought maybe he could; the gigantic man looked strong as Atlas but not very quick. But what about Curt then? Both men were sure to have guns on them. Even if he got out of the van, he'd only be offering himself up as a moving target.

He heard Percy laugh quietly to himself and looked at the gigantic man.

Percy hadn't moved much since settling back into his seat a couple of hours before, but now he lifted one side of his shirt-tail, revealing a nasty-looking pistol tucked into the belt of his black jeans.

"It's not worth it," Percy said. "You wouldn't get ten feet, m'man."

Okay, John thought. *Not that way, then.* He sat back into the well-oiled leather seat.

"Where are we?" he asked. "Been driving for a couple of hours at least."

"At least," Percy said. He looked tired and bored. "Sorry, man. Sucks for us, too."

Outside, John heard the gas stop pumping, and then the metallic scrape as Curt removed the nozzle from the tank.

"Hey," he said to Percy, "I have to go to the bathroom."

"Couple more hours," the man said. "Then you can piss all you want. Moan, too, if the notion takes you."

"How about a phone call then?"

The giant chuckled. "Ah shit, you're funny."

Chapter 15

Before Phylum headed south, he'd had to take care of a few things in New York, his normal base of operations. Those few things had included: withdrawing enough money from his account to pay for whatever might need buying—it was bad form to leave a credit trail when you were in Phylum's line of business; picking up three of his favorite suits from the Vietnamese cleaner on 5th; finding long-term care for Arbus, his 2 year-old calico; and beating the ever-loving shit out of Kimbo Perkins, the douchebag who'd been nailing Phylum's sister for the better part of two years. The last item on the list had been the only one he'd really needed to be present for—the rest he could have taken care of easily enough over the phone. But beating the ever-loving shit out of some greasy, know-it-all, conman fuckface always felt better in person. The administration of said ass whooping had been followed by the ultimatum that Kimbo either blow town immediately and never come back, or spend the better part of the next decade paying a team of surgeons to reverse the gender reassignment Phylum would happily perform on his worthless ass, and *gratis* at that.

All of those tasks crossed off his mental to-do list, Phylum climbed into his black BMW X1 and headed south, feeling content and relaxed.

* * *

The drive to Charlotte was fine, pleasurable even. Mostly, Phylum stuck to the back roads as he wove through central and then southern Pennsylvania, into West Virginia, Virginia, and then down out of the mountains into North Carolina itself.

Before leaving home he had entered Barron's address into his Garmin GPS, and the gadget's British-accented female voice guided him along. He pulled off Interstate 85 a few miles from Barron's home and fueled up, going inside just long enough to purchase a six-pack of Diet Coke and a family-sized bag of Cool Ranch Doritos, which he swore by. Loaded for the proverbial bear, he continued on his way.

His reason for being here was odd in some ways and totally normal in others. The voice on the phone, which belonged to the man Phylum had come to think of only as Mr. "It's Me," had told him there was a man in Charlotte named John Barron who needed to be "taken care of," which Phylum had always thought a strange way to express the concept of murder. So that part was just about normal, and Phylum had no problem with it.

Although he knew very little about the company for which he worked, he understood the basic operating principle: someone has a problem he wants "taken care of"; he calls Mr. It's Me; Mr. It's Me calls Phylum. Who the initiating party *was* didn't much matter to Phylum. What did matter was that when he got back to New York, there would be another $250,000 sitting in his bank account. That's all there was to it. Easy Peasy Japanese-y.

And it shouldn't go unstated that Phylum liked his job. He'd been doing it at an exceptionally high level of success for much longer than any of his contemporaries had lasted, in part because Phylum had killed most of his contemporaries. Competition being bad for business and all that. Phylum had what some might have considered to be principles, but they were uniquely his own, constructed over the duration of a childhood that had nearly destroyed him.

His father had been abusive, his mother a drunk, and Phylum himself—at that point in his life he had been Eric Wilson—a marginalized loser who'd never managed much in the way of friends. There had been beatings in the parking lot after school, trays of food upended over his head in the cafeteria, and thumbtacks left on his seats.

And then all of that had ended rather abruptly.

It had ended when Phylum's tormentors began to suffer a series of very unfortunate mishaps. No one had been able to prove anything, but everyone knew who was responsible for Mark Sefferin's brakes failing, for Kyle Parker's fall down the basement steps at his sister's graduation party, and for Katie Bartlett washing up dead and naked and repeatedly raped on the bank of the Crum Creek not two days before the graduation party her parents had planned. Yes, they all knew, but there was no proof, and then one day, he started hearing the kids at school referring to him as Phylum. Curious as to why, he'd cornered a sophomore girl in the ladies room and demanded to know. After wetting herself, she told him that a couple of the kids in biology class had been joking about how no one even thought he was human—that he wasn't even in the same phylum as humans.

That had made Eric smile, and then he had stopped being Eric and became Phylum for good.

* * *

He left the BMW in a Harris Teeter parking lot and headed toward Barron's complex on foot. The Beemer was a little flashy to take on a job like this, and he didn't want to attract the wrong kind of attention.

The complex was walled and gated, and there were, for some reason, a few reporters loitering around the entrance, drinking coffee and smoking cigarettes. So Phylum made his way into the woods where he would have some shelter and hopped the wall.

He'd seen this kind of place before, plenty of times. It was the sort of situation in which only the very young or the very apathetic would choose to dwell, a roughly circular track of identical buildings, all arranged around a central pool, gym-facility, and poorly-maintained tennis courts. Phylum passed people as he walked, searching for Barron's building—college students, moldy oldsters who probably worked at Wal-Mart or in the local Hobby Lobby...

Ah. Phylum stopped, checked the notepad in his breast pocket and climbed the stairs to the second floor of the building. He stood in front of Barron's door for a moment, looked around, shrugged and then knocked. He put a smile on his face and waited, but he heard nothing from inside. He knocked again and waited for a few more seconds, then let his smile fall.

He figured there was no use breaking in. He was here to kill this guy, after all, not to do his fucking laundry. It would just have to be tonight. Thus decided, he left.

Chapter 16

At a little past nine o'clock that night, Rose knocked on the door of John's apartment, listened for anything from within, heard nothing. *Hmm.* She was starting to feel confused and concerned.

The night before, after ditching her ride with the Mexicans in the Firebird, Rose caught on with a long-hauler passing through Charlotte. The first hints of dawn were showing—a lightening of the sky by degrees, from black to dark blue—and Rose knew she was on the verge of a bad situation. She didn't know what she'd been expecting to happen when they reached the city, but passing into, through, and then out of Charlotte-proper to the north, the eastern horizon now taking on a pink-stained hue, Rose had felt nothing more than the vague sense of anticipation that had held onto her for the past several weeks.

And then, maybe five miles north of the city…

"Hey," she'd said, sitting up straighter in the shotgun seat of the wide cab, "can you let me out here?"

After the truck pulled away, Rose had found herself standing on the side of a four-lane expanse of asphalt called Harris Boulevard. Not too far down the road, lit by bright roadside lamps, she could see the white and red sign of an Outback Steakhouse jutting from a declivity. Further down, past the restaurant, was a well-lit plaza of shops with another brightly-lit sign reading: HARRIS CROSSING PLAZA.

None of it meant anything to her, but at the same time, it *did*, and she'd found herself walking with a sense of purpose.

Across Harris Boulevard, dodging a couple of speeding cars, through the almost empty lot of a Harris Teeter supermarket, and then half a mile down another wide street.

And then into the Davis Oaks apartment complex.

So close, her mind had whispered, *so close now, so close...*

Following a winding road around the well-treed complex, past the pool, lit a brilliant and unnatural blue, past the darkened clubhouse, and then, minutes later, climbing the stairs to a green door on a second-floor landing. 208 on the door, the numbers silver, faux-elegant.

Everything inside of her had cried out for her to kick down the door, to dispatch whatever poor soul lay beyond, to reclaim her life...but the horizon flared with the first light of sun, and Rose knew that in moments she would grow tired and torpid. It would be dangerous to do this now. And so she had resolved to return the next night, retraced her steps, pried up the door of a storage unit not far from the apartment, and slept on the concrete floor until the sun had gone back down.

Now she was back, but something was different.

No longer did she feel any special attraction to the apartment, not as she'd felt burning inside of her during her long trek up from Jacksonville. For the last couple of days, she had been drawn like a magnet to this place, pulled completely against her will toward a fate she didn't understand. And now that she was here, standing in front of this door, she knew instinctually that something had changed. No longer could she detect the nearly radioactive power that had summoned her here, but just as a physicist might gauge with a Geiger counter, she sensed that the source of the power had passed this way, could still intuit with the primal, unthinking part of her that this was a pooling-place. There was no denying the strength of the force that had guided her here.

Out of her bag she took a wallet-sized black rubber bundle and unfolded it, pulled forth a thin file and a tube-shaped prong about the width of a paper clip. A glance both ways, then she went to work. Thirty seconds later the lock rolled over and she was in.

She shut the door behind herself.

Dark.

Her eyes were good in the low light, but it had been bright on the landing and it took her sight a moment to adjust. *There, better.* Things were starting to come into focus now, the outlines of furniture and walls blue in the almost black.

Rose listened, but heard nothing, strained for anything, breathing, the rustle of sheets, but it was totally silent. The apartment was empty.

With her right hand, she reached out and searched the wall near the door, found a light switch, and flicked it up.

Seeing the space laid out before her, Rose felt a powerful and inexplicable rush of loneliness. The room was furnished sparely, almost spartanly: a thin-backed couch in front of a small television, a desk against the wall with the chair pushed in, some papers scattered around, a lap-top computer folded over on itself.

On the breakfast bar separating the living room from the kitchen was a single framed photograph of a man and a woman, both older, the man with a full dark mustache and black hair streaked with silver, the woman dark-haired and olive-skinned, wearing a flower-print dress.

Rose picked up the simple silver frame and ran a finger gently over the glass. The couple looked familiar, but only passingly so, as if she might have seen them once in an old movie, or in a dream. She replaced the frame on the white Formica bar.

The walls of the living room were off-white and devoid of decoration. No art; no photos. Plain and unremarkable. The apartment reminded Rose of a model home, but then it occurred to her that no semi-competent interior decorator would make a space so soulless, not if they wanted to make a sale.

There was a sliding glass door onto a small balcony, and Rose stepped to it and drew the hanging white blinds into place. No need to risk being seen while she reconnoitered.

Safely sheltered from any would-be prying eyes, she turned and regarded the room critically.

What the hell? her mind complained. It was like no one actually lived here at all. Why had she been so powerfully drawn to this place, then? And there was no doubt in her mind that this apartment was precisely where she'd been pulled.

Maybe another room.

On the far side of the living room, opposite the front door, was a door, standing slightly open, and Rose started toward it. *Bedroom,* she thought, *check the bedside table.*

She stopped in mid-step, puzzled.

There was no way she could know that the room behind the door was the bedroom. If this was a two-bedroom apartment, it might be a study or a den, or even the bathroom. But it was the bedroom. Standing there, still ten feet from the door, she realized that she even knew what the bedroom looked like. A queen-sized bed pushed midway between the two bordering walls, a dark faux-oak bedside table, a matching chest-of-drawers facing the foot of the bed, the kind of cheap furniture one might buy at Wal-Mart or Target. In fact—and there was no way she could possibly know this—the bedside table and chest-of-drawers *had* come from a Target, a Target in Columbus, Ohio.

Rose walked slowly to the door and gave it a push.

The room was exactly the way she'd envisioned.

* * *

Five minutes later, she sat down on the futon with a journal and a sheaf of loose papers. Some of them she'd found in the desk, a couple more in the bedroom, piled on top of the bureau. The journal she'd discovered hidden away in the top drawer of the bedside table.

The paper on top was a folded over bit of newspaper. Printed across the top was the headline: CHARLOTTE TEACHER HEALS STUDENT. Puzzled, Rose read the rest of the article, which had been clipped from the *National Enquirer*. When she was finished, she sat back and put her feet up on the coffee table.

John Barron? The name was oddly familiar, but, like the picture on the breakfast bar, she didn't know from where. And a healer, at least reputedly? Something about that made sense.

Lost in thought, Rose got up and went into the kitchen, opened the fridge, and without looking, reached in and pulled out a beer from the top shelf. She twisted the top off and drank deeply—

The cold beer still in her mouth, she froze.

Shaking a little, she put the beer down, the article forgotten. A drip of beer ran from her bottom lip and onto her chin. Rose reached out her left hand and tore a paper towel from the dispenser screwed to the wall. She wiped her mouth, then reached down and opened the cabinet under the sink and tossed the towel in the trash.

And stopped again, suddenly breathless.

Half of her brain was paralyzed, shocked into uselessness. The other part of her, the reptilian, instinctual part that had been dealing with bizarre occurrences for her entire life, still seemed to work.

From all appearances, she had been drawn from hundreds of miles away to an apartment she didn't recognize, but somehow knew intimately. In the brief time she'd spent inside the apartment, she had seen a picture of two people she could almost place in her memory, and she had read an article about a man whose name sounded more than familiar.

Which left her where?

Rose took a sip of the beer and sat back down on the futon. She was surprised at how unrushed she felt; in much the same way she'd been led here, the way she'd found the papers in the bedroom, the way she seemed to know her way around this apartment as if she'd lived here for years, she also knew that this John Barron wasn't coming home, at least not anytime soon.

She opened the journal. And nearly recoiled in shock.

Staring up at her from the page was a face she recognized. The rendering wasn't anything to write home about, just an amateurishly sketched representation, but there was no mistaking the sunken eyes, the week's worth of scruff, and the tattoo... On the neck of the man in the drawing was a black sun, and issuing from it, a fan of dark red rays. She'd killed this man in Florida, not a day before she'd felt compelled to leave the beach house.

Hands shaking slightly, she flipped back a page. Another sketch, this one of an old woman wearing a pearl necklace. Rose had found her walking on the beach with her little dog and a glass of white wine and torn her throat out behind a sand dune. *Oh, Jesus.* Rose let the pages sift through her fingers, seeing face after face, a catalogue of her victims. And then one drawing in particular stopped her and she hitched in a quick breath.

"Oh, no," she whispered.

In the sketch, a little girl slept soundly in a farm-style bed, the covers pulled up to her chin. In the foreground of the drawing was a cross that bisected the view both vertically and horizontally, and Rose knew the view was through a window. And she knew what the sketch could not show her, that it had been snowing that night—a blizzard, in fact—and that the little girl's blood was sweeter than anything Rose had ever tasted...

Enraged, Rose stood and threw the journal across the room. It hit the wall and fell behind the television, fluttering down like a bird that has flown into a window. Wanting to be out of this place, out in the night, Rose stuffed the papers from the coffee table into her bag and stepped toward the door.

She was almost gone when she saw the small white square of paper sitting on the edge of the breakfast bar.

Written on the paper was a name, Mary Ann Shaw, and one other word: Call. Beneath that, a phone number. It was the one thing in the apartment that signaled a connection between Barron and any other person. She stuffed the paper into her pocket and turned again to leave.

That was when a man's voice said, "Well, now, who the fuck are you?"

Chapter 17

Phylum stood in the doorway of Barron's apartment, a Glock 17 in his right hand, and regarded the woman standing in the living room. She was youngish, somewhere in her late twenties or early thirties, and she was, Phylum thought, about as drop dead fucking hot as a female could get without combusting. He felt movement below his belt and grinned, waiting for the woman to panic.

But she didn't. Instead, she just stood there, looking at him implacably. Phylum felt his grin falter.

"What are you doing here?" he asked, stepping into the apartment and closing the door behind him.

"I could ask you the same question," the woman responded. Damn, she even had a nice voice, low and husky, like one of those chicks from the phone porn places. Of course, most of them were fifty, filthy, and fat as fuck, holding the phone with one hand while they shoveled KFC or Taco Bell into their faces with the other.

He nodded. "I'm here looking for John Barron. I don't guess you're him."

She smiled, actually *smiled*, at that. She wasn't supposed to be smiling, goddamnit. He was huge, and he was holding a fucking gun. What was wrong with this girl? She shook her head. "No," she said. "Not him. But I'm looking for him, too, I think."

"Any idea where he is?"

"No," she said. "If that's all, I was just leaving."

Phylum reached behind him and flicked the deadbolt on the door. "Not quite all."

Her eyes widened and then she nodded resignedly. "I figured as much."

"How do you know Barron?" Phylum said, stepping closer.

She stepped back, edging toward the breakfast bar, putting it between them. "I don't," she said.

"Then why do you want to find him?"

She looked at him stonily, measuring him. "You ask too many questions. That's a good way to get yourself hurt."

He surprised himself by laughing. "Hurt? That's good." He took another step closer and she retreated an equal distance. Now they stood on opposite sides of the bar, him in the living room, her in the kitchen. She was trapped.

"Look," she said, her eyes never leaving his, "I don't want to kill you, but I will if I have to. Just back off and let me go, and we'll go our own ways. Deal?"

Oh, she was *fantastic*. "And how are you going to kill me?" Phylum said. Now he was edging around the bar, entering the kitchen, the gun still at his side. The woman had stopped backing up and stood facing him in the tight kitchen, the counter behind her. Nowhere else to go.

She smiled again, and he saw that her teeth were very white. "I'm going to rip your throat out with my hands and then drink your blood," she whispered. "If you make me."

"My god," he whispered, raising the gun and pointing it at her chest. "I think I'm in love."

There was a sudden banging on the door, and a muffled voice yelling, "Mr. Barron, this is the police. Are you okay in there? Open the door!"

Phylum's head turned in the direction of the door for the briefest of moments, and then he was ducking as the microwave oven, one of the old ones—it must have weighed thirty or forty pounds—came sailing toward him. It smashed into the wall behind him with tremendous force and drywall dust cascaded down all around Phylum. The door of the microwave, which had come open on impact, clipped the hand holding the gun as it fell to the floor and the Glock discharged with a deafening *CRACK*.

"Fuck!" Phylum yelled, trying to regain his balance. He stood and looked back into the kitchen, but the woman had hopped the breakfast bar and was heading toward the sliding glass door out to the balcony.

He raised the gun and fired twice. One of the rounds punched through the glass door, and it exploded outward with a shimmery cough. The second bullet caught the woman high in the back, just to the side of her right shoulder blade. Not a kill shot, but a crippling one.

Gotcha, Phylum thought. But the woman never stopped, never so much as paused. She gained the balcony, braced her hands on the wooden railing, and then vaulted over the edge.

"What the fuck?" Phylum said aloud. And then the door flew open and two uniformed cops were suddenly in the doorway.

"Put the gun on the ground!" one of them yelled—screamed, really; Phylum could hear the panic in his voice. The other stood behind the first, gun pointed at Phylum's chest.

Still thinking about the way the woman had gone over the second floor balcony, Phylum very calmly raised his gun and shot both of the cops. He aimed low because he knew they'd be wearing body armor and a direct hit center-mass would do little more than knock the breath out of them, maybe break a couple ribs if he was lucky. He hit one of the cops in the crotch and the man fell, his mouth open in a silent scream. The other, Phylum hit in the shin, halfway between ankle and knee, and the bone snapped like a toothpick, dropping the cop to the floor. This man's scream was *not* silent, and the shrill sound did Phylum's heart some good.

As he walked past the two writhing men, he shot each in the head. Three minutes later, after a cursory check of the grassy area below Barron's balcony, he had scaled the back fence of the complex, where he'd entered earlier in the day, and was trotting across Harris Boulevard toward his car. When he climbed in behind the wheel, he was still shaking his head. Who the fuck had that crazy bitch been? There was only one thing he knew for sure: she wasn't like any person he'd seen before.

* * *

After his encounter with the woman at Barron's apartment, Phylum had taken it upon himself to do a little research. Sitting in his car in the parking lot of a McDonalds twenty minutes outside of the city, Phylum booted up his MacBook and connected to the internet via a wireless card. He surfed over to Google and searched for information on John Barron. The number of hits was awe-inspiring, nearly two million, and all seemed to have been generated over the last couple of weeks.

Barron, it seemed, had supposedly healed a girl who was mortally injured in some kind of hit-and-run jackassery at the school where he worked. According to the articles he read—and these were articles from reputable sources like the New York *Times* and the Washington *Herald*, the girl's head had, for all intents and purposes, been spread across the road like jam on bread. And then she had been back in school a couple of days later.

"Huh," Phylum grunted, ripping open a pack of salted peanuts and upending it into his mouth. "Weird, man." He went back to his search.

Fifteen minutes later, he'd managed to gather a few other seemingly salient pieces of information.

People were by turns worshipful and exceedingly skeptical about the healing; after the incident at his school, Barron had been laid-up in a local hospital for a number of days, convalescing after suffering some kind of physical breakdown of his own; Barron had been attacked during his stay in the hospital by a cancer patient; the Catholic Archdiocese had been called in to investigate the veracity of the healing and had pronounced it false. That struck Phylum as odd. Barron didn't seem to be using the purported healing to garner attention, money, or fame. In fact, from all reports, the exact opposite was true. There were no direct quotes from Barron in any of the articles, and several referenced the man's reclusive behavior. In short, just the way the Church might *want* to see a man acting in the wake of such a "miracle." Denying the authenticity of the healing seemed a stupid move in what should have been a win-win situation for the Catholic Church.

And then there was what Phylum had observed inside of Barron's shitty little dwelling. *Nothing.* No plush furniture, no fifty inch flat-screen TV. It wasn't the home of the kind of man who borrowed money from Mr. Prince, in other words.

* * *

Phylum dialed Mr. It's Me and was gratified when the man answered on the first ring.

"You shouldn't call me," the man said, sounding uncharacteristically annoyed. In all the years Phylum had been taking calls and receiving jobs from the man, this was the first time he'd ever initiated contact. Phylum's business operated on much the same premise as the United States armed forces had for years: don't ask, don't tell. When he got a call from Mr. It's Me, the understanding was that Phylum would complete the job without question. It was an arrangement that had worked well for a long time. But this job was different.

On the surface, it had made little sense to begin with; he had been hired to bump off some regular Joe in North Carolina. Not New York or L.A., not Vegas or Atlantic City. Those were the kinds of places Mr. Prince's customers regularly did business. So from the very beginning, Phylum had assumed Mr. It's Me was hiring him on behalf of some other party. Now, given what he had learned during his brief foray into the World Wide Web, he was sure of it.

"Yeah, well, them's the breaks."

"What do you want?"

"There was a woman in Barron's apartment. Someone else looking for him. She wasn't normal."

There was a pause on the other end of the line. "Explain."

"I shot her in the back with a Glock 17 from about fifteen feet away, and then she jumped off a balcony two stories off the ground and still felt good enough to run off, no problem."

"Don't worry about her. Just take care of Barron."

"He's gone," Phylum said. "Hasn't been back to his apartment all day. And I want to know who this woman is."

"Never mind the woman," Mr. It's Me reiterated. "Can you find Barron?"

Phylum laughed. "Of course I can *find* him. But I want to know who wants him dead."

"That's not part of our agreement."

"No," Phylum agreed, "but this isn't a normal job, is it?"

There was silence for a moment as the other man turned thoughts over in his mind. "No," he finally said. "That's not part of our agreement."

Phylum exhaled. "I want you to understand a very basic fact," he said, his voice level and still agreeable. "You are not very smart. In fact, you're about the dumbest motherfucker in the world. Not to mention the dumbest motherfucker in Reston, Virginia."

He waited for the words to sink in. Six months ago, Phylum had taken it upon himself to do a little research into the real identity of Mr. It's Me. He'd done so for no other reason than that he had begun to resent the way the man seemed so comfortable ordering him around. Phylum was no trained monkey. It had cost him nearly twenty thousand dollars, but Phylum had learned from a contact inside the FBI that the number that always popped up PRIVATE when Mr. It's Me called his cell phone actually belonged to a forty-three year-old schmuck named Harold Colson who lived with his wife and two children in a suburb of Washington, DC. He'd been waiting for the right time to use the information.

He heard the other man's breath click dryly in his throat.

"Are we communicating now?" Phylum asked.

"Yuh-yes," It's Me said, the cocky, self-assured tone completely gone from his voice now. It had been replaced by the whiny, panic-stricken quality Phylum so treasured; it told him that the natural equilibrium had once again been reestablished. The wolf. The sheep.

Mr. It's Me told him everything.

Chapter 18

The pain was bad, but not as hot and sharp as it had been immediately following the confrontation with the hulk in Barron's apartment. Moving gingerly, Rose slipped off her blouse and turned around, craning her neck backward to get a look at the gunshot wound in the grimy mirror.

After her leap from the balcony, Rose ran blindly, thinking about nothing other than getting into the woods and away from a conflict she wanted no part of. It wasn't that she was afraid. If she'd wanted to, she was fully confident that she would have disarmed and killed the man who had walked in on her in Barron's apartment. She may have taken a bullet or two in the process, but the outcome would have been all but preordained. But then the cops had shown up, and Rose's two millisecond evaluation of the situation had told her she had only one viable option: run. She'd gotten what she came for, and she didn't need the kind of trouble knocking at Barron's door. There were at least two cops out there, and if they'd reported the gunshots there would be two dozen more in ten minutes. Operating under those conditions, she might be able to kill three or four of the cops before they took her down, but she didn't think she would get away.

When the bullet entered, it had done quite a bit of initial damage, she decided. Not a hard-cased round. Something softer. A dum dum, the kind of round designed to inflict a maximum of damage by mushrooming and then rattling around inside the victim instead of simply going in and then coming out, leaving a straight trail.

"Damn," Rose muttered and spit a red string of saliva into the sink. The bullet must have clipped her lung. She reached her left arm across her chest and over her right shoulder, felt the wound, noting the ragged edges, the craterous width of the hole.

"That's going to scar," she muttered. Already, she could see the edges of the wound beginning to draw back together, closing in over the bullet still lodged in her flesh. This had happened to her before, and the itch of the bullet as her body tried to push it out a rift in her skin that no longer existed was impossibly aggravating. Better just to get it over with.

Rose dug into the wound with her forefinger, bringing a fresh wave of white hot agony, and dug for the bullet. Not finding it, she pushed the finger deeper, up to the second knuckle, felt something hard, hooked it with her fingertip, pulled it out.

Panting, Rose let the bullet clink into the filthy sink. It came to rest on the rusty drain screen, gore smeared and flattened at the tip from where it had impacted the bone of her shoulder blade.

"Motherfucker," Rose whispered, then turned and examined the wound again. Free of the bullet, the wound was closing more quickly, the skin knitting itself back together, leaving a pale white scar. After a few days, the scar would itself be all but gone, but never completely. It would just be another memento of this goddamned life into which she had been born. She pulled her blouse back on, grimacing as she lifted her right arm to fit it through the sleeve.

Anyway, despite the unanticipated interference at Barron's apartment, there had been forward movement. Rose dug her hand into the front pocket of her jeans and pulled forth the small square of paper she'd stashed there.

Mary Ann Shaw.

Alright then.

* * *

Rose tracked Mary Ann Shaw down in exactly the same way John had done only days before. She had a name and a phone number; all she needed now was an address.

Easy.

Though she could have taken the long way around and scanned through the white pages, Rose didn't want to waste any more time. Instead, she walked across the street to a shady looking motel fronted by a flickering white and black sign proclaiming it THE RAVEN MOTEL. Inside, a young man with a scraggly patch of black hair on his chin was sitting in front of a computer. Rose could hear voices coming from the monitor and knew he was watching a show online. She asked the young man if he would mind if she used his computer for a moment.

When he said that was against company policy, Rose tore his throat open with a slash of her hand and fed on him. Even as the first salty, coppery-tasting gouts of blood moistened her throat, Rose felt the pain in her back begin to ease.

* * *

Half-an-hour later, Rose pulled up outside of Shaw's home in the bruised and rusty Toyota Corolla she'd lifted from the lot outside The Raven Motel. She killed the engine and climbed out of the car.

The house in front of which she stood was small, but very neatly kept. A rectangular lawn, fastidiously edged and recently mowed, fronted the place. A bed of brightly-colored flowers ran the length of the façade, and white rope-lights outlined the path from the street to the front door. Several of the windows glowed a soft yellow. *Good,* Rose thought, *she's home.*

She walked to the front door, pulled the screen door open, and knocked. There was no sound for a moment, but then footsteps pounded toward the door.

"Who is it?" A man's voice.

"I'm here to see Mary Ann," Rose said in a neutral voice, readying herself. When she heard the bolt turn, she twisted the doorknob and shoved as hard as she could. There was a dull *thud* as the stout wooden door connected with something solid, a skull, maybe, and then a louder sound as a substantial body hit the floor. Rose pushed into the house and shut the door quickly and quietly behind herself.

A man with thinning blond hair half-sat, half-lay on the floor of the small foyer. He wore checked flannel pajama bottoms and a gray bathrobe. A nasty cut on his forehead leaked blood into his left eye as he squinted up at Rose. He reached up with one hand and clapped it over the wound, yelped in pain.

"Where is she?" Rose said.

The man shook his head and started to stand. Rose planted her foot in his chest and pushed, sending the man catapulting backward into the wall. He fell to the side with a moan, knocking over a small table as he did so and then falling on top of it. There was a *crack* as the table collapsed beneath his weight.

"If you don't tell me where she is," Rose said patiently, "I'll kill you."

"I don't know—" the man said, and Rose cancelled the statement with a kick to his face. The man's head snapped back and into the wall, plowing a crater in the plaster. He slumped, legs caught beneath him so that he was kneeling. Blood flowed from his mouth and nose, and his nose pressed against his face at an irregular angle.

"Oh Jesus," he moaned, and spat. A wad of blood and saliva splatted to the floor and a strand of rosy spit stretched from his lower lip and dangled down to his bare, nearly hairless chest.

"Mary Ann Shaw," Rose said, squatting down so that she could look the man in the eyes. "Here?"

He shook his head, eyes rolling wildly in their sockets. He coughed, and a bubble of blood grew and then popped on his lips, showing his cheeks with a fine drizzle of red. Some got on Rose's hands and upper arms.

"Where then?" Rose asked, but he didn't hear. Very slowly, his head fell back against the wall, his eyes closed. Unconscious.

"Shit," Rose said, standing. She searched the house quickly, going room to room, opening closet doors, checking under the beds, but there was no one else home. Done with her tour, she went into the kitchen to wash the blood off her hands. She was drying her hands with a paper towel when she saw the dry erase board mounted on the wall next to the refrigerator.

Written on the board in black marker, just below a reminder to pay the phone bill and pick up some milk at the market, was: APRIL 21st—LOCK-IN WITH KIDS AT FIRST PRESBY.

"Ah," Rose said.

There was a sound behind her and she barely got out of the way before a fireplace poker smashed into the wall where she'd just been standing, digging a deep dark rut in the white paint.

Rose whirled around to face her attacker.

"Get out," the man snarled. Neither his mouth nor his nose had stopped bleeding, and his chin and chest were slick with fresh blood. It looked like someone had flayed his chest. He held the poker in both hands and brought it back for another swing. "Go now," he said. "Just get the fuck out!"

Rose regarded him coolly. She brought up a hand and tapped the dry erase board, gave the man a small smile. "Have what I came for anyway."

He saw what Rose meant and screamed, swung the poker at her head. Rose caught it in mid-swing and snatched it from his hands, then, in the same motion, spun and brought the poker down on the defenseless man's head. There was a soft and empty sound as bone collapsed beneath the force of the blow and the man fell to the ground, motionless. A stream of blood pumped slowly from his lacerated scalp and spread on the floor in a wide pool.

Rose dropped the poker and searched the kitchen for a phonebook. She found one in a cabinet next to the dishwasher, located the listing for First Presbyterian Church, jotted the address down, and left the house.

* * *

It took her a little longer to locate the church than it had to find Shaw's home.

After parking the Corolla out of sight, she walked to the front door, found it locked, and so walked around the outside of the building. From inside, she could hear the muffled sound of music and laughter. At a rear entrance she heard approaching voices and pressed herself against the side of the building, behind a row of high hedges.

Two young boys, no older than sixteen, walked into view.

"Over there," one of them said and pointed, his voice hushed.

"Where?" the other said.

"Behind that tree."

"Don't you think she'll be able to see us?"

"Naw, dude. There are, like, eight thousand other people in there. Like she's gonna even notice we're gone for five minutes. I mean, Dorian and Joe are practically fucking in the rec room. I mean, did you see what they were doing? She had her hands down his pants, man. Right there, in the middle of everyone!"

"Okay," the other said, obviously reluctant. The boys walked to a tree not far from where Rose crouched, and she heard a *snick snick* sound, recognized it as the sound of a lighter, and then there was the smell of marijuana smoke.

"Pass it over," one of the boys whispered.

A door suddenly slammed open and light flooded from the inside of the church.

"BOBBY SHAY AND TONY DOMINGUEZ, WHERE ARE YOU?" a woman's voice called. "I KNOW YOU'RE OUT HERE, AND IF I DON'T SEE YOU FRONT AND CENTER IN TEN SECONDS, YOUR PARENTS ARE GETTING A CALL."

"Shit, man," Rose heard one of the boys whisper frantically, "crush that fucker out. I'm dead shit if my parents hear about this. Come on, let's go."

There was a flicking sound and a shower of red sparks and the joint skittered to a stop next to Rose's foot.

"We're right here, Miss Shaw!" one of the boys called. "Just wanted to get some fresh air!"

Rose tensed. It was *her*.

As the boys walked back past her, Rose found herself needing to make a choice. If she took the woman now, she'd have to deal with the two boys. No big deal, but if they put up a fight, she didn't want to have to kill them. On the other hand, she might have to wait all night for another chance like this.

Fuck it.

Rose waited until the two boys were almost at the door, then cupped her hands around her mouth and called out, "Miss Shaw! Is that you? Come quick, please!"

There was a whispered exchange, only part of which Rose could hear.

"Bobby...who else...there?"

"Dunno...didn't see."

"...inside. Get Mr..."

The sound of something heavy being dragged over concrete. Rose peeked around the corner of the building and saw the slender shape of a woman silhouetted against the light in the open doorway.

"Who is that?" Shaw called.

Rose said nothing.

After a moment, the woman walked slowly down the short flight of stairs to the grass and started heading hesitantly toward Rose.

Rose waited until the woman was within ten feet of her hiding place, then stepped quietly out from behind the hedges.

"Who is that?" Shaw asked, squinting into the darkness.

Rose said nothing, but stepped toward the woman, closing the distance by half. By the time Shaw really began to understand that something was wrong, Rose had her by the arm in a vice-like grip.

"Come with me quietly and you'll be fine," Rose said. "Try to run and you're dead. And after I kill you, I'll kill every one of those fucking monsters inside the church."

There was a moment of silent consideration from Shaw, and then the woman said, "Oh my god, *you.*"

When Rose pulled her in the direction of the car, she came without a struggle.

Chapter 19

John woke in a bed and sat up, shucking the sheet and thin blanket that had been covering him. In a half-second, the last day's events played back in the front of his brain: the abduction, the van ride. That was all he remembered, actually. He'd accepted the offer of a Diet Coke in the van as he was beginning to nod off in his seat, and now suspected that one of his captors had slipped some kind of sleeping aid into it.

The first thing John noticed was that he felt good, alive, immediately awake. Usually it took him an hour to really get going, but right now he felt...what?

Rested, he thought. *Incredibly well rested.*

He registered the texture of the sheets under which he'd slept, and under which his legs still lay. Silk. And the mattress, which John thought must be king-sized but seemed much larger, was somehow soft and firm at the same time.

I've never felt anything like this, he thought. *This is amazing.*

Reluctantly, John threw back the covers and slid his way to the edge of the bed, dropped his legs over the side.

His feet didn't touch the floor, didn't even come close. Instead, they hung a good foot above the polished wood. John dropped down and saw, really *saw*, for the first time, the room in which he'd awoken.

"Holy crap," he whispered.

He took the room in the only way he could, in stages.

It was a good thirty feet wide, and at least as long. The ceiling was domed, twenty-five or thirty feet at the highest point, painted with a fresco of a blue sky smudged here and there with clouds that were marshmallow white at the center, but stormy gray, almost black, at the edges. The four-poster bed sat squarely in the center, bordered on every side by huge gulfs of space. The bed's posts reached halfway to the ceiling and each was topped with an inward looking gargoyle.

When he'd managed to get his mind around the proportions of the space, John began to take in the things that filled it.

The bed, of course, which was, indeed, much larger than any bed he'd ever seen. Beneath it, a richly colored Persian rug that looked ancient, hundreds of years old, almost threadbare in places, but still deep in its hues.

In the middle of one of the gray stone walls, a fireplace, the lintel a full six feet tall, gaped like a toothless mouth. In front of the huge hearth, a plush tan couch and a pair of matching high-backed chairs, all arranged around another Persian rug.

A chestnut bar stood against another of the walls, a full liquor cabinet behind it. Five stools sat in front, neatly pushed in. Glasses twinkled from their wall-mounted rack.

A state-of-the-art entertainment center and a black leather couch took up the corner nearest the windows. John saw low racks running along the walls to either side of the entertainment center and it took him a moment to realize that the racks were filled with thousands of DVDs and compact discs.

The entire wall to the right of the entertainment center was made of glass, floor to ceiling. The scene beyond it was pastoral. Grass stretched off, interrupted here and there by the occasional tree. At the far end of his vision, a low bank of darkness. It was evening and the light was fading, but if John really strained his eyes… *Trees*, John thought. But how far? Half a mile? Maybe further. Acres and acres of empty, perfectly manicured grass.

His mind went to Connie. She would be wondering where he was, thinking that he had decided not to come. John could imagine her daughter sick in bed, his childhood bed, probably, shivering even beneath the quilts his mother would have given Connie to put over her. John rested his hands on the glass, feeling powerless.

There was the sound behind him of a door opening and John turned around.

A woman stood in the doorway. She was tall and thin and wore a sharp-looking black suit and heels. Dark hair cascaded down over her shoulders.

"Good," she said, her lightly-accented voice echoing in the huge space. "You're awake. There's someone very eager to meet you, John."

Chapter 20

Albert Navarre, born Alberto Antona Navarro sixty-seven years ago in the tiny Texan town of Maguarichi, was dying slowly. The fact of his impending death did not disturb him—there was no fear of what would come after, or what *wouldn't*. There was no crying, no simpering, no begging some hypothetical God for more time. It wasn't the idea of ceasing to exist that offended Albert. More so, it was what his death would *symbolize*.

Defeat, final and irrevocable.

Did it matter that this final defeat was one that each life eventually had to endure? Albert had considered the question for many years and, after substantial thought, decided that it did *not*. He, after all, was no normal man; the rules that applied to everyone else should not, therefore, restrict him. And so he had determined that they would not. He was unique, and would find a way to avoid the most equalizing of all events.

For nearly thirty years he had searched for a solution, and for the entirety of the period during which he conducted his search, Albert had known well the enormity of the task he'd set for himself. The grail after which he quested was the subject of more failed searches than any other.

In the fledgling stages of his attempt to locate the fount of long-life, he'd encountered more stories and legends, all of them dead-ends, than he could sort through by himself.

There were the old favorites: the Holy Grail, a chalice that, according to legend, had caught the blood of Jesus Christ at the

Crucifixion; the Fountain of Youth sought so arduously by Juan Ponce de Leon; the Corazon del Dio, a magical emerald supposedly hidden away in a cave in the Brazilian rainforest. But there were hundreds of others as well, enough that Albert had eventually resorted to hiring an assistant to do the research, to go about the painstaking business of crossing each bogus lead off the list.

His search had taken him all over the world, and when his delicate condition had rendered such travel first impractical and then impossible, he had hired others to conduct his search for him. Money, for Albert, was no obstacle. Yet even with all of his resources, the years had begun to wear down his optimism. Lead after lead dismissed. Legends debunked. His assistants came back shaking their heads, or sometimes they didn't come back at all.

But he had continued his search with the stubborn persistence of a man who was *called*. Three weeks ago, his blind faith had been rewarded.

That a man like John Barron existed was no revelation to Albert. What did shock him was how easily John had fallen into his hands. That such a man should not only live *right here* in the United States, but also have his presence, his *nature*, so clearly announced to the world! Reading account after account of Kyra Metheny's healing in the papers, Albert had become convinced that in Barron lay his salvation. He had focused in on the man, waited for the press coverage to die down, and then he had sent two of his men to corral the healer, to bring him here, to Helena's Heart, the palatial home in which he'd lived for the last five years, and which he'd rarely left over that time.

Albert tapped his cigarette ash into a crystal ashtray and stood up with some effort. His desk was on the other side of the big room, and as he moved slowly toward it, he pulled a thin silver cylinder behind him on a small dolly. A plastic tube ran from the tank to a mask. Oxygen, for his emphysema. He didn't need it now, but by the time he reached his desk, he'd be wheezing like he'd just run two miles up the side of a mountain.

A knock at the closed door stopped his progress as he approached the desk.

"Yes," Albert said, then immediately dragged from the mask, his wind spent. The door opened.

His granddaughter stepped into the room and waved Barron through the door.

"Thank you, Sasha," Albert said. "You can go." He took another puff from the mask.

Sasha pulled the door closed as she left, leaving Albert and Barron alone in the huge room. Albert walked the rest of the way to his desk and collapsed into the chair behind it. He placed the mask over his face and took several deep breaths as he watched Barron's gaze pan around the room, taking it in. This room, Albert's library, was one of the biggest in the house. Circular, it was fifty feet wide and high-domed. Four levels of shelves were inlaid into the walls and were home to thousands of tomes, mostly on the occult.

Albert removed the mask from his face. Barron looked at him expectantly, hands in his pockets. Albert gestured to a chair on the other side of his desk and Barron sat, his eyes never leaving Albert's.

"You look just like any other man," Albert finally said. "Amazing. You'd think there would be something…"

Barron shrugged. "Something what?"

"Different," Albert said. "Something different. A marking, maybe, something obvious. On your face, or on one of your hands. Where it couldn't be missed. Something to declare to the world your…nature."

Barron laughed ruefully. "Couldn't have that," he said. "Someone might kidnap me." He stared boldly at Albert, and there was no missing the raw anger in his eyes.

Albert nodded. "I'm sorry about that. It couldn't be avoided."

"Well," Barron said, "that's not exactly true, is it? You could have, for instance, not ordered your thugs to pick me up. *Then* it could have been avoided, no?"

Albert spread his hands expansively and smiled. "But then you wouldn't be here, with me."

Barron didn't respond, just looked down at his hands.

"Look," Albert said, then found himself short of breath, placed the mask back over his mouth, and took a hit of the sweet oxygen. "I understand that you're angry about what I've done, bringing you here."

"You understand?" Barron said. "That's a crock. Three weeks ago, my life was my own. I could go to work, sit and watch TV, screw around on the computer, whatever. Now…now I'm being held against my will in some kind of Xanadu. I don't think you understand much at all, Mr. Navarre."

Albert nodded. "You know who I am?"

"*Everyone* knows who you are."

"Ten years ago, maybe. Not now. The only time my name comes up anymore is in conjunction with this or that business venture, and then only as a side-note."

Barron looked at him evenly. "You fell off the earth. When I was a kid, your name was all over the place. I don't think I've heard a single word about *you* since I was in college. The last thing I remember hearing is that...I think it was that you'd funded the construction of an AIDS research clinic in Africa."

Navarre held up the oxygen mask. "Life's little ironies. I spent most of my life trying to help others, and then *this*."

"Cancer?" John asked.

"Emphysema."

"How long do you have?"

"To live? Oh, *years*. If you can call this life at all. I wake up in the morning and have to be helped to the bathroom. My nurse helps me into my wheelchair, my cook makes me breakfast, I take pills, I read a book, sign papers... And then I go to sleep and do it all again the next day." He paused, then added, "But maybe now that will all change. For now, go with Sasha. She'll get you anything you need. My house is your house, Mr. Barron, and I want you to think of yourself as a guest here."

Navarre pressed a button on his desk and the door opened immediately and Sasha stepped into the room.

Barron stood, glowered at Albert. "What else would I think of myself as? *A prisoner?* Perish the thought." He turned and walked out of the room.

Sasha waited behind and Albert said, "Anything he wants."

She nodded and shut the door.

Albert leaned back in his chair, feeling the pain in his chest, but feeling something else, too. Something he hadn't felt in a long, long time.

Hope.

I could feel it coming off of him, Albert thought, *just coming off of him in waves.* He shuddered and closed his eyes, trying to calm the fluttering thoughts in his mind, but he was so close, so close now.

Chapter 21

It was interesting, Phylum thought as he broke down the Glock into its component parts for cleaning, the little gifts life delivered when one was proactive. His phone call with Mr. It's Me had been informative to say the least, and for the first time in years, Phylum was really feeling something. If pressed, he wouldn't have called it purpose—he wasn't that philosophical—but he might have said that he was feeling "amped," or "stoked." Those were the kinds of words kids had used to talk about enthusiasm when he was young, and Phylum still defaulted to that kind of vocabulary in his own mind.

What he had learned from Mr. It's Me was this: Phylum's directive—bumping Barron off—had originated with a business man named Peter Pokorney. As Phylum had suspected, Pokorney had no ties to the usual organizations that sought out the services of an individual like Phylum—the mob, a high profile loan shark, and the rest of the like—but what he hadn't seen coming was the true nature of Pokorney's interest in seeing John Barron dead.

Peter Pokorney was a member in good standing of the Catholic Church. He had a wife and four grown children, a thriving import-export business, and vacation homes in the usual rich motherfucker locales: Vail, Bermuda, Malibu. He also had a thirty-year grudge against a man named Albert Navarre, a name Phylum recognized peripherally, but didn't know from where. Apparently, Navarre had run afoul of Pokorney during a business dealing in the early 80s, something to do with oil rights somewhere—Phylum's attention span when it came to banalities had never been a strong suit, and at this point he'd gently encouraged Mr. It's Me to get back to the point—and, long story short, Navarre's tampering had cost Pokorney millions.

Now, more than three decades later, Pokorney had caught wind of two things: one was that Navarre was extremely sick; the other was that Navarre thought John Barron, who had lately been presented in the news as a faith healer or some such ridiculousness, would be able to save him. As such, Barron had to die, not for anything he'd done directly, but because killing him would harm Navarre.

And so Pokorney had contacted Mr. It's Me, and Mr. It's Me had contacted Phylum, and so the world worked and had worked forever. Only…something had changed for Phylum; not because of the possible involvement of religion—no, he was still *more* than happy to kill Barron and fully intended to honor his contract to do so. He wanted the $250,000 and felt certain that, despite the conversation he'd had with Mr. It's Me the night before, the money would still find its way into his bank account, just as planned. What had changed had to do with the woman he'd shot in Barron's apartment the day before. It was the nature of what she was that had captivated Phylum's attention.

For the first time in his adult life, a stage of his existence that had been defined by the very simple precept that Phylum was the wolf and the rest of them—which was how Phylum thought of everyone else save for his sister—were sheep, the balance had been disrupted. He didn't understand the precise nature of the woman he'd encountered the day before, but there was no avoiding the simple truth of the matter: Phylum was fascinated. More to the point, he was *offended*. That there was another wolf out there, maybe even a *stronger* wolf, was an obscenity, and it was a condition he would not suffer.

And so he would kill the woman. He knew that she was also after Barron, so the math was pretty simple: find Barron—which he had to do anyway if he still wanted the money, and he did—and he'd find the woman.

That was what had brought him here, to Five Forks, a shitty little town in Virginia. He had checked into the Five Forks Motel the night before, and then driven early in the morning to the address Mr. It's Me had given him over the phone. If Phylum had been unable to find Barron in Charlotte, he'd be here, nabbed by Navarre's people. The need to break into Navarre's home to complete his assignment would complicate things slightly, but Phylum didn't mind. It had been a while since he'd been required to stage a head-on home invasion, and he anticipated finding out whether his skills had atrophied.

From the edge of the woods he had scoped out the palatial home in which Barron was supposedly being held, then returned to his motel room to plan.

As he dabbed oil onto a rag and began to work through the pieces of the pistol one by one, Phylum's mind wandered back to the woman. Her hair, her eyes, the swell of her breasts. Yes, he thought, he was going to kill her, but maybe not right away. He wanted to fight her again, to get her into some contained place and really go at it. No guns this time. Hand to hand. Fists and teeth and nails.

He set down the barrel of the pistol and picked up the spring, ran the rag over it, imagining the fight, the battle, thrusts and parries, roundhouse kicks and uppercuts, blood and sweat, the raw clash of bone on bone. He felt himself growing hard.

And when it was all over with, when the woman was his to do with as he pleased, would he fuck her? Oh yes, he thought. Most certainly.

Even beaten down and tied up, he thought she'd fuck like a cornered lunatic.

Chapter 22

As they had driven last night, two things became clear to Mary Ann. The first was that Doug was dead. The other was that, in time, this woman, this *creature*, would kill her, too. She would use her until she was no longer needed, and then she would shoot her, or cut her throat, or something worse.

After taking her from the lawn outside the church, the woman had led Mary Ann to a rusted-out Toyota parked in the deepest shadows of the parking lot. She'd shoved Mary Ann in behind the steering wheel, and then gone around to the passenger seat.

Sitting there as the woman made her way around to the other door, Mary Ann had nearly jolted with a sudden realization: *this might be my only chance!* When the woman grabbed her outside the church doors Mary Ann was so firmly enmeshed in her own terror that running never seemed an option. But now…

In the space of two seconds her brain mapped out a plan.

Open the door, back through the church lawn — *keep away from the church, she'll kill every one of them if you lead her inside* — to the sidewalk on the other side of the hedges. From there, the nearest businesses were, what, a quarter of a mile? Could she stay ahead that long? Could she even run that far? And if she found a business open at this hour, what then? Call the police, she guessed —

The passenger side door opened and the woman climbed in beside her, closed the door, leaned back, and smiled at Mary Ann.

"In way of introduction," the woman said, "I'm Rose. You don't need to tell me your name—I already know it. There are keys in the ignition. Start the car and drive."

Mary Ann stared at her, wanting to talk, wanting to run, but all she could do was swallow dryly.

"Start it," the woman—Rose—said, putting her hand over Mary Ann's on the wheel. "Start the car. I won't tell you again."

Mary Ann groped blindly for the key, found it, twisted. The little car thought it through for a second, then started with a burp that settled into an uneven growl.

"Where?" Mary Ann started to say, but then she saw something on the woman's sleeve, something red, and her hand flew to her mouth, where it hovered, quivering, like a giant moth.

The other woman looked down and saw the blood, smiled grimly. She said, "I won't tell you that you're wrong. If it's any consolation, it didn't take long, and it wasn't what I wanted."

Tears came to Mary Ann's eyes as she thought of Doug. *Sweet Doug, patient Doug.* The man who had gotten her through two miscarriages. The man who had proposed to her on one knee at the North Carolina State Fair five years ago outside of the Tunnel of Love. The man who had stopped smoking and drinking because he knew his indulgences frightened her. The man who rolled over in the night and draped his arm around her stomach, pulled her in tight…

Dead.

Mary Ann's hands tightened on the wheel until the plastic squelched and her knuckles went white as bone. "You bitch," she said past clenched teeth, feeling the hot salty tears running down her face. "I'll kill you." A sob tore itself from her then, and the rage was suddenly gone, replaced by a black, empty mineshaft of loss.

"Yeah, well," Rose said. She wasn't looking at Mary Ann and seemed uncomfortable. She shifted in her seat, picked a nail. "We can talk about this later if you still want, but now you have to drive." In her voice, the barest note of sympathy.

Mary Ann wiped her eyes. And she drove.

"How do you know John Barron?" the woman asked, looking intently at Mary Ann.

Mary Ann said nothing, just stared ahead at the dark road.

"I found your number in his apartment," Rose said. "Tell me what you know about him."

But Mary Ann was swimming inside her own mind. "This can't be happening," she whispered. "No, no..."

"Hey!" Rose yelled and grabbed Mary Ann's wrist, squeezed. "Concentrate. Tell me what you know."

Still shaking her head, Mary Ann found the strength to say the two words she could find. "Fuck you."

Apparently understanding that she wasn't going to get any information out of Mary Ann, at least for the time being, the other woman sat back in her seat.

* * *

Occasionally, Rose gave directions, told her to take this or that exit, but none of it made any sense to Mary Ann. The route seemed haphazard.

But it was okay, because Mary Ann was coming back to herself. Minute by minute, mile by mile, she was getting to where she needed to be.

At a little after three in the morning, they stopped for gas in a small town in southern Virginia. By this time, they had been driving for almost four hours, and Mary Ann was getting tired. *Coming down*, she thought. It was almost unfathomable that she should be able to feel this way. Doug was dead and she was tired. But the thought did little to change the basic complexion of things.

She'd been sitting in the car while Rose pumped gas, but now she opened the door and got out, earning an angry look from her captor.

"What are you doing?"

"I need to pee," Mary Ann said, "and I'm tired. If you make me keep driving, we're going to end up wrapped around some tree."

For a long moment, Rose considered Mary Ann's words, then she nodded toward the small station building and said, "Go ahead. Don't take long. I'll be watching."

She headed straight for the bathroom, head down, drawing a look from the clerk behind the counter. Once inside, she sat down on the closed toilet seat, buried her head in her hands, and cried, sobbing in throat-scoring bursts.

A gentle knock at the door stopped her. She sniffed back tears and said, "Yes?"

"You okay in there?" A male voice. The clerk.

Mary Ann opened her mouth and then immediately shut it with enough force that her teeth actually snapped together. *What had she been about to do?* If she told the clerk that she needed help, to call the police, as she'd been about to do, she'd only be thrusting him into harm's way. There was no way she'd be able to explain the situation, not in a way that would let him know the danger he was already in. No, she couldn't do it. She wouldn't. There was enough blood on her hands already. Doug's blood. She wouldn't cost another man his life.

"Y-yes," Mary Ann stammered. "I'll be out in a moment."

There was a brief pause, as if the clerk considered pressing the matter, and then footsteps moved away from the door.

Mary Ann stood in front of the sink and splashed water on her face, then used a handful of brown paper towels to dry her skin. She dropped the soggy towels into the wastebasket, then looked at herself in the mirror, not liking what she saw.

When she left for the lock-in at First Presby at around eight in the evening, she'd looked, she thought, like a perfectly normal thirty-five year old woman. For the past few years she'd been noticing more and more wrinkles at the corners of her eyes, and the first gray hairs had started appearing here and there in the black when she was still in her twenties, but now the woman she found herself staring at was a stranger.

Dark purple smudges of fatigue and shock under both eyes, which were red-rimmed and bloodshot from crying and driving. Her mouth was turned down, and there was a seemingly endless network of lines and wrinkles in the skin around eyes. Her hair was a frizzy mess.

She stared at herself in disbelief. How could so much change in so little time? How? Everything you worked so long and so hard for, the house, the car, the job, the man you thought you'd spend your life with, make babies with. All gone in moments, sucked away from you by some huge cosmic vacuum cleaner, as if God had looked down, seen you happy, and said, *Oh, sorry, that wasn't supposed to be yours...*

Mary Ann felt herself shaking her head, tried to exercise control over her body, but was powerless to end the motion. From deep within her, a sound was working its way to her mouth, and though she didn't know what it would sound like when it came out, she knew she didn't want to hear it. If she let that sound escape her lips, it would kill her, it would tear her apart from the inside out like a bomb. So she shut her eyes and clamped her mouth shut as hard as she could, and all that came out was a puffy humming, and then that stopped and she opened her eyes and found that she could breathe again.

She wiped her eyes with the inside of her wrist and was about to turn from the mirror when she caught sight of the window in its reflection.

The window was small and at shoulder-height, but if it would open, she could fit through. She tried the crank, found that it wouldn't budge, saw the lock, disengaged it, and then tried the crank again.

The window swung smoothly out.

* * *

As Mary Ann dropped to the ground, a hand settled on her arm and she screamed, clapping a hand to her mouth to stifle the sound. Rose.

"I don't blame you," Rose said, a frown in place. "But this is your one free pass, Mary Ann. Try it again, and I'll hurt you so you'll never forget it." After a moment, she added, "All I need from you is information. If you tell me what I need to know, you'll be okay. I'll let you go. But if you try this shit again..."

She led Mary Ann back to the car and they got in, Rose behind the wheel this time. Before she put the car in gear, she cracked the window and then lit a cigarette, blowing out through the narrow gap.

Rose put the car in gear and pulled out of the gas station parking lot. For a while, they rode in silence, then Mary Ann said, "Why are you doing this?" She posed the question in a calm, quiet voice, not wanting to provoke some kind of attack or rebuke. Inside, she boiled; outside, she froze. She didn't look directly at Rose because she thought that if she did, she wouldn't be able to hold herself together.

Rose didn't answer immediately, just drove, eyes on the road ahead. Finally, she said, "You know." She glanced briefly at Mary Ann, then turned back to the road.

"I knew that you would come for John," Mary Ann said truthfully, hoping Rose would hear the sincerity in her words.

More silence, then, "Do you know why?" The look Rose gave her was almost shy; hers was the face of a woman not used to asking people for answers.

"Not with any certainty," Mary Ann answered, choosing her words carefully. As much as she wanted not to tell this monstrous woman anything that would help her track John down, she was also thinking clearly, surprisingly clearly, and knew that her continued health depended on retaining her usefulness. "Do you have any idea?"

"Very little," Rose said. "I know I'm drawn to him, this John Barron, and I know that my intentions when I do find him are...less than benign. I can *feel* that. What I don't know is *why* I need to find him. If I find him and kill him, will something change? What caused this all to start up so suddenly?" Rose slapped the steering wheel, then flicked her cigarette out onto the road.

After a moment, Mary Ann said, "I can't tell you the answers to all of those questions."

"What can you tell me?"

Mary Ann clasped her hands in her lap. "How old are you?"

The question appeared to take Rose by surprise. "Thirty-four, why?"

Putting a check next to item number one on her mental list, Mary Ann said. "Other than the new compulsion to track John down and kill him, has anything else changed for you recently? Have you started...*feeling* anything you didn't used to feel?"

Rose glanced at her through slitted eyes. "What are you doing?"

"Trying to give you what you want."

The Toyota's steering wheel was covered by a rubberized leopard-print sleeve. Rose stroked it softly with the tips of her fingers, and Mary Ann saw a haunted look play over the other woman's face.

"You want to have a baby," Mary Ann said almost under her breath. "Don't you?"

Rose snatched in a shocked breath. "How did you know that?" The haunted look on her face had changed to one of fear. Pure crystalline fear.

"It's just something I've always suspected."

"What do you mean?"

"You're not unique, you know," Mary Ann said. "There have been others like you before, and when you're gone, there will be another to take your place. Like everything else in this world, you're just part of a cycle."

Rose shook her head impatiently. "But the baby," she said. "Why would you say that? Tell me." After a moment, she added, "Please."

A pinprick of anger started in Mary Ann's heart. She tried to snub it out, but suddenly it was in her throat and in the middle of her brain like a poisonous snake. She wanted to throw up. She wanted to beat this murdering monster with her bare fists. She smiled, and it was a cold, deadly smile.

When Mary Ann spoke, she didn't know her voice. It was as if her body had filled with something, something red and black and somehow radioactive, and if it didn't come out, she'd die, drown in it. "You go to my home and kill my husband and take me from my job and threaten my life and you think a 'please' is going to win me over? Are you stupid?" She snorted a laugh.

Rose said nothing, just kept her eyes on the road.

After a while, Mary Ann tired of looking at the woman and slumped in her seat. She felt empty, deflated, and sleep approached like an inky black wave.

Just before she drifted away, it occurred to her what she'd really meant to say when all those other things came out.

"I wanted babies, too," she murmured, her eyes still closed, her anchor sunken deep in the realm of sleep.

Chapter 23

"It's almost like fate, you know," Navarre said to John, then took a pull off his oxygen tank. The two men sat in an enormous dining room at one end of a table crafted beautifully out of teak planks. A few minutes earlier, Percy, the giant, had knocked on John's door to inform him breakfast was being served. He had been ushered into this room and found Navarre waiting. "I've been looking for you for most of my adult life, and now, when I need you most, you're here."

"And happy about it," John muttered, then looked up at Navarre. "You know, I do have a question for you, though. You've gone to all this trouble—sending your thugs to kidnap me, transporting me to, well, wherever the hell this is—but you haven't made me do anything yet. That seems odd."

Navarre laughed. "I have my reasons."

"And they are?"

Navarre seemed to consider whether to answer John's question. "Do you know what tomorrow is?"

John thought about it for a moment—with all that had happened since the incident with Kyra, the passing of time had taken on a liquid, uncertain quality—then said, "Easter."

Navarre said nothing, just looked at John as if waiting for John to answer his own unasked question. And then John suddenly understood. "The day when Jesus was resurrected. A day of healing."

"And the day on which more confirmed healings have been recorded than any other. Will it make any difference?" Navarre said to himself, then sipped from a glass of orange juice. "I don't know. I hope so. Either way, it can't hurt."

"Can't hurt *you*," John said, and Navarre nodded, signaling that he understood.

"You'll be cared for by my private physician here, in the house. I read about that unfortunate incident with the cancer patient while you were in the hospital. I won't put you in that position again."

John looked down at his hands. "And what if it doesn't work? What if I put my hands on you and nothing happens?"

"It will," Navarre said, cold certainty in his eyes, "as long as you do it willingly."

"So...you're going to force me into doing something willingly? Are you familiar with the concept of irony, Mr. Navarre?"

Navarre smiled and spread his hands. "Let me ask you, do you understand where you fit into the big scheme of things, John? Do you know what you are?"

It was the very question Mary Ann Shaw had attempted to answer for him just a day ago in the park, but for all John had learned, he found he really didn't know much at all.

"I know bits and pieces," John said.

Navarre nodded and looked down, drew on the oxygen tank. "You are part of a cycle that goes back more than two thousand years. In all that time, there have been maybe fifty healers like you. Fifty. Think about that."

"I'm honored, really, but it doesn't seem to have done much for my circumstances."

"But it *has* for thousands and thousands of others. People like me, who need you."

"So I exist for *you*, not for me."

"You exist to be what you are, the same as me and everyone else."

"Wow," John said, sitting back in his chair, "now that was some poetic shit. I mean, it sounds vaguely like rationalization on your part, don't get me wrong, but still, *poetic* shit."

The old man smiled. "I understand your reluctance to accept all of this. If I were in your place, part of a lineage traceable to Christ himself, I might feel...overwhelmed as well."

Now John couldn't stop himself from laughing. "Traceable to Christ? Are you joking? Are you seriously implying that I'm a—a *blood relative* of Jesus Christ?"

"Not at all," Navarre said, then added, "I'm saying that the soul inside of you, the soul that has jumped from body to body for over two thousand years, *is* the soul of Jesus Christ."

John gaped at the man for a second, then slapped the table with both hands and laughed. "Oh, my god," he whispered. "You really don't know how crazy you are, do you? You really *believe* that."

Navarre smiled serenely and drew once again from his oxygen mask.

* * *

Back in his bedroom, John thought about *Macbeth*. Why, Monica had asked John's sub, had Macbeth hired the murderers to kill his friend Banquo? The answer was not what the sub had said, that great men had to pass off duties to the smaller people. The answer was that Macbeth had, as the result of his own ignorance about the nature of his existence, felt he was protecting himself against a cruel universe bent on taking from him what he felt was his by right. In a world where men made and lost their own fortunes, Macbeth had been duped into believing that fate dictated his actions, and that fate, therefore, exculpated him for the commission of his heinous deeds.

It was a truth that had always caused John to both pity and despise Macbeth's character, but now he saw that he had been confronted with his own prophecy—not by three bearded sisters on the Scottish moors, perhaps, but a prophecy no less. The question was, what was he going to do about it? Give in and do as Navarre demanded? Or take his life into his own hands, maybe for the first time in the thirty-five years of his existence, and dictate his own actions?

It struck him as ironic that, now that he was confined and unable to truly do anything, he suddenly found himself not just wanting but *needing* to be elsewhere. He needed to be with Connie, and not only for her daughter, but, if he was being honest, for himself, too. If there was any chance she would have him…he had to try. But now he was stuck here, and there was no end to this ordeal in sight.

Sitting in the comfortable chair in his gilded cage, John thought about all of these things, but what he thought about most was how horrible he'd felt during the days after he woke up in the hospital.

If he went along with Navarre's wishes and something actually did happen—and despite his prior skepticism about his own abilities, John thought something *would*—John would undoubtedly suffer a physical trauma similar to the one he'd incurred at Kyra's healing. That would lay him up for days, and maybe even weeks. John remembered how he'd felt lying in the bed in Presbyterian Hospital, sick and exhausted, helpless. It wasn't a sensation he was eager to invite into his life again, and certainly not for the likes of Albert Navarre.

On the other hand, if he did what he wanted to do, if he made a *run* for it... Really, what was the worst Navarre's people could do? They couldn't kill him if he tried to escape; Navarre would no doubt deal out swift justice to any man who injured or killed the man who represented his only hope for a normal life. All they could do was lock him up somewhere, and that wasn't too far from where he was stuck right now.

John stood and walked to the window, rested his forehead against the glass, and closed his eyes. He tried to picture as much of the house as he'd seen; every hallway, room, and door. That wasn't much, really, not in a house as big as he thought this one was, but he believed that, if he could get a moment to himself outside this room, he might have a chance.

Which left him with his first job: escape this room.

* * *

There were three potential ways out of Albert Navarre's home. One was in the back of a hearse—or, more likely, the back of Curt's van. That one was understandably unappealing, and John couldn't help but remember his initial thought that Curt might be the kind of guy who enjoyed taking liberties with dead people.

The second option was what John had, in his mind, dubbed "the graceless exit," a smash and run job. There were several variables at work in that option, however, not the least of which was the fact that John had not the slightest idea where Navarre's goons lay in wait. He could break a window and hop down into the waiting arms of Curt out on a smoke break. There was just no telling. Plus, that option had another major drawback. Once he was out of the house, where would he go? From what John had been able to see, the house was entirely surrounded by grass. Green, flawless grass, in every direction. Anybody leaving or approaching the house would be detected in moments.

He raised his head and looked up at the distant, dark line of trees. How far, he thought again. A mile? More? Even if he did get out of the house unseen, how long would it take for someone to see him scampering across the empty field? Not long, John thought. Before he was halfway to the trees, someone would be out to scoop him back up in a Hummer or on an ATV.

So that was out, at least as his first choice.

What John thought just might work was more subtle. Standing in front of the window, his eyes closed, John began to formulate his plan.

* * *

It was early-afternoon. An hour ago, he'd been served lunch in his room, and John had wondered if Navarre had somehow detected his desire to reconnoiter a little on his way to the dining room. There were cameras in John's room, after all—at least one that John could see, and who knew how many more—and maybe one of Navarre's people had seen him looking around the room a little too interestedly. In the end, John figured, it didn't really matter; that a prisoner would desire to escape was hardly the kind of conclusion it took a rocket scientist to reach.

John walked into the bathroom and splashed water on his face, making sure to get some on his t-shirt. Hoping there wasn't a camera behind the vanity mirror, he began to run in place, lifting his knees high toward his chest, pumping his arms. Two minutes later he was sweating, and after five sweat was dripping from his neck and face. His breath came in ragged gulps, and John could only hope he had enough left in the tank to move fast when the time came.

"Okay," he panted, regarding himself in the mirror. "You can do this." He grabbed his chest, opened the door, and stumbled into the bedroom.

The response was almost instantaneous.

Whomever Navarre had viewing the monitor in John's room was focused and efficient. This was a part of the plan John had been unsure about; even if there was a live body looking at a monitor somewhere in the house, there was no way to tell if that person decided to go to the bathroom or take a smoke break.

As it was, though, the door slammed open mere seconds after John hit the floor, still clutching at his chest, his eyes pressed shut. John could hear the sound of pounding feet and squeaking wheels, and then voices.

"Come on, get him up. Call Carol, tell her he's having what looks like a heart attack. Tell her to prep the AED. We'll be there in one minute." Strong hands slipped under John's knees and armpits and he was lifted onto the stretcher. He could hear the staticky squawk of a radio, then a man's tight voice telling Carol to get the defibrillator ready.

And then he was moving, the gurney swerving wildly as the two attendants ushered him out of the room where he'd been held prisoner for the last twenty-four hours and then down a long stretch of hallway. John's head was to the side and he risked cracking his eyes, saw white wall sweeping by. Then they were in the foyer, where John had seen the AED when Curt and Percy had brought him to Navarre's library the day before. There were others in the house—John assumed the place was so well stocked because of Navarre's declining state of health—but he'd hoped this was the closest. So far, so good.

Through his cracked lids, John could see one other person in the room, a woman he assumed was Carol. She knelt in the middle of the marble-floored foyer, the brief-case sized defibrillator in front of her, blatting instructions in the robotic voice John knew from the training he underwent yearly as a teacher at Denton. Right now, the device was telling Carol to remove the protective covers from the contacts and to open the victim's shirt.

"Bring him lower," Carol yelled at the two men handling the gurney. John felt a jolt and then he was being lowered until he was only a foot or so off the ground.

"Call Dr. Gleason," Carol snapped at one of the men, and he took off running. Now it was just Carol and the other man, whom John had not yet seen. Deciding to take a risk, he opened his eyes, hoping neither Carol nor the man would notice.

Carol was still kneeling on the ground, and the AED was saying, "*Charging, charging,*" over and over. The man was kneeling beside her. He was obviously a techie, not too big or strong-looking. He wore a short-sleeved Hawaiian shirt and khaki pants. He was sweating, bothered into a state of near panic.

The AED stopped saying charging and started in on a new mantra: "*Ready. Apply contacts. Ready. Apply contacts.*"

"Lift his shirt up," Carol said to the man, and he dragged John's sodden t-shirt up to his chin, baring his chest.

"What now?" the man said.

"Back up." Moving quickly and efficiently, Carol slapped the two contact pads, from which rubber-insulated wires trailed back to the AED, onto John's chest, one below his left nipple, the other on his right pec, then she hit a button on the AED and it said, "*Do not touch patient. Press green button.*"

John opened his eyes again, feeling terror singing in his veins. If she pressed the button while the AED was still attached to him, it could stop his heart. Carol and the man were looking at each other, the AED between them.

Carol said, "Check his heart rate. If we do this wrong we could kill him."

The man's hands flew up in a gesture of helplessness. "Like I know how to check someone's fucking heart rate. You do it. You're the one with the nursing degree."

She huffed and bent over John, extending one hand to his neck to check his pulse. Then she turned her head back toward the man and said, "Go see what's taking Martin so goddamned long. Think you can handle that?"

The man stood, and John heard him muttering under his breath as he headed for the door at a trot. Now it was just John and Carol.

"Okay," Carol muttered to herself. "Okay, okay, okay. Heartbeat, but jagged rhythm. Arrhythmia. Jolt him back on track. Okay, okay." She turned back to the machine, and as she did, John ripped the contacts from his chest, slapped them onto her exposed arm, then, in the same motion, brought his hand down on the green button on the AED's console.

There was no snap of electricity, no high pitched whine. Instead, Carol's body went rigid for a moment, and then she collapsed onto her side, convulsed once, and then was still.

John stood up and pulled his t-shirt down, then walked quickly to the front door and pulled it open. Behind him, he heard Carol moan, and he felt a surge of relief that she was still alive. He stepped out into the sunshine.

* * *

There were three cars parked in the crescent-shaped driveway. One was the van in which Curt and Percy had driven him here, one was a black Mercedes convertible, and the last was a hunter-green Range Rover. John made his way down the line, trying doors.

The Range Rover was unlocked, and there was a key in the ignition. John climbed in and turned the key; the engine roared to life instantly. He put the truck in gear and pressed down on the gas. Ahead, the driveway joined up with a long, straight lane bordered on both sides with towering trees. Turning off the crescent and onto the straightaway, John accelerated. Before him, the driveway went on for as far as John could see.

He never saw the van.

One second he was driving confidently ahead, his spirits starting to rise as he contemplated freedom. The next, he was sideways, then upside down, then smashing to a glass-shattering halt as the Range Rover came to rest against the gigantic trunk of a tree. He brought a hand to his head and it came away bloody.

Out of the passenger side window, he could see the crumpled grill of Curt's van, steam rising from the blown carburetor. He could smell burning circuitry and smoke and knew he needed to get out of the Range Rover.

The windshield had shattered on impact, and John pulled himself out of the truck, cutting his hands and arms on broken glass as he did so. He crawled as far as he could, then collapsed onto his side, willing himself to stand, but unable to do so. He didn't think anything was broken, but his side hurt badly and his breath wouldn't come back. *Just a minute,* he told himself. *I just need a minute.*

"Hey," a voice said from behind him, and John turned to see Curt standing above him. There was a gash above the man's right eye, and blood covered the side of his face. "Nice try," Curt said. "But no cigar, fucker."

Chapter 24

Rose was getting weaker.

For the last several hours she had tried to ignore the ache in her stomach, the fuzziness in her mind, but she couldn't put it off much longer. If it hadn't been for the gunshot wound she'd sustained in Barron's apartment—a wound that would have killed any normal person within minutes—everything would have been fine, but when her body was healing, the demands on her system were great, and that system needed to be *fed*. The motel clerk the day before had provided her with some energy, but she'd used it up quickly and now felt the first waves of need washing over her.

She knew what the progression would be from here. It would start with the feeling she had right now of growing torpidity, like all she wanted to do was curl up somewhere dark and sleep. But that would just be the beginning. In hours, she would start having trouble breathing, her heart would slow in her chest, her vision would grow darker and darker…

An hour earlier, just as the light was beginning to fade from the sky, she had pulled into a hotel in northern Virginia, just off I-95. It had been a long day's drive, and her eyes were bleary and grainy from the road. Navigating during the day had been an exercise in torture, and Rose's head pounded from the effort of keeping her mind focused on the task. It had been years since she'd made such extensive use of daylight hours, but with her quarry on the move, she had seen no alternative.

Mary Ann was asleep in the passenger side seat, and she didn't wake up until Rose climbed back into the car after checking into the motel. Rose could see the hate and frustration burning in the woman's eyes, hate for what Rose had done to her husband, frustration because she had missed her chance to run while Rose was in the office.

Now, they sat quietly in the room, Rose in a chair, Mary Ann on one of the beds, her hands and feet secured with duct tape. Helpless as she was, though, Mary Ann hadn't stopped looking at Rose since she woke up, her eyes wide and intense, almost smoking with pent up anger.

Rose had been thinking about what to do with the woman. Her usefulness was almost exhausted, and Rose had only held on to her for this long out of hope that Mary Ann would be able to offer additional insight into Rose's situation. Soon, she'd kill Mary Ann and feed on her, but not yet, not while there was still an outside chance she could be useful.

Rose stood and walked to the television, picked up the remote and switched on the TV. It was tuned to MTV, and some hideous reality show was playing.

"I'm going out," she said to Mary Ann, looking at the woman but not making eye contact. "I won't be long, so don't get any ideas. In fact..." Rose grabbed the roll of duct tape from where it sat on the bed-side table and walked over to Mary Ann. "Hold still," she said.

She grabbed Mary Ann by the shoulders and pushed her back against the headboard, then looped tape around Mary Ann's chest and around the bars of the bed-frame. She made several loops around Mary Ann, then stood back and appraised her work. "Good?" she asked. "Comfy?"

Still, Mary Ann said nothing to her, only stared at her with those eyes full of silent rage and loathing.

"Okey dokey," Rose said. "Only one more thing." She grabbed a pillow off the bed, shucked the pillow case off, then wrapped the dusty-smelling fabric around Mary Ann's lower face and duct taped it into place. "Just in case you feel like making a ruckus," Rose said. She dropped the roll of tape on the bed and walked to the door. "Back in a jiff," she said, then left.

* * *

When the woman left, Mary Ann closed her eyes and began to sob, the sounds muffled by the pillow case jammed into her mouth, the fabric dusty and stale tasting against her lips and tongue.

Cut this shit out, she told herself. *You do not have this luxury right now. Who knows how long she'll be gone.*

Slowly, Mary Ann pulled herself together, taking deep breaths through her nose, which was still exposed. When her shaking had diminished to a manageable tremor, Mary Ann closed her eyes and thought.

She was taped to the bed. That was the first problem. The second was that the woman had not only taped her wrists together; she'd also taped Mary Ann's wrists to her thighs, passing the tape under her legs and over her wrists. The only movement Mary Ann could really manage was in her fingers, and they felt numb and far away, like soldiers about to pass out of radio range. Trying to regain feeling in her hands, she flexed her fingers, curling them and then stretching them out, and gradually she began to feel the prickling sensation of blood returning.

Next, she tested each of her bonds, one by one. Her legs were tightly wrapped around the ankles, no problem to take care of if her hands were free, but really, she thought, useless in the long run as long as her wrists were taped. Next, she tried pulling away from the headboard, straining her stomach muscles against the tape. There was almost no give, and the wood around which the woman had passed the tape felt strong, not brittle with age, as Mary Ann had hoped.

Okay, she thought, *you're not going to pull free. You need something. Something sharp…*

Looking around the room, her eyes lighted on a glint of silver from the bedside table. She squinted and bent her head as far as she could in that direction. *What was it?* And then she saw. It was a paper clip binding together the pages of the local attractions menu that had been resting on the bed when they walked in. Mary Ann could remember the woman picking it up and tossing it aside.

Now what? The pamphlet was some three feet away from Mary Ann, a distance that might as well have been two miles, bound as she was. She felt despair hovering just above her heart and pushed it away. *No, goddamnit. Not yet.*

Her eyes lighted on the duct tape, which the woman had tossed on the bed as she was walking out. Mary Ann reached out a foot—she'd been wearing sandals when the woman grabbed her and had taken them off when they entered the hotel room—and grabbed the roll between the first and second toes of her left foot.

She leaned forward as far as she could and saw what she'd hoped to see. As so many people did out of habit, the woman had bent the tape to the side after she'd ripped the last strip off, leaving perhaps half an inch of the sticky underside exposed. A flare of timid excitement rose in Mary Ann's heart. But the hard part was still ahead, and Mary Ann thought it was probably going to cost her. Still, it was this or nothing, and at this point nothing wasn't an option.

Using the bed to help her, Mary Ann slid the roll of silver tape between her toes until the folded back section where the sticky underside was exposed was just above the nail of her big toe, then, gripping the tape tightly between her toes, she began to shimmy her butt in the direction of the bedside table. The tape binding her to the headboard was tight, and as her body shifted, it dug into her upper arms and put pressure on her chest, constricting her rib cage and, beneath that, her lungs. But she pressed on.

It'll be over soon, she thought, *a minute, maybe. I can hold out that long if I have to.*

Her breath beginning to wheeze in and out of her nose, Mary Ann swung her left leg over her right and, with all of her strength, stretched her left foot toward the bedside table. Groaning with the effort, she saw the roll of duct tape clenched between her toes stop eight inches from the pamphlet, maybe ten. Not enough.

"Goddamnit," she whispered, the word muffled into meaninglessness by the gag. Her face was slick with perspiration and she felt blazing hot all over. Her chest was screaming for a full breath of air.

Once again, she began to move, squirming along the bedspread, moving her rear end closer to the edge of the bed inch by inch. The tape had been tight around her chest before, but now it cinched even tighter, and Mary Ann began to wonder if she'd be able to reposition herself even if she did manage to grab the pamphlet. It wasn't beyond the realm of her oxygen starved imagination to picture herself stuck in this tortured position when the woman came back from wherever she'd gone.

Probably to kill someone else's husband. Mary Ann felt new, fresh anger surge into her body. She jerked another inch to the left, then another. She thought she could reach it now, extended her left leg toward the bedside table once more…and the turned-back triangle of tape came down on the near corner of the pamphlet.

For a second Mary Ann didn't so much as breathe. Then she pushed down with her foot as hard as she could, securing the tape, she hoped, on the paper and then lifted. The pamphlet rose into the air with her foot, dangling from the corner of tape like a kite. Her heart was beating hard, and her vision was growing staticky. Mary Ann realized that she was on the verge of fainting and felt red, horrible panic growing in her brain.

Gingerly, she set the pamphlet down on the bedspread, taking care not to detach the paper from the tape, and began to squirm back into her original position on the bed. With every inch she moved, she felt the tape loosen on her chest, like a vice releasing. And then she was back, and she could breathe again. For a while, that was all she did, drawing big, greedy lungfuls of air into her nose, not even minding the dusty smell of the pillowcase anymore. The air could have smelled like manure and it still would have been heaven.

Mary Ann lifted her feet and used her heels to pull the sheaf of papers toward her butt. Charley-horses bulged in her hamstrings, but then she leaned hard to her left and her hands felt paper.

An absurdly powerful feeling of pride washed over her. Even if the woman came back now, even if this was as far as Mary Ann got, she was fighting. And if she got free, if she got out of this place, she would kill that woman if it was her last act on earth.

Moving carefully, Mary Ann rotated the papers between her fingers until her fingers felt metal. She shucked the paperclip off the sheaf, bent the shaft upright, and started to work on the tape binding her wrists.

Chapter 25

John lay in the dark room and tried not to move. His ribs throbbed terribly, pulsing with every heartbeat, and when he tried to move it felt like there were bones grinding in his left hip. And then there was his head. He'd whacked it on the driver's side window when Curt T-boned him with the van, and he thought he'd opened a pretty good cut in his temple. After Curt had brought him back into the house, a nurse had steered him into this room and tended to the shallow cuts on his hands and on his face.

The door opened and a wide slat of light from the hallway illuminated the room. John covered his eyes, groaning at the pain in his side that resulted from even that small movement. He heard gentle footfalls approaching, then a voice.

"I have some pills for you," a woman said. "They're for your pain."

John said nothing, but let the woman slip the pills into his mouth, then sipped from the glass of water she offered. When she took the glass away, he rested his head back on the pillow and closed his eyes. Behind his lids, he saw Connie, the girl he had once known when his life still held the undefined promise of the future. Without his even knowing it, hope for something more had begun to germinate inside of him again in the days since they had talked. Even knowing that there would be a terrible physical toll to pay for healing Connie's daughter, there was no questioning the newfound sense of forward-looking purpose in his life. But now, he knew, there was nothing he could do to avoid what Navarre had in mind.

He wondered what exactly would happen to him when he touched Navarre. With Kyra, it had been his head. He could remember the growing sense of frictive warmth in his brain and then the supernova of agony as the process of healing her broken body shifted into full effect. With Navarre, would it be his lungs? An image leaked into his mind: him, lying half-conscious in bed, wheezing for air through lungs that had, in the space of moments, grown hard and black.

How long would the crippling effects of the healing last this time? Two days? Two weeks? And after that, what? A lifetime of imprisonment here, in Navarre's home? What of Connie, her daughter, his parents?

A soft, warm sadness spread through him, and then John was asleep.

*   *   *

He woke up some time later, unable to remember where he was. Then he moved to sit up and almost screamed from the pain.

It was light outside—that was the first thing he noticed. Early morning light, yellow through the gauzy curtains. He ran his hand over his ribs and stomach and felt thickly wrapped bandages there. Tape. Undoubtedly he'd cracked a rib or two, maybe broken them outright. He'd suffered a similar injury as a teenager and still recalled how the injury had seemed to linger forever. This wasn't going to help his chances of escape.

"Oh, shit," he muttered, the thoughts of escape bringing into his mind the conversation he'd had with Navarre the day before at the breakfast table.

Today was Sunday. *Easter* Sunday.

The door opened and John saw an older man in a gray suit standing in the doorway. He was carrying a leather physician's bag. "You're up," he said to John.

John said nothing in return, just remained quiet as the man set his bag on the floor, then bent over John and examined his head and ribs.

"I can't give you any more pills," he said, straightening. "I wish I could, but Mr. Navarre..."

John smiled grimly. "Right. He needs me lucid."

"You're lucky," the doctor said. "That crash could have done more than crack a couple of your ribs."

"I *feel* lucky," John said, then added, "can you give me a hand, please?"

The doctor helped John sit, pulling gingerly on John's proffered hand. The pain was hot and sharp, like someone had inserted a steak knife between two ribs and was trying to pry them apart. Finally, though, John was sitting.

"What time is it?" John asked.

"Quarter past ten," the doctor answered, then set about ministering to John's injuries. He cleaned the wounds on John's face and hands, then wrapped them with fresh gauze. For John's ribs and hip, he couldn't do much. "Sit straight as you can," the doctor said to John, then prodded at his rib cage. The flesh was tender but basically okay until the doctor pressed against an area just a few inches above his hip, then John sucked in breath and straightened.

"Not broken," the doctor said softly. "Just nicked."

"You can't give me anything at all?" John said. "Not even Tylenol or something?"

The doctor shook his head apologetically. "And if I were you, I'd put any escape plans on hold for a while. There's...quite the presence outside this door right now."

John grinned. "That's okay. I was planning on going out the window anyway."

The doctor stood and pulled back a curtain, revealing wrought-iron bars outside the window. "Good luck with that." He packed up his things and then left John to think about what the rest of the day might hold in store.

Chapter 26

Rose was driving again, and she felt like she had a couple of days before, sitting between the two sleeping Mexican children as the pickup approached the outskirts of Charlotte. She felt like she was close, close once more to John Barron, the man who held some strange claim on her life that she couldn't understand.

For a few brief hours, she had thought the Shaw woman might be able to furnish her with some answers—she seemed to *have* them, even if she was unwilling to surrender them to Rose—but then Rose had come back to the hotel to find her gone. In its own way, what the woman had done was impressive, really. She had taped Shaw tightly. Not a doubt had existed in her mind as she left last night that the Shaw woman would be there when she returned from her hunt. Instead, all she'd found on the bed was torn tape and a bloody, bent paperclip. How long had it taken to cut free of all that tape? Hours, Rose guessed.

For a while, Rose had considered going after her. She couldn't have too significant a head-start, after all, and she had undoubtedly headed south, toward home. Rose knew she would likely find Mary Ann at a bus depot, or down the highway somewhere. But in the end, it just wasn't worth the trouble. Rose had come here, to this netherworld of bumfuck Virginia, for a reason, and other than the meager wisdom Mary Ann may or may not have been able to furnish Rose with, there wasn't a substantial reason to go after her. It was a loss, and Rose felt—knew—that letting the woman go was potentially a grave mistake, but nothing was turning out to be as easy as she would have hoped.

So she had left the hotel and headed west, her blood still singing from the kill she'd made last night, her skull almost vibrating with the nearly magnetic power yanking her toward her fate, toward, she now knew, John Barron. For a while, the blood-high she'd been riding had been enough to counteract the weakening effect of being up and around during the day, but now she realized that she might be in trouble. Her vision was by turns crystal clear and hazy, and sometimes, when she blinked, she saw not one but two scenes in front of her, as though she were seeing through two sets of eyes simultaneously.

In much the same way, her thoughts were only half her own. She kept catching snatches of thoughts and overheard conversations. Partly, that was why she couldn't stop now—something was about to happen, she sensed from those overheard thoughts, and whatever it was, she couldn't allow it to occur. So she allowed herself to be pulled forward by the magnet in her head, giving into it more fully than she'd ever done before. She wanted this all to end.

Where the power was pulling her was bizarre. Ahead, in the bright light of early afternoon, she saw a sign for FIVE FORKS, a town she'd never heard of before. Of course, it was a little late to ask for things to start making sense, so she followed along the winding, two-lane road, winding her way deeper and deeper into a nature preserve of some kind. She had to drive slowly and found herself blinking often and shaking her head to clear it, but several times she barely managed to avoid wrapping the car around a telephone pole, or crashing into the scant oncoming traffic.

Then she saw it, a pair of stone pillars flanking a black iron gate. Into the stone were carved the words, HELENA'S HOPE. Rose had to stop herself from pulling the Corolla over and getting out; that would have been too obvious. From the looks of the gate, this was a rich person's house. No doubt there were cameras staring down at the little car even now. So she continued for another hundred yards, then pulled the car off the road and into the woods as far as she could go, about thirty yards. Not so far the car would be impossible to find if someone really looked, but far enough that no one driving by would be able to see it.

She got out of the car, making sure the revolver she'd stolen in Florida was tucked into the back of her jeans, and she stood still, listening, taking everything in. Her thoughts were growing more and more fuzzy, and she found herself needing to double and triple check her own impulses and instincts, which was unfamiliar and disquieting. She heard insects singing, the rustling of leaves and underbrush, and somewhere ahead, not too far off, she heard the sound of an engine. She began to move in that direction.

* * *

If she'd been asked to do so at this particular moment, there was no way Mary Ann could possibly have articulated what she was feeling. On the physical side, there was pain. The contortions she'd been forced to put her body through during her escape had been brutal, and they had left her wrists nearly useless from picking at the tape, the muscles of her ribcage fiery-sore from the effort of staying upright without the aid of her hands and feet for balancing. And then there was the exhaustion itself. How long had it been since she slept? A day and a half? At least. It was hard to make herself think back that far, because thinking of sleep made her think of…made her think of Doug.

And this, of course, was the worst part of it. Her physical state was a joke in comparison. In time, her body would heal. But the part of her that had been Doug Shaw's wife, that had been the mother of his unborn children, that part would *never* recover, and she didn't want it to.

After leaving the hotel room, she had hidden behind a dumpster to consider her options. It hadn't taken long. She could have called the police—probably *should* have called the police, really. But if she had done that, they would have needed to take her into custody. They would say it was for her protection, and they would probably have been telling the truth, but holed up in their Podunk station, she would have felt helpless, impotent. Kneeling behind the dumpster, feeling water sinking into the knees of her jeans, blood warm on her fingertips where the paperclip had worn right through her skin in burning lines, she knew that *impotent* was the last thing in the world she wanted to be right now.

So she had opted for plan B. And that had almost gotten her killed.

Rising from her spot behind the dumpster, she'd seen a number of cars in the motel's parking lot, at least a half dozen. If she'd been the heroine of an action movie, she would have broken one of their windows with a rock and then hotwired the engine. But she wasn't a hero, not anything close to it. Confronted with a bundle of colored wires, she was confident of nothing save for the fact that she would quickly render a car undriveable. Shit, even if she *did* manage, by some cosmic coincidence, to get the fucking engine started, she had no doubt that a mile down the road she'd press on the brake as she approached a stoplight only to find the brake pedal squishy and unresponsive beneath her foot. Hotwiring a car was not an option. Which left her with the office.

From where she was standing, she could see that the lights in the office were still on, though she knew from the clock in the hotel room that it was well past five in the morning. Maybe the morning clerk gets here that early, she thought, to start the coffee, maybe to prepare a continental breakfast. She hoped the opposite was true, however, that the night clerk was still on duty. If so, maybe he'd be asleep on the job. There couldn't be much to do in the middle of the night in a place like this.

Moving quickly, Mary Ann skirted the parking lot, staying out of the lights as best she could. Soon she was standing behind a tree, facing the office from about twenty feet away. She peered through the window and saw no one, only the bad orange and brown décor of a place that hadn't been refurbished since sometime in the mid-70s, a beige counter, and an abandoned spinney chair in which the clerk *should* have been sitting. Beyond the counter, she could see the dark gap of an open door, but she couldn't see into the room beyond. Could the clerk be in there? If so, why weren't there lights on?

Because he's asleep, she thought. *Asleep on one of those rollaway cots they bring to your room when you're too crowded.*

Eyes frantically skipping from side to side, scanning every inch of the parking lot and the office, Mary Ann crept to the office door, took a steadying breath, and put her hand on the doorknob. She began to twist the knob, then stopped, her heart suddenly jagged in her chest.

The clerk isn't at the desk because there's a chime that tells him when someone comes through the door, the voice yelled at her. *Don't touch the door.*

Mary Ann took her hand off the knob and looked up. Through the glass, she saw a string of silver bells hanging from red yarn. They were affixed to the top of the door, and if she had yanked open the door, as she had just been prepared to do, they would have jangled madly, letting anyone within hearing distance know someone was there.

Gently then, she thought. She put her hand back on the knob, turned it slowly, and eased the door open, her eyes locked on the bells, willing them to continue to dangle limply. When there was enough room for her to squeeze into the office, she slipped through the crack, then eased the door closed behind her. As the door fell back against the jam, there was the tiniest of tinkles from one of the bells as it knocked against the glass, then nothing but silence.

Standing now inside the front door, Mary Ann took in her surroundings.

No more than ten feet away, the counter stood chest high. Beyond that, the far wall of the office. A wooden cabinet hung open, room keys on display. Just to the left of the counter, the door she'd seen from outside. She listened for a moment, straining her ears for the softest of snores, for anything that might suggest the presence of another person, but all she heard was the insistent hum of an air conditioner.

Walking on tiptoes, Mary Ann moved to the counter and peered over it. And saw what she'd hoped to see. Behind the counter, on a little table pushed up against the wall, sat a wallet and keys.

A rush of hope rising in her chest, Mary Ann walked around the counter, grabbed the keys, closing her hand gently around them to make sure there was no clink of metal, and then turned to head back to the door. She was at the edge of the counter when she heard the sound, soft and wet, coming from the room beyond the darkened door.

She paused, half of her yelling at her to *get out, get away, run!* The other half needing to see whatever was inside that room. The second half won out, and she looked through the doorway.

It took a moment for her eyes to adjust to the dim light, but then, as somehow she'd known she would, she saw the woman—Rose—

kneeling beside a prone man, her head buried in the hollow between his shoulder and neck. She rocked back and forth as she fed, and through the horrible slurping sounds, Mary Ann could hear the sound of crying. Rose's crying.

Kill her, the voice inside her head whispered urgently. *She's distracted. She'll never even know you're here until it's too late.*

But Mary Ann had a feeling that was wrong. First of all, there was nothing to kill her with. Bare hands weren't going to be enough for this job. If she'd had a gun, that would have been one thing, but unarmed…

Her eyes never left the door until she was back outside of the office, then she pressed the unlock button on the clerk's keychain, waited for the flash of headlights, and got into the car. Moments later, headlights off even in the darkness, she coasted slowly out of the motel parking lot.

*   *   *

That had been hours ago. Now the sun was up, and she was pulling off the road and into the woods where a moment ago Rose's Corolla had disappeared. She saw the car up ahead and killed her own engine, then got out and started walking.

In the distance, she could hear the sound of an engine, maybe a high-powered lawnmower, maybe a wood-chipper. She thought of the sign she had passed just before turning off the winding country lane. HELENA'S HOPE. The sounds were coming from a house up ahead, Mary Ann thought. A wealthy person's house, from the look of the gate and the landscaping she'd glimpsed.

She hoped the residents were ready for company.

Chapter 27

Lying on his stomach, hidden by trees and the dense underbrush, Phylum watched the dark haired beauty climb out of the Corolla and stand for a moment, seemingly considering the landscape all about her. Almost like an animal, a fox or a wolf, she turned her head from side to side, testing the wind, smelling, seeing. After a moment, she put her hand to the small of her back—feeling for the pistol Phylum knew was stashed there—and set off toward the house he had reconnoitered earlier. Quietly, he pushed to his feet and followed her.

It didn't take long to see that there was something...off about his prey. This wasn't the same woman he had encountered in Barron's apartment. Although she showed no ill-effects from the round he'd placed in her back, or from the leap from Barron's balcony, the woman walked uncertainly, almost clumsily, not like the predator he'd sensed that she was. Before she'd gone a hundred yards, the woman's hands and arms were striped red from snapping branches, and she had tripped several times over fallen branches and vines. If Phylum hadn't known better, he would have assumed he was following a drunk woman.

Which was why taking her was so easy.

Choosing his footing carefully, stepping on exposed dirt and rocks, not on the fallen leaves and twigs that littered the forest floor, Phylum approached the woman from behind and brought the butt-end of his Sig Sauer down on her head, hitting the exact spot he'd aimed for, close to the base of her skull. She went down as though her power had been cut and Phylum caught her before she hit the ground.

"I gotcha," he whispered and looked down at her beautiful face. "Don't worry, I gotcha."

Less concerned now with making noise, Phylum carried the unconscious woman quickly back to his car and deposited her in the back seat. Given the force of the blow he'd delivered to the base of her skull, an area that assured maximum forceful impact between the brain and skull, he was fairly certain she'd be out for some time, but then again, this was the woman he'd shot dead in the back and then watched catapult off the side of a second-story balcony without breaking stride. Why take chances?

He taped her with the roll of duct tape he always kept in his trunk, working first on her wrists, then her ankles, and then, for good measure, her knees. When he was done, he grabbed a pair of stainless steel handcuffs from the trunk. He affixed one of the cuffs to her right wrist, the other to the convertible's frame. If she had enough time to figure out a way to escape he had no doubt she'd be able to do so, but he wasn't planning on being away long. Satisfied, he took one more look at the woman's face and then closed the BMW's door.

*   *   *

Mary Ann waited until the man was out of sight and then came out from behind the tree where she'd been hiding. She could hear the man moving away through the woods toward the house and she knew his mission had something to do with John, but this…this was where she needed to be.

As she approached the car, she peeked through the back window. Rose lay prone on the seat, her eyes still closed. The man had taped her thoroughly, and Mary Ann could see the silver loop of a handcuff attached to the car's roll bar. At least for the time being, Rose was secured.

She moved to the trunk of the car, hoping the man had left it unlocked. She hadn't heard him arm the alarm or the tell-tale click of a lock engaging, and to her satisfaction, the trunk opened when she depressed the button release. From the inside, she grabbed what she had seen as she hid behind the tree, then moved to the rear passenger-side door and tried the handle. It lifted with no resistance, and Mary Ann eased the door open. Rose never moved. Whatever the man had done to her, the woman was deeply unconscious. Mary Ann thought that was a shame.

The first blow was to Rose's chest, and although Mary Ann could only raise the hunting knife so far before her clenched fists encountered the roof of the car, she still managed to muster enough force that she felt the blade slide cleanly through skin and muscle and cartilage.

Rose's eyes shot open, and in them Mary Ann saw a fearful questioning. She felt her own mouth twist into a snarl.

"This is for Doug," she said, and then pulled the knife free and brought it down again. And again.

And again.

Chapter 28

A male nurse and one of Navarre's thugs came for John later that morning. The nurse pushed a wheelchair ahead of him, and when he stopped the contraption in front of the bed on which John had been sitting, John followed the path of least resistance and sat down in it.

For the last several hours, John had run through the various possible outcomes of the situation. Depressingly, there were only two. The first was that he tried to escape again and Navarre's people picked him up before he'd gotten more than a hundred feet outside the house. Even more likely, before he got out of this *room*. His last attempt hadn't been much of a rousing success, and in his current physical condition, John doubted he could do more than hobble pathetically anyhow. So that was option one.

Option two offered the same end result—John held captive and forced to heal a rich man he didn't know or care about—but it was easier. Much easier. In the end, easy—even an easy that came with weeks of bedbound illness—won out.

The nurse wheeled him out of the room and down hallways whose walls gleamed bright white in the April morning sunshine. Through each window, John could see the green of grass and trees. He could imagine the smell of the air. On property that required as much upkeep as this place apparently did, John had no doubt that, were he standing outside, he would smell musky, damp mulch and the deeper odor of fertilizer run heavily through with manure.

The thought triggered memories of his childhood on the farm in Pennsylvania. He remembered Two Bucks, the old palomino his father used to keep around the place for John to ride when he was a kid. John remembered how he had loved to brush the old horse, working burrs and stray twigs from his mane and tail. Back then, in the simplicity of his childhood life, John had even enjoyed the mundane task of shoveling Two Bucks' stall and laying new straw down.

Of course, those days were long gone. Nothing was simple anymore. Everything carried a weight, a consequence.

A sudden grief squeezed John's heart in its grip as a memory of Connie replaced the image of the old horse. Here was Connie in Boston, in the place she had been born, and which she had loved so well. The place where she had wanted him to stay with her. The place he had left her, without anything approximating an explanation. And now she was in Pennsylvania, waiting for him with her sick child, a girl who might only have days to live. He had told her he would arrive today, but from the looks of things, there was no way that would happen. He had a feeling he was going to be stuck here for a very long time.

The nurse came to a door and knocked. It was opened from within by a man wearing a black suit, his hair slicked back from a preposterously large forehead.

"He's ready," Forehead muttered, opening the door wide enough for the wheelchair to pass through.

As the nurse pushed him into the room, John saw Navarre propped up in a king-sized bed that occupied most of the far wall. Nailed above Navarre's head was a wooden cross six feet tall, an agonized Christ nailed to its transverse arms.

"A little dramatic, no?" John said.

Navarre raised the oxygen mask to his lips and sucked deeply, then said, "Perhaps, but you never know. Not on a day like this."

John nodded. "Good point. Be a shame if I made you all better and then it fell on you, though. I hope your holy decorator used good hardware." He smiled at Navarre, shocked at the reproach he was feeling.

Navarre gestured at the nurse behind John and the man guided the chair over to the bed. "What happens now?" Navarre asked.

John feigned surprise. "Oh, I thought you knew. I'll need a gallon of gasoline and a match. You have to be on fire for this to work."

That made Navarre laugh, but he only got out one pained chuckle before the laugh deteriorated into labored coughing. The nurse moved to him and held his arm, steadying the old man as he hacked into his cupped hands, moaning in pain between snatched, shallow breaths. When he managed to get his breathing back under control, he sat back heavily in the bed, eyes rolling up to the ceiling. In spite of himself, John found himself pitying the man.

Navarre's head lolled to the side and his eyes locked on John. "What I wouldn't give to be able to laugh again without needing a nurse here in case my lungs decide to shut down once and for all." Tears ran down Navarre's cheeks and John could see him struggling to hold back his emotions.

"Okay," John whispered, approaching the bed. He sat down in the chair that had been pulled up there and leaned toward the old man, hissing in a breath at the pain in his ribs. "If I try to help you—if I do whatever I can, and I'm still not sure that's anything—will you let me go?"

"What do you have to go back to?" Navarre said. "You have to know that you're better off here. Safer, too. If you understand what you are, and what else is out there, looking for you, you know that I'm right. If you stay here, you'll never want for anything. You will be protected."

John shook his head. "What would you be thinking right now if you were in my position? I'm a man, not a pet. I'm a teacher. I have parents, people I love, people I'm responsible for. People I need to try to be responsible for. If you keep me here, I'll keep trying to escape. I won't stop, no matter what you do to me. You wouldn't stop, either, and you know it."

"If you heal me," Navarre said, "if you make me healthy again, I'll release you. On one condition. That you come back here if I get sick again. If you agree, don't think this is something you'll be able to back out of. You won't."

John was nodding, a feeling of hope warming him for the first time since he had almost managed to escape the day before, since Curt had blindsided him in the van. "Okay," he said. "I will. I give you my word."

"Okay then," Navarre said, his face pale and sweaty, his breath whistling through in his throat. "It is agreed. When you have recovered, you're free to go. My men will take you home."

"No." John shook his head. "I have to go somewhere else—"

There was a concussive blast from somewhere in the house, and John felt the floor tremble beneath his feet. A moment later, an alarm blared outside the room.

Chapter 29

Having reviewed all possible strategies for attack, Phylum decided that sometimes there was something to be said for simplicity, so he opted for the front door. Of course, that was easier said than done.

He assumed that somewhere inside the castle-like house there was a room full of monitors displaying various shots of the compound. The trick was to figure out what areas a security consultant in charge of setting up such a camera system might deem most vulnerable. Because having too many cameras on a system was inefficient—who could monitor two hundred views and not miss something?—Phylum knew that there would only be twenty, maybe thirty, to cover the entire grounds, and some of those would have to be dedicated to the interior of the house. That left a finite number to cover the exterior.

Some of those, he knew, would be posted at the entrance to the long, oak-lined driveway, probably in one of the tree-limbs overhanging the HELENA'S HOPE sign. One or two more likely provided views of the drive itself as it made its way toward the house. If Phylum had been the one in charge of setting up security for the house, he would have posted four panoramic cameras on the roof, one pointing in each direction. The house was surrounded by sprawling fields of uninterrupted grass, so any interloper making a break for the house from the woods would be spotted immediately. In addition to the unseen cameras, there were two security guards making periodic rounds of the property's periphery, skirting the edge of the forest.

In short, the security set-up for the house was good. But Phylum was better.

Patiently, he waited for the guard to pass by, emerged from the spot where he'd been hiding behind a tree, and wrapped his arms around the man from behind. With one hand he grasped the man's left shoulder, with the other he cradled the man's chin, and then he jerked in opposite directions, snapping the guard's neck. He dragged the man into the woods, took his jacket and ballcap, and quickly emerged, strolling leisurely in the same direction the man had been walking.

Gradually, he redirected toward the circular turn-around just outside the front door of the house, still moving slowly, inconspicuously. He took his hand out of his pocket. In it was a grenade. Never breaking stride, he pulled the pin and tossed the grenade toward the door, the way a paperboy might toss a newspaper.

The device hit the marble stoop and bounced twice, then rolled to a stop in front of the door. When it exploded, the door blew inward, as did a good portion of the masonry surrounding it. Phylum drew his pistol and entered the house through the hole he'd created.

While the security system around the house may have been competently installed, the security operatives themselves were panicked. They came at Phylum in a full frontal assault—there was no strategy to the attack whatsoever. All he had to do was take cover behind a marble pillar in the foyer and wait for them to come. And come they did, one after another. Less than a minute after he tossed the first grenade, Phylum had dispatched four guards. He pulled the pin on another grenade and tossed it down the hallway.

This explosion did much more damage than the first. Fragments of marble flew like razor-sharp projectiles, slicing through doors and paintings and curtains. Phylum heard an agonized scream and spared a small smile.

Gun raised, he moved deeper into the house.

* * *

When the first explosion shook the house, the reaction inside the room where John had been brought to heal Navarre was urgent and immediate. All but one of Navarre's bodyguards left the room at a dead run. The other drew a pistol from a shoulder-holster and pointed the gun at the door, his left hand cupped under the right to steady the weapon.

In rapid succession there was a series of shots, and John knew he was hearing the uneven rat-a-tat of semi-automatic pistol fire. There was no pattern to the shots, just a random clatter. And then, over the course of a minute or so, the shots began to die down— not all at once, which would have been good news, but gradually, as if one by one, the shooters were being dispatched. There was one final crack of gunfire, and then, for a moment, silence.

That silence was shattered seconds later by the sound of something small and hard skittering over marble. John immediately understood.

"Oh, shit," he said to himself, then shouted, "get down, there's going to be an—"

The explosion came from just outside the room and it was deafening. Bits of wall and floor rocketed through the small room and punched holes in everything. John was saved only by the fact that he had thrown himself flat on the ground. He heard the one bodyguard who had stayed behind cry out in pain, and then, somewhere in the back of his consciousness, he heard another sound. The sound of glass shattering.

Still stunned from the explosion, his hip and injured ribs screaming holy hell, John lifted his head and looked through the smoke at the outward-facing wall. The window there had disappeared completely, blown from its frame by the blast. Without so much as a look back, John leapt to his feet and vaulted through the window and onto the grass outside, moaning softly to himself from the pain, hearing the crunch of broken glass beneath his feet as he landed and then broke into an unstable, weaving run.

He had barely cleared the corner of the immense house when he heard the pops of two gunshots behind him. For a second—he seemed unable to stop himself—he skidded to a stop. Navarre and his bodyguard. Dead. There was no doubt. But this was also not the time to think about it.

Ahead, John saw the turn-around and the cluster of cars. This time, he found keys laying on the seat of the first one he tried, a black Escalade. He turned the key, threw the vehicle into drive, and slammed his foot down on the gas.

From behind him there was another volley of shots and John heard bullets slapping into the back of the truck, but the Escalade was picking up speed and then it was out of pistol range. When he reached the gate at the end of the drive, he never slowed. The wrought-iron gave before the tank-like force of the truck and then, with one more jerk of the wheel that guided him onto the road, he was gone.

Chapter 30

Rose had almost managed to work her wrist free of the handcuff, using her own blood as a lubricant, when the man—the one who had attacked her in the woods and knocked her out, she assumed—pulled open the door of the car. She was weak, more so than she had ever been, and had already passed out twice for brief periods since waking to find Mary Ann crouching above her, driving the knife into Rose's body over and over again. The pain had been like nothing she'd ever experienced before. In the past, there had been times when her victims had managed to defend themselves, whether with a knife or a gun or, once, a baseball bat, but those were situations she'd always managed to cut short. Maybe she'd taken a slash to the arm, or a blow to the ribs—most recently, of course, there had been the bullet in her back—but never had she found herself on this side of the equation, lying helplessly as she was brutalized.

But even as Mary Ann had plunged the knife down again and again, a part of Rose's mind, the portion where her basic sense of humanity lived, had understood why the woman was taking her revenge. The man she killed in Shaw's home, Doug, had been Mary Ann's love, her partner in life, the father of children neither of them would ever have now. Rose had destroyed that possibility, just as she had done so many times before. She was a monster, a murdering monster, and Mary Ann deserved her revenge.

Her insides were on fire, her abdomen and chest a bloody mess of torn flesh and muscle, but the pain wasn't the worst of it. The worst was that Rose was still deteriorating, not getting better. There were simply too many wounds for her body to heal itself as it normally would. She had resigned herself, over the past twenty minutes, to the truth—that she could very well die. In a way, it was calming to know that this sad excuse for an existence might nearly be over. But she was damned if she would die taped and handcuffed in the back of this blood-smelling car. All she had wanted to do was drag herself into the woods, into a creek bed or beneath a tree, and close her eyes until it was over.

But now he was here, and maybe, maybe there was a chance. He was bending over her, the look on his face not one of shock, but of perplexity. He'd had plans for her, no doubt, and now those plans were going to have to change. He looked unhappy about it.

"Help," she whispered. Mary Ann had sliced her up nice and good. Rose doubted if there was an organ in her body that wasn't punctured or lacerated in one place or another. She'd have been dead before the woman left had she been normal.

The man leaned over her. "Come again?" he said.

"Blood."

He nodded. "A lot of it," he said. "Someone really doesn't like you."

She tried to shake her head but it only lolled to the side and stayed there. "Drink. Blood."

He looked down at her, considering what he thought he had heard her say. "You want blood to drink?"

"Yes," she tried to say, but then a wave of black swept over her, and as hard as she tried to fight against the tide, it took her away.

* * *

When she next came to awareness, the car was moving. She was still in the back seat, and beneath her she could feel the sticky coldness of congealed blood.

She realized that something had changed. She felt...stronger. Not much, but a little. Wincing at the agony the motion caused, she turned her head to the side and saw the man. He was sitting in the driver's seat, his hands on the wheel. Around one of his hands was wrapped a hank of bloodstained fabric. For the briefest of moments, Rose understood what he had done and wondered why. Then she was gone again, swimming in the darkness.

* * *

"Wake up," the voice said, and Rose opened her eyes.

She was sitting on the ground, her back against the car. The man squatted in front of her, an unconscious woman at his feet. She wore expensive clothing, pinstriped slacks and a white blouse. There was a trickle of blood on her temple, where Rose assumed the man had hit her. Her respiration was shallow.

"Can you?" the man asked.

Rose tried to speak and managed, "Think so." She fell onto her side and shimmied painfully toward the unconscious woman. When she was close enough, she cradled the woman's head in her hand and tore out her throat with her teeth.

And then she drank until she could drink no more.

Chapter 31

John killed the engine and opened the door of the Escalade. There were two other cars in the driveway, an old Ford pickup and a Toyota Prius. In front of him, the stone farmhouse was dark. The only light came from the crescent moon overhead.

Slowly, he crossed the dooryard, gravel crunching under his feet. As he reached the porch, the door swung open and he saw first the barrel of a shotgun and then the man holding it.

"Dad," he said.

Tim Barron lowered the shotgun and came toward his son, saying, "I don't believe it."

* * *

"Connie?" John asked as he and his father walked into the kitchen.

His father held a finger to his lips. "Upstairs, asleep. She's only been getting a couple hours a night with Katie the way she is. Let's not wake her up just now, okay?"

John nodded and opened his arms as his mother stepped toward him for a hug. "Hi, Mom," he said.

"Hi, sweetie," his mother said back, her voice muffled in his neck. When she let him go, there were tears in her eyes.

"I'm in trouble," John said. He sat at the kitchen table. His mother sat next to him, and his father was making himself busy putting together a pot of coffee.

"Bad?" his father asked, turning around to look at John, who nodded slowly.

"Tell us," his mother said. She wore a blue flannel nightgown and her hair was crazy from lying in bed, but John didn't think he'd ever seen anything so comforting. A sudden wave of emotion swept over him, and he began to talk.

He spoke for a long time, pausing occasionally to answer a question from one or another of his parents, and when he was done, he felt as though he'd said everything there was to say. His father slid a mug of coffee in front of him and Tim sipped it as his mother and father processed. More than anything, he wanted to tell them how crazy he knew it all must sound, and once he even started to do just that, but his father raised a hand and waved him off.

"So, if I'm hearing you right," his father said, "this woman will be coming for you. She'll be coming here."

"If I stay," John said. "Wherever I go, she'll find me eventually."

There was a voice from the kitchen door, behind John. "Who will find you?"

John turned and saw Connie. He felt his breath catch for a moment. Connie wore old, faded sweatpants and an oversized t-shirt, one of his father's, with KENNETT SQUARE MUSHROOM CAPITAL OF THE WORLD stenciled across the front over a flaked off image of one of the fungi for which the region was so well known. Her brown hair was pulled back in a ponytail, and other than the few wrinkles around her eyes and mouth, she looked exactly as she had last time John saw her, all those years ago.

"Hi," he said, and stood. She came forward and hugged him.

"You came," she whispered into the crook of his neck.

"I did," he replied, "but before long, you might wish I hadn't." They sat down at the table and his father poured Connie a cup of coffee.

"This is my fault," she said, looking distraught. "I asked you to come here, and now…your parents are in danger." She glanced at John's mother. "I'm so sorry, Isabel. All you've done is show me kindness, and this is what I bring in return."

John's mother shook her head. "This has nothing to do with you, sweetheart. This is," she paused and looked at John's father, "an old matter. Tim?"

Tim Barron rubbed his eyes and took a sip of his coffee. "Okay," he said, closed his eyes, and then spoke. "You know that we adopted you?" he asked John, who nodded. "And you know that your birth mother died during delivery?" Another nod. "That's part of the story, and really, it's the only part we thought you'd ever need to know. The rest of it doesn't have to do with you, really, at all."

"Go on," John said.

"You birth mother had twins," his mother said. "For a while, we had foster custody of you both."

"A sister," John murmured. "It was a girl, wasn't it?"

"Yes," his father said. "But from the very beginning, there was something wrong with her. We only had her for a few weeks, but even then we knew that she wasn't normal."

John shook his head, not understanding. "I don't understand. What do you mean?"

This time, his mother answered. "She was always hurting you. We'd walk away from the crib for just the briefest of moments, and when we came back, you would be crying and there would be marks on you. Scratches. We thought it would stop, but it didn't, and we got scared." She paused. "And it was more than that. She would scratch us, too, and she never stopped crying. It was more than just a matter of being fussy—that's normal—it was *meanness*. Meanness like I wouldn't have believed was possible in an infant. You were the exact opposite. Sometimes, you were so calm and well-behaved I just couldn't believe it. What baby doesn't cry? Ever? Maybe you were sick a little more often than most babies, but that was it."

After a moment, she added, "Even back then, I remember thinking that it was like the two of you were parts of the same whole, that you'd gotten everything good, and she'd gotten everything bad. It's a terrible thought, and one I hated myself for having, but I couldn't shake the feeling that maybe, somehow, it was true."

Quietly, John asked, "So what happened?"

His father shrugged and said, "It was a difficult process, because DSS prefers to keep siblings together, but when we filed papers for adoption, we just...well, we just kept you."

"And my sister went back into the foster care system?"

His mother nodded.

"Was she adopted?"

"I don't know," his father said. "I tried to check a few times, but that's not information they give out. Once we gave her up, we surrendered any right to know what was happening with her."

John gave a rueful little laugh. "Well, I think we know now. She's coming home."

* * *

Later, Connie led John to the bedroom that once, what seemed like a thousand years ago now, had been his. As quietly as possible, she cracked the door and John peeked in. Connie's daughter lay in bed, John's old quilt pulled up to her chin. It was dark in the room, the only illumination the light spilling in from the hallway, but John could still see that the little girl looked like Connie. High boned cheeks, soft brown hair. But he could also see that she was pale, and that the form of her body beneath the frayed patchwork quilt was too slight, too small.

"She's beautiful," he murmured.

"Yeah," Connie said. "She is. My Katie..." She eased the door shut and they went back downstairs and sat on the couch in the living room. Connie pulled her feet up and tucked them beneath her. John angled himself toward her and rested his arm on the top of the couch. It was late—or early, depending on how one looked at things—and John's parents had gone back to bed for another hour or so of sleep. The house was quiet, the only sound an occasional crack or creak as the house settled.

"What are you going to do?" Connie asked.

John thought for a moment, then said, "I wish I had a good answer for you. I came to help your daughter, but my being here is...dangerous for *all* of you. This woman who's after me—" he snorted a laugh, "my *sister*, is a killer. I don't think she'd bat an eye at killing each and every person in this house."

Connie stared thoughtfully at John for a second, then said, "In the visions and dreams you have, the ones where you see through her eyes, do you ever feel what she's feeling?"

"In a way. Loneliness, sadness. Frustration. Why?"

She shook her head. "I don't know. It's just that...I guess it's just that, when we were together all those years ago, I knew that I loved you, and I knew that you loved me, but...I always felt like there was something missing."

"Missing," John mused. "What?"

She shook her head, searching for the word, then finally said, "Abandon, maybe. There was something holding you back, a wall. Even if you didn't quite understand it, I could see it, and I could see what it was doing to you. And to us."

John huffed a laugh. "Thanks."

"I don't mean that to be insulting. But think about it. Have you ever felt free, whole, like you were fully who you were meant to be? When I think about our time together—" she paused, "it's like you were always looking over your shoulder, waiting for the sky to fall. That wasn't it, of course. I know that now. You were waiting for her to show up, and even if you didn't understand some of the things you were doing, they were all to protect the people around you."

John thought about his inability to stay in one place for more than a year or two, about the way he had ended things with first Connie and then, years later, with Suzie, and about how coming home, even for a day or two, felt *dangerous*, not just for him, but for his parents. "What are you getting at?"

She shrugged. "I guess what I'm getting at is that your sister probably feels the same way, like there's something essential missing from her life. And maybe she feels like the only way she can fill that hole inside of her is by killing you. Maybe...in order to have a normal life, she needs some of the *goodness* that went to you when you were born."

When John didn't respond immediately, she added, "Maybe the same is true for you, that you'll never be able to live your life completely until she's dead, until some of her darkness balances out the light inside of you."

"We're twins," he said, "halves of a whole, like my mother said. Neither one of us can be complete until we've...*devoured* the other. Either way, one of us has to die."

"Maybe," Connie said pensively. "But maybe not."

"What do you mean?" John said, his eyes narrowing.

She shrugged. "It might be nothing—"

"Come on," he said. "Give."

And so she did.

Chapter 32

As Phylum drove, the woman talked. She was stronger now and able to sit up front with him, although she rode slumped against the passenger side door. Her wounds, which had been grievous, were healing, the flesh seeming to knit back together at a pace *just* too slow to see with the naked eye. One of the gashes left by the brutal attack had entered the woman's chest just below the collar bone; when Phylum first saw it, the wound gaped open and seeped blood, but now he could barely tell where it had been. The first few ounces of blood he'd given her, his own, had kept her alive, but she had only really started to come around after feeding on the woman Phylum had cold-cocked coming out of the gas station a few hours later. If he hadn't been willing to accept his initial instincts about the true nature of this beautiful, dark woman, he was ready now.

Why he was doing all of this for her was hard to put into words. He just knew that he didn't want her to die, not now, not at anyone's hand beside his own. Everything he was doing, he knew, was the result of sloppy thinking and poor judgment. The job he'd been hired to complete was simple — kill John Barron. But after his encounter with this strange and fascinating woman in Barron's apartment and then the revealing conversation with Mr. It's Me, wheels had started turning in his mind. Normally, he was very good at ignoring the thoughts that weakened the resolve of lesser men, but now he found that he didn't want to push these thoughts aside. He was truly conflicted, perhaps for the first time in his life.

That the directive to kill Barron had been handed down by a group affiliated with the church bothered him. That was a large part of the problem. He hated the church, hated what it stood for. As far as Phylum was concerned, the church was nothing more than a money-making machine that granted shitty people *carte blanche* to do awful things and then, through the magic of "God," be forgiven for it. His father had been that way, first when he was beating Phylum's mother and drinking his way through their monthly mortgage payment, and then when he decided Phylum's mother had had enough—or maybe when she had stopped resisting the way he liked—and started in on Phylum himself.

And then, on top of all the church and daddy issues, there was Mr. It's Me, as well. To cut right to the point, Phylum had decided that Mr. It's Me was quite a tremendous lump of cow shit. Here was a man who sat in his chintzy house in Reston, Virginia and made calls, to people like Phylum, that ended lives. Not that the lives mattered to Phylum—no, that wasn't the issue at all; he was more than happy to kill and kill, right up until the proverbial cattle found their way back to pasture. He liked his job. Killing made him feel *good*. What he had grown tired of was taking orders from shitsacks like Mr. It's Me. And that's why Phylum had a bit of a problem on his hands.

Here he was, driving north toward Pennsylvania with this woman who appeared—it could really no longer be denied—to be an actual, no-shit *vampire*, and he was seriously considering bailing on the job he'd been hired to do.

What it came down to was whether Phylum was willing to give up his current line of work, and he was beginning to think he just might be. There would always be men who would pay to have other men killed. That was just how the world turned. Leaving Barron alive would mean leaving the United States, but he had enough money to be comfortable for a while. For quite a while, in fact.

A green highway sign came up, telling them they had 55 miles until the merge with I-95.

"We're getting close," the woman said. "Just a little while longer."

* * *

Two hours later the sun was just coming up and they turned onto Route 1, heading toward Philadelphia. The woman was awake now, and although she still appeared to be weak, she was looking at him with perplexity.

"What's your name?" Phylum asked.

She appeared to consider whether or not to tell him the truth, then said, "Rose."

"Mine's Eric. Most people call me Phylum. Your choice, Rose."

"Okay then, Eric, do you mind if I ask you a question?"

He glanced over at her and grinned. "I'll save you the trouble. I saved you because you're like me."

"Like you? What do you mean?"

"Wolves," he said. "We're both wolves."

After a moment, she nodded. "Yes, I suppose we are."

"Do you know how many wolves I've met in my life?" he said. "I mean, the genuine article. Not the poser CEO pieces of shit who shop from *Soldier of Fortune* magazine and play war-games in the woods during the weekend. People like us? None. Not one. Until you."

"And how did you know I was a wolf?"

He was surprised she had asked. "I knew the first time I met you, Rose. In Barron's apartment. You weren't afraid. *Everyone* is afraid of me. They're all sheep. I could tell that you thought I was a sheep, too. It shook me. I won't lie about that."

"So that's why you've done all this for me? Saved me in the woods, brought me a kill, driving me north?"

"That," he said, then grinned at her, "and strategy. I was hired to kill John Barron, and I'm still deciding whether or not to go through with it. I was told where he would be, but you...you just fucking showed up. I thought maybe you'd know where he'd gone now."

"But there's something else, too," she said. "Another reason you kept me alive."

He nodded. "Maybe there is," he said, eyes focused on the road ahead. "But that's my own business."

* * *

Using an assumed identity he often utilized while on the job, Phylum checked them into a Super 8 motel at a little after ten o'clock that morning. As the sun had risen higher in the sky, Rose had become less focused and responsive, and then had blacked out altogether.

He parked as close as he could to their door and half-carried Rose inside and lay her on the bed. She showed little sign of stirring, but for good measure—he had to admit that the long night and day had taken their toll on him also—he bound her wrists with duct tape from his trunk, then taped her hands to the headboard. If she woke up, she might be able to escape, but she would make a lot of sound going about it.

When he had finished, he lay down on the other bed and fell fast asleep on top of the covers.

Chapter 33

After breakfast, John took his father aside and asked if they could take a walk. They needed to talk about something.

More out of remembered routine than anything else, John started off toward the cinderblock growing buildings. The morning was cool and the air was clear. By noon it would have warmed significantly, but for now the chilly spring air felt wonderful against John's face and arms.

"If this is about last night," his father began, "I understand why you're angry with—"

John raised a hand and waved it off. "No, it's not that. I don't blame either of you for not telling me. It's not something you could have known would matter. This is about something else, Dad."

"Okay," the older man said. They had turned off the gravel driveway now and were making their way across a rolling hill toward the mushroom buildings, about a hundred yards off. "What is it?"

"You know why I came here?"

His father nodded. "For Katie. Connie told us you'd spoken."

"Right. And you know what it's going to do to me if...if whatever this is actually works?"

Now a look of sadness spread across his father's features. "I guess I have some idea. Does that frighten you?"

"Honestly, no. I mean, I'm not eager to feel that way again, but I have no doubts. You know?"

"I think so."

John considered his words and then spoke again. "If I'm going to stay here and do this thing, it's going to put all of you in danger, and I can't do anything to protect you. If it works and I'm able to—to *heal* Katie, I might not even be conscious afterward. And this woman, my sister, is coming for me. She might even be close now."

"We know that," his father said. "We're ready."

John shook his head. "No, Dad, you're not. Based on what I've heard, this woman may have killed dozens, even hundreds of people. She isn't normal. She's like—well, she's like a *vampire*, Dad. She'll kill all of you without thinking twice about it, not because she needs to, but because you're in the way of her getting what she wants."

"You," his father said. They had arrived at the cinderblock building and they stopped now and faced each other. In the distance, John saw smoke drifting lazily from the house's chimney. It all looked so calm and idyllic, and he wondered how he could ever have thought it was okay to bring this kind of trouble to his parents' front door.

"Me," John reiterated. "So that's why, if I'm unconscious afterwards, I want you to give me over to her. No fight. No struggle. Just tell her you're going to hand me over. Do you understand?"

His father's face went white and he stepped back. "No," he whispered. "I can't *believe* you'd ask me to do that." He moved back toward John and grabbed both of his son's hands. "Your mother and I love you, John. You're everything to us. When we took you in all those years ago, it was a *miracle*. We never thought we would be able to have children, and then there you were. And now you ask me to…to just give you up? I ought to hit you."

Tears were coursing down the older man's cheeks and he dug in his pockets and came out with a battered yellow pack of American Spirit cigarettes. "Tell your mother about this and I *will* hit you," he said, then lit the cigarette with a match.

"Dad—"

"Don't," his father said, raising a hand. "You're my son, and having you was the best thing that ever happened to us. I understand where you're coming from, and I know that's a good place, but please, if you ever ask me to give up my own son again, I—I think I've already made enough threats of corporeal punishment, but to reiterate, I *will* knock your shit down. Pardon my French."

Now John laughed, and it was a good feeling. He couldn't remember the last time he'd really laughed. "I'd like to see you try," he said when he was able.

His father drew on his Spirit and smiled. "Don't poke the sleeping dragon, John."

* * *

Feeling unsure and more like a phony than he ever had in his life, John opened the door to Katie's room and stepped inside. Connie came in behind him and closed the door.

As before, Katie was asleep, curled on her side. In the dim sunlight filtering through the closed plantation blinds, John could see the girl shaking, and the dark circles of illness and fatigue beneath her closed eyes.

"What now?" Connie whispered.

"Got me," John said, shaking his head. "Let's just see what happens."

Moving on tiptoes, they approached the bed and knelt down beside it. Katie made an unintelligible sound and then cuddled deeper into the covers. Connie reached out and stroked the girl's hair back behind her ear, whispered, "Hello, my love."

John closed his eyes and tried to find an inner calm, but all he could feel was fear. Fear for what would happen to this beautiful young girl if what he tried didn't work, and fear for what might happen to all of them if it *did*.

He breathed slowly in, then out, trying to drop his shoulders down and release the tension he felt all over his body. Dimly, he could recall the heightening of the senses he had experienced just before touching Kyra Metheny and he tried to will the same thing now. But there was none of that. Just the sound of the clock on the wall, the labored breathing of the girl lying in front of him, the…the ticking of the grandfather clock in the living room downstairs.

And then, all at once, it came over him. His body relaxed and the pressure in his chest released. He opened his eyes, reached out, and took the girl's hand.

This time, there was no explosion behind his eyes, no starburst of pain in his head. Only a slow, steady throb all over, in his arms, his legs, his spine. As he held on to Katie's hand, the pain became agony and then grew into something new, something strange and alien, as if he were now sharing his body with another entity, crammed into a too-small skinsack with a vicious, murderous creature that wanted only to kill him.

John heard someone cry out and vaguely understood that the sound had come from him. The girl's hand jerked from his grasp and he fell, felt his head hit something, and then there was, for a time, only black.

* * *

When he came to, his mother was sitting beside his bed, her head tilted back against the wall. He felt terrible, as if he were suffering from the worst case of flu he could imagine. Twice he tried to speak, but was unable. Finally, he found his voice and said, "Mom."

His mother jerked awake and was instantly by his side. She put her hands on his face, felt his forehead, bent and kissed his burning skin. "Oh, dear God," she said, revealing the Catholic upbringing that had never truly left her. "Are you okay, Johnny? How do you feel?"

"Like shit," he whispered. "Katie?"

His mother tried to speak, but her voice eluded her. That was okay, though. John didn't have to hear her words to know what she was already saying with her eyes. She clasped his hands in her own and smiled down at him through the tears on her cheeks.

"Good," he whispered. Then he closed his eyes and fell back asleep.

Chapter 34

Mary Ann stood before her house, utterly exhausted, swaying unsteadily. Yellow police tape had been strung across the steps onto the modest porch, and more crisscrossed the front door in an X. The house looked empty and still and unlived in. Mary Ann supposed that was the truth.

Slowly, every step shooting bolts of pain into her knees and feet, Mary Ann started forward, across the lawn. Halfway to the front door, she stopped, stood still for a moment, and then collapsed to her knees in the grass, her head falling forward, her hair over her face. And she wept. She wept for Doug, and she wept for herself. Her hands, still in agony after her exploits in the hotel room, dug into the soft, moist grass, pulling handfuls of blades free, releasing them in crushed clumps.

All the way here, she had been anticipating this moment, not with eagerness but with dread. Returning to her house, to the home she had spent with Doug for so many years…finding his body removed, a dark stain spread over the floor where he'd lain, where Rose had killed him. Or, worse, finding his body still there, still early in the long cycle of decomposition, perhaps not smelling too badly, not so soon, but bloated with gas…

His dead body, eyes fixed, skin bloodless, had been the only thing she could think of as she walked away from the hotel where Rose had held her prisoner, her shoeless feet naked to tiny shards of rock and glass; the only thing she could think of as she walked mile after mile along darkened country roads, her feet cut and bleeding; the only thing she could think of as she finally arrived at an all-night truck stop and begged, wishing for tears but unable to bring them, for anyone to take her south, to take her home. One of the ten or so men sitting at the J shaped counter had indeed been traveling south and said he would take her, but not until the lone waitress had fed her a meal and cleaned the wounds on her hands and feet. After that, for a while, Mary Ann knew she had slept, and the trucker had only woken her once they'd arrived at the outskirts of Charlotte.

Slowly, slowly, Mary Ann got hold of herself. Wiping weakly at the tears on her cheeks, she looked up, back at the front door of her house, and prepared herself to go inside.

"Mary Anne?"

Her head snapped left, to where the voice had come from, sure it was Rose, that the woman had come back for her. Having killed John, she'd come back for Mary Ann; she should have known. But it wasn't Rose. It was Hillary Lamb from next door, and she was running across the lawn toward Mary Ann, her long blond hair flying out behind her, her eyes wide and shocked. She fell to her knees and wrapped her arms around Mary Ann, pulled her into a tight embrace.

Mary Ann pulled back from the woman, said, "Doug—"

"None of us knew where you were," Hillary said, cutting her short. "Doug's at Northeast Medical Center in Concord."

Not understanding, Mary Ann could only gape at her neighbor and shake her head slowly back and forth.

"Come on," Hillary said and stood up. She helped Mary Ann to her feet and pulled her toward the house. "Let's get you cleaned up. I'll drive you."

Mary Ann pulled away from the other woman. "Doug's dead," she whispered.

"No," Hillary said softly, grasping Mary Ann by the upper arms, "hurt badly, but not dead. I heard yelling and called the police. The cops and paramedics got here five minutes later. He was bleeding and unconscious, but it looked worse than it was. He's going to be okay."

Comprehension dawned slowly on Mary Ann. Doug, alive. Not dead. It was like adding two and two and coming up with eight. Nothing made sense. Doug was dead. Doug was alive. Doug was at Northeast Medical Center in Concord.

"Take me now," Mary Ann said, grasping Hillary's hand and dragging the other woman toward her car. "Take me."

And so Hillary did.

Chapter 35

The clock on the dashboard read 7:55 when Rose turned onto the gravel driveway and switched off the headlights of Phylum's BMW. After a short debate, Rose had convinced him that she needed to do this alone and Phylum had agreed to wait for her at the hotel. If she wasn't back by morning, he was to assume her dead.

She pulled halfway down the driveway, then killed the car's engine and climbed out of the car, wobbling a little as she stood. Although her wounds were healing rapidly, she was still weak. Too weak, she thought, to be attempting anything like an out-and-out assault on a house full of people. Phylum had said that she was a wolf, but a wolf was the last thing in the world she felt like tonight. A cub, maybe. A wounded, weak wolf cub. But that was okay. She wasn't here to do any killing. Not tonight.

She walked slowly toward the house, sticking to the shadows cast by the various trees in the dooryard. All of the curtains were drawn, and behind them Rose could see only the suggestions of shapes, none of them moving. They were expecting her.

Suddenly, floodlights mounted to the outside of the house flicked on, bathing the yard in brilliant white light. Rose squinted against the light and raised her hand to block it.

There was an explosive blast and a cataclysm of pain engulfed her side and hip. Rose cried out and fell. Another shot rang out and she heard pellets tear into the tree behind her.

And then a tired-sounding voice. "Dad, no more!"

Rose scrabbled behind the tree and sat there, feeling warm blood leaking down her side and stomach and into the crotch of her jeans. Already weakened from Mary Ann's attack, her body was unable to stop the bleeding. She would be dead in minutes.

"Hey!" the voice yelled again. "Come out where we can see you. We won't shoot."

She tried to speak and blood dribbled from her mouth. She spat it out and yelled, "How do I know you won't?"

"You don't," the voice called, and in it Rose could hear a terrible fatigue, "but nobody here wants to kill anyone. I know it's me you want. I just want to talk to you."

Rolling onto her uninjured side, Rose pulled herself around the tree and into the open. Whether they shot her again or not, she was finished. She tossed the pistol that had been tucked into her jeans out into the yard and lay down on the grass, staring at the house.

Two men stood on the porch. Two other people crowded in the doorway behind them, a woman and a girl. Rose felt her eyes drifting closed and saw, for just a moment, the baby. She smiled and reached for it, wanting only to touch its hair, to smell its skin.

Violently, she shook awake and gasped for air. It was hard to breathe now. She worked her way into a sitting position, supporting her weight on her arms, and looked back toward the porch, where only one man was standing now, the barrel of the shotgun trained on her.

The man on the porch called out, "Johnny, be careful."

"Hi," a voice said from much closer. Rose looked up and saw a face emerging from the shadows. Or maybe not from the shadows. It was hard to see now. Everything was getting fuzzy and dim.

"Do you know who I am?" his disembodied face asked. It was closer, and she thought he was kneeling over her. She could make out his features. Brown hair, brown eyes. Like hers. He looked so tired, and even through the pain and the fear in her brain and gut, she felt sorry for him. Sorry for him because he was like her. Broken. Incomplete.

"Jo—" she started to say, but her mouth was full of blood again. She coughed and spat, then said, "John."

"What's your name?"

"Rose."

And then—she couldn't help it—Rose began to cry. She cried for everything she had done, for everything she had been *compelled* to do. She cried for the lost lives of children, for Mary Ann and her husband, and she cried for herself.

"It's okay," she heard a voice say from far, far away, and then she felt arms around her, holding her, and the feeling of warm comfort was like nothing she'd ever known.

Suddenly, without warning, there was bright light, *light everywhere*, and Rose felt the pain lessen, then disappear altogether. The last thing she saw was the baby, the beautiful baby, and then there was no more.

Epilogue

Kennett Square, Pennsylvania—Two Weeks Later

1

When he got out of the hospital, John decided to stay in Kennett Square for a few weeks. He no longer felt the fear and anxiety that had ruled his life for so long, and all he really wanted to do was read, eat, sleep, and spend time with the people he loved.

Connie had decided to stay on for a while, too. Over the time she had spent with Tim and Isabel Barron, they had become like parents to her, and John could tell that the affection was mutual.

Katie's improvement was shocking. When Connie brought him home from Riddle Memorial Hospital, the first thing John saw was his father giving the girl a tractor ride around the back field, the girl laughing wildly as she bounced and jounced on the hard metal seat. John could see that his father was laughing along with her, and that did his heart as much good as the two weeks he'd spent recovering.

Connie helped John get his belongings—a couple of books and a few changes of clothes—inside, and then John went to the kitchen to say hello to his mother. She was cooking, and the whole house was redolent of caramelizing onions and garlic. When she turned and saw her son, a smile came to her face.

"My boy," she whispered, drawing him into an embrace. "He's home."

"I am," John said, hugging her back just as tightly as she held him. "I'm so sorry for all of this. I know it had to be horrible for you and Dad."

She shook her head against his shoulder. "Nonsense," she said. "This was no more your fault than the sun setting, or the changing of the seasons. You get over that, okay?"

"Okay," he murmured into her hair. "I'll try."

After a while, his mother held John at arm's length. "It's all over, no?"

John nodded. "Looks like it. I tried this morning on a sick girl in the waiting room, but no dice. Really, though, I didn't have to try. I just…feel different. I feel free."

She smiled again, then her face darkened. "And the other one?"

Just moments after John had collapsed after grabbing hold of Rose's hand, an enormous man none of them had ever seen before emerged from the thicket of trees at the mouth of the driveway and carried Rose off. Though John had been unconscious, his father was certain that he saw the woman breathing.

"We don't have to worry about her," John said. "All she wanted was what I wanted, and I think I gave it to her. I think I was able to give it to both of us."

"And it nearly killed you," she scolded. "I don't know what you were thinking, Johnny. You were already so weak."

He shrugged. "Either way, she has what she needed from me. Somehow, I got part of her, and she got part of me."

She nodded. "Good. Now we can get down to business."

He laughed. "What are you talking about, Mother?"

"Babies."

There was a banging behind them and John turned to see Connie standing just inside the swinging screen door. "What babies?" she said.

John's mother raised both eyebrows and shook her head. "If I have to answer that question, both of you need help."

John blushed and slapped her lightly on the arm. "For god's sake, woman. Connie, I need a beer."

She smiled at him, and he could see color in her face, too. But not embarrassment. "A beer sounds good," she said, then added, in a whisper, "for starters."

For starters, John thought, following her outside, where a tin pail sat, overflowing with cans of Budweiser. *It's about time.*

2

Baja California — One Year Later

Gabriel Corderman — Gabe to his few friends and Gabey the Baby to the seemingly endless succession of bullies who had haunted his days during middle and high school — had not come all the way to Todos Santos, a tiny fishing village not too far from Cabo san Lucas, to get his chops busted by rude American assholes. Not getting his chops busted by rude American assholes was, in actuality, the very reason he had chosen to leave his small Iowan town of Millersberg at the first possible opportunity.

And yet here he was. And here again, for the fourth or fifth time this week, was the rude American asshole. That was all right, though. These kinds of people passed through. People who had come down to spend a couple weeks in Cabo and found the resort town a little too polished for their liking. So they rented a car, took a drive, made their way up the coast to see some of the real Mexico, or the slightly-less-unreal Mexico. These assholes, usually pretentious pricks from New York or Los Angeles or some such place, would stay until the rustic charm of Todos Santos wore off, usually no more than three days, and then scurry back off for the comfort of Cabo.

What made this particular situation different was that Gabriel felt it was very important not to let this particular asshole figure out how much of an asshole Gabriel thought he was, with his chronic under-tipping and marked unwillingness to say "Thank you." Because this guy was scary. Not just big—though he *was* big—but hard-looking, the way Aryan brothers always look in prison movies. Gabriel could tell that the guy had tried to tone down the scariness factor by dressing for the climate in Bermuda shorts and a short-sleeve linen shirt, but the clothes did little to mask the creature wearing them.

With a sigh, Gabriel put the beer and the virgin daiquiri on a tray and headed back to the outside table where the asshole was sitting with the woman.

"Your beer," he said, setting the bottle down in front of the man, whose eyes were hidden by reflective Aviator sunglasses, "and your daiquiri." He set a cocktail napkin in front of the woman and placed the drink atop it. "Can I get either of you anything else?"

The asshole said, "No alcohol in that daiquiri, right?"

Gabriel nodded. "It's virgin, just like you said."

"That's it then," the asshole said, and Gabriel turned to go.

The woman's voice stopped him. Though he'd been seeing the man and woman for nearly a week, he'd never heard her speak before. Some kind of abusive relationship, he'd assumed. None of his business. She was hot, though, almost painfully so. Even with the pale, straight scars just barely visible on her shoulders and chest.

"Thank you," she said and favored him with a look and a small smile.

Gabriel smiled back and saw, for the first time, the woman's belly. That explained it, then. She was pregnant.

"No problem," he said. "If you need anything else, just give a shout."

"We will," she said and looked out at the water. Just before Gabriel turned back around to go inside, he caught one last glimpse of the woman out of the corner of his eye. There was something about the way she stared out at the horizon, some sense of serenity, that he had never seen before. It was nearly painful to observe, so he walked back inside, thinking to himself that he had been wrong to think of her as merely attractive. That was missing the point of a woman like this, entirely.

She was the most beautiful creature he had ever seen.

3

From Melbourne *Herald-Sun*—Melbourne, Australia

Birth Announcements

Bryce Connor Parsons and Samantha Stevens Parsons were born April 22nd, 2011 at Lee Hospital in Melbourne. Bryce weighed 6 pounds, 1 ounce, and was 19 inches long; Samantha weighed 6 pounds, 5 ounces, and was 20 inches long. The twins' parents are Kyle and Piper Parsons of Melbourne. The two healthy babies and their parents send thanks to family and friends who continue to support and care for them.

About the Author

Mark P. Dunn was born in Pennsylvania but has lived most of his adult life in Ohio, Maine, and North Carolina, where he teaches high school English at a small private school. Mark is married to the photographer Piper Warlick, and the two care for their two daughters and a veritable menagerie of animals, ranging from dogs to cats to chickens. Mark's previous novel, *A Girl in Mind*, was published by Five Star Mysteries in 2006, and he has also published horror and suspense tales in various magazines and anthologies. Currently, he is at work on a third book, a supernatural thriller set in the wintery woods of Western Maine.

CPSIA information can be obtained at www.ICGtesting.com
Printed in the USA
LVOW11s2238240616

494069LV00001B/18/P